CURVY GIRLS CAN'T DATE BILLIONAIRES

KELSIE STELTING

Structural Edit by Sally Henson

Copy Edited by Tricia Harden

Sensitivity and Proofreading by Yesenia Vargas of WriterMom

Cover design by AngstyG

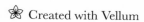 Created with Vellum

For Sarah. May you always use your beautiful voice to speak for others and yourself.

ONE

THE WORST PART ABOUT A BREAKUP? Wanting to text them and then realizing you can't because every moment you shared no longer matters. Especially since the guy I wanted to text was already with another girl—and had been since we'd broken up. That fact was made even worse at 3:45 in the morning.

The only thing that made waking up before the birds any better was a white chocolate mocha and a cinnamon bagel from Seaton Bakery. I waited in the parking lot in my sputtering car while my mom went inside for our breakfast trade. We cleaned their bakery once a week in exchange for free breakfast each day. (Not sure who fared better in that deal.)

I lowered my phone and dropped it in the cupholder, feeling just as tired but much more acutely aware of the ache in my chest. I hated that we were done, but I hated that I needed him even more.

When would I stop wanting to text him? How long would it be before I stopped picking up my phone to call him only to realize I shouldn't?

They say time heals all wounds, but if it worked this slowly, I needed to find another solution. For now, I'd settle on the delete button. My finger hovered over his contact info, his name with the red, white, and green hearts around it.

The pain in my heart grew stronger, and I hurried to press delete. He was gone from my list. I just wished his name could be gone from my heart as easily.

Through my permanently cracked window, I heard the bakery door clang shut. Mom approached my car carrying two to-go cups and two white paper bags. As she got closer, I opened my door (because the window wouldn't roll down) and took my breakfast from her. "Thanks, *amá*."

"Enjoy, *mija*."

With half a smile, I nodded and lifted the cup to see what she'd put on it today. Using a black

Sharpie, she'd written, *Eres fuerte* with a heart for a period. *You are strong.*

As she went back to her car, I took a sip of the coffee. The sweet flavor immediately made me relax. This would be a longer day than most—especially considering I had to go to school after cleaning what Mom said was a mansion. To be fair, most places felt like mansions compared to our one-bedroom apartment.

After getting into her car, she pulled out of the bakery's gravel lot. I drove behind her, hearing the rocks crunch and pop under my tires. We started down Emerson Highway until we reached a neighborhood where the houses got bigger and bigger.

Half of me marveled at the homes while the other half resented them. Why did they need so much space? The owners probably weren't using all those extra rooms to take in foster children or store goods to donate. Just one of those houses could fit my entire extended family, plus some. And yet here we were, cleaning for them, making their lives easier.

Ahead of me, my mom slowed and turned into the beginning of a driveway. I stopped behind her at a security gate like the one Zara had, and she spoke into a speaker box before the wrought iron slid open, revealing a winding driveway lined by sycamore trees. Even in the pale light, I could make out the leaves' faded hues of orange, yellow, and red.

At the end of the drive was the biggest mansion of all. A massive fountain spurted water in front of what had to be at least twenty thousand square feet of gleaming windows and perfectly landscaped accents.

Mom had warned me the day before that this house belonged to an Emerson Academy family. I just hoped whoever owned it didn't have a student in my class. That they had kids in elementary school and I'd never have to face them at the Academy. I already caught enough grief for being on scholarship. I didn't need any more for what Mom and I had to do to get by.

Mom circumvented the driveway that circled toward the front entrance and drove toward a separate garage. The one for servants. We'd cleaned enough rich peoples' homes to know we weren't allowed to mar their perfect image with our old clunkers that might leak oil on their pristine cement.

She got out of her car and went to the trunk for our supplies while I swallowed the last sugary drops of my mocha. I'd need all the caffeine I could get my hands on today. Plus, I had to steel myself before going inside. If this was what the outside of the house looked like, I hated to think of what chandeliers lay inside that could pay my college tuition or crystal serving bowls that could float us for months.

I shoved my empty cup in the cupholder and got out to help Mom. She passed me the handle to the cart we used to bring cleaning supplies from place to place. I began pulling it toward the open garage door, but she put her hand on my forearm. "Jordan, wait."

I turned and looked at her, confused. We needed to get as much work done as possible before I had to get ready for school. "What's up?"

She waited until my full attention was on her eyes, completely serious. "This is a big job, and it could mean finally paying off Juana's medical bills." She gently touched the charm at the end of her silver necklace, just like she always did when she talked about Juana. "I need this to work."

My chest clenched as I nodded, too afraid to even hope to get out from under the crushing medical debt. "I'll do my best, I promise."

Her lips tugged down. "There's more."

Confused, I set the handle of the cart back and gave her my full attention. "What's going on, amá?"

"The client—he has a son. Your age."

My stomach clenched. A son? At least that cut Merritt Alexander and her crew of mean girls out of the mix, but that didn't leave a lot of options... "Who is it?" *Please don't be Kai Rush. Please don't be Kai Rush.* I couldn't go much lower than cleaning for an actual billionaire.

"It doesn't matter who it is." Her hands ran over my shoulders. "Let's just make sure we do this right."

She meant the gesture to be comforting, but now I was just nervous. "What's going on?"

She held the charm of her necklace, looking at our pile of cleaning supplies. "Things have been tight since I started my business, and if this doesn't work, I don't know what we'll do."

Now I was less worried about the mystery boy and more concerned for our home. Maybe it wasn't the right time to start a business. "Can't you go back to work at Lucinda's? She always took care of us."

"She made sure we didn't starve, but I wanted more for us than just getting by." She shook her head, frowning. "When I went on my own, she told me to never come back."

I gasped. The woman who'd been like a second grandmother for my entire life had cast my mom off like that? Cast me off? "Why would she do that?"

"She's a proud woman," Mom said. "She feels like she gave us everything. She doesn't understand why I'd want more for myself. For us."

I opened my mouth to argue, but Mom simply shook her head. "We can't risk this job. Please, whatever you do, do not date this boy."

That's what this was about? I scoffed. "Amá, you know I'd never date an Emerson rich kid." And a boy who probably hung out with models and the social elite would never consider dating a poor, plus-sized girl like me.

With that, I picked up the handle and started walking toward the house. Me falling for the boy inside the mansion was the last thing my mom needed to worry about. Public humiliation? Definitely. A secret romance? That was a waste of her mental energy. We had a job to do.

TWO

A BUTLER LET US INSIDE. A butler. Wearing a suit. Who apparently worked at four in the morning.

"Welcome, Ms. Junco," he said to my mom. "Miss Junco," he said to me.

She smiled at him, but all I could do was stare at the house's entryway. An abstract art chandelier hung from a ceiling so tall it might as well have been the sky. Art lined the walls as well, like someone had meant to place the installation in a gallery and whoever owned this house decided it belonged here instead.

I didn't have time to gawk, though. The butler —Robert, he called himself—was leading us through the mansion, telling Mom the plan of attack. We were to start with the kitchen and dining quarters today, the living areas tomorrow, and so on until the entire home was cleaned in the span of a week. Cleaning this place would take us that long, and I hoped Mom was prepared for that amount of work on top of the other small jobs she'd acquired for us.

But if this guy paid like he should (well and in cash, unlike the trades Mom made with other clients), she was right. Our bills would be covered and then some.

"This is Mr. Rush's office," Robert said, pointing at a room with glass French doors. Inside, a tall, thin man with a thick head of graying hair worked in front of five computer monitors, lines of code pouring down each screen. "However, if you have questions, they should be directed at me. He likes not to be disturbed."

I barely caught what Robert said though, because my mind was fumbling over one word: Rush.

This was the Rush mansion?

As in the popular gaming app, *Rush+*?

As in our school's resident billionaire, *Kai Rush*, lived here?

A glance into the expansive living room

confirmed the truth. Over the fireplace with floor-to-thirty-foot-celling built-ins was a photo of Kai and the man I'd seen in the office.

The blood drained from my face. This was the client Mom had landed?

How?

And more importantly, *why?*

This had to be a joke. A prank. Something that would land us on a reality TV show looking like fools.

Suddenly, the creak of our cleaning cart's wheels seemed so loud on the marble floors, like they were a giant glaring buzzer letting me know I did *not* belong here.

Robert led us into a kitchen even larger than the one at school, with more ovens than two people could ever use and the kind of cabinetry so fancy it masked the refrigerator. There were no magnets holding up photos and old receipts here. No room for a mess. Honestly, this room already looked spotless.

"The chef, Mr. Wallace, will arrive at six to begin breakfast," Robert said, folding his hands in front of him. "If you need anything, I will be in my office, which is down the hallway to the right."

There was another office for the butler?

But then again, what else would there be? They could have had an entire football stadium inside and a helicopter pad on the roof for all I knew.

Mom was acting like none of this bothered her. Like she wasn't repulsed by all of the waste happening in this "house" where only two people lived, wait staff not included. In my opinion, billionaires might as well have been villains. They were holding on to exorbitant wealth that could have made such a difference in the world—kept children from starving, built houses for widowed mothers, supported any number of meaningful causes, but they sank it into mansions like this instead. Just thinking about it made my blood boil. I'd rather work fifty jobs like Seaton Bakery, trading for food, than spend another second making life even easier for billionaires like the Rushes.

Mom was already going through the cart, gathering buckets and the cleaning solution for the countertops. How was she not completely appalled?

Glancing over my shoulder to be sure Robert had already left, I whispered, "We're not seriously doing this, are we?"

"Did you not hear a word I said this morning?" She walked to the sink and flipped on the hot water.

Lowering her voice, she added, "We should be thankful to have this job. *I* am."

"Which means I'm the only one not being grateful to shine marble floors."

She frowned at me over the top of the cart. "I didn't raise you to be like that."

I sighed. "You're right." I should be grateful. Having Juana's bills paid off might mean we could get into a different apartment, that my mom could take a weekend off just to relax here and there. Still, I resented the fact that the Rushes would be the ones to help us do it. Mere pennies to them were lifelines to us.

I took the dust mop from the cart and began on the opposite side of the kitchen so I'd stay out of Mom's way. She was the hardest worker I'd seen and could move so quickly it was almost like magic.

We worked in silence for the next couple of hours until the chef came in and introduced himself. A drool-worthy personal trainer eventually passed through the kitchen as well.

After he walked out, Mom leaned against her mop handle and whispered conspiratorially, "Kai might be off limits, but him? Hubba hubba."

I winked at her. "He can train me any time."

She laughed and continued working, but my

heart twitched painfully as I realized that was the first time I'd been attracted to anyone since Martín. My fingers itched to reach into my pocket and dial his now-deleted number for the millionth time, even though he'd moved on.

I hated myself for wanting to get back together with him, even if he'd found another girl so quickly after breaking up with me. The scary thought crept into my mind that he'd already found her before ending things, and I beat it back. I so couldn't go there.

"Look at the time," Mom said. "You better get changed."

I glanced at the clock over the stove, still not trusting myself with my phone. I had about half an hour to get into my uniform and make myself look like I hadn't just finished a housekeeping shift.

I had better hurry. "I'll head out to the car."

She shook her head and grabbed my drawstring bag from the cart. "You can use one of the bathrooms."

I lifted my eyebrows. "You're sure?"

She gave me a soft smile and whispered, "They have fifteen. I'm sure one's open."

Was she exaggerating? I definitely couldn't tell from the size of this house.

Mr. Wallace, the cook, pointed his spatula over his shoulder, "The one down the hall is for our use. Go ahead."

Our use. The *help's* use. I didn't know how my distaste could grow even more, but it did. Mr. Rush kept us in servants' quarters and had us watched by his butler. He was making sure we knew where we belonged: on our knees, scrubbing, below the king he thought he was.

F-U-know-what that.

I walked down the hall like I was going to the designated bathroom, but then went up a set of stairs. This floor seemed less imposing than the ground level, even though it had the same abstract art pieces lining the walls. I carefully opened a couple of doors until I found a bathroom that looked like it was for guests.

My first thought was that the last cleaning service hadn't done a great job. The toilet paper wasn't creased into corners like my mom always did, and the towels were lazily folded. Pride swelled in my chest. My mom and I may have been poor, but we did honest work for honest pay. And we did it well.

I took off my JJ Cleaning polo and khaki pants, then pulled on my pleated uniform skirt. Even with the back unzipped, I had to tug it over my wide hips before I could zip it up and have it fit around my narrower waist. Curvy girl problems.

I sat on the closed toilet lid and bunched up my pantyhose before pulling them over my feet. That was the nice thing about expensive hose—I'd worn these the entire school year, and so far, no runs. I kept my fingers crossed that they would last through my senior year.

I switched out of my sports bra that was comfortable to work in and into a push-up bra before going to my makeup bag. Mom always said half the battle is showing up as the person you want to be. I wanted to be polished, presentable—the professional doctor I hoped to be someday.

A little mascara and matte lipstick worked wonders with the clear complexion Mom had passed on to me, but this curly hair was a challenge. I was busy creating a half French braid to hold it away from my face when the door opened.

Standing in front of me was none other than Kai Rush, an amused smirk growing on his face.

My hands flew to my chest as my braid unraveled, and I stepped back, stammering, "I—I—"

I what? I didn't know what to say, so I stayed silent.

"I wasn't expecting to find you here," he said.

He might have seemed amused, but the power of his presence caught me off guard. I'd never seen Kai this close before, but now he had me pierced under his casual intensity. And he was tall, taller than I'd thought him to be simply passing him in the hallways or sitting across the cafeteria.

He raised dark, arched eyebrows, and I realized he was waiting for a response.

Still covering my more-than ample chest as best I could, I nodded toward my JJ Cleaning polo with the logo facing up. "My mom and I are your new cleaning crew."

His dark, angled eyes scanned my half-naked body, making me feel fully exposed, before turning to the mirror and examining himself. "Welcome aboard."

He feathered his fingers through his smooth hair and then plucked at an invisible piece of lint on his uniform. His attire had clearly been custom-tailored, the way the suit jacket framed his trim shoulders. Not the way mine hung loose because I had to buy a size up so it would fit my bust.

Kai adjusted his tie and then smirked at me. "See you at school, Jordan."

THREE

THE DOOR CLICKED SHUT behind him, only half as loud as my anxiously pounding heart. Kai Rush had seen me in my bra. And not the sports bra. No, this was the lavish one that pushed up the girls with a tiny pink bow in between my cleavage.

I covered my face with my hands. Not only was I his maid, I was also an embarrassment. If Mom found out I'd been in a client's bathroom, exposed, she would be so disappointed.

Kai hadn't had the decency to turn around and walk away, but I at least hoped he would keep the encounter to himself.

I tried to still my fretful heart as I finished dressing, gathered up my things, and went back downstairs. When I made it back to the kitchen, Mom was half inside the oven, scrubbing.

"Amá," I said quietly, careful not to startle her. I'd bumped my head more than a few times the same way.

She disengaged herself from the oven and smiled at me. "You look nice."

I barely managed a twitch of my lips. "Thanks. So, I'm heading out. Need anything else?"

Shaking her head, she said, "No, I'm fine. I have another job after this. Should be home around eight. Will you make supper?"

I nodded. It was the least I could do for how hard she worked for us.

She kissed my cheek, and then I walked back out the front door. The butler somehow appeared, as if he'd been watching me the entire time. Well, where was he when Kai was walking in and seeing me in my bra? Huh?

As I left the front entry, I caught sight of Kai's Tesla pulling through the gates. One day, just out of curiosity, I'd looked it up. The black car driving away from me right now cost upwards of two hundred thousand dollars. That fact made me detest the boy who drove it even more.

And Mom was worried about me falling in love?

Not a chance. He and his dad stood for everything I despised. They practically bathed in hundred-dollar bills while Mom and I wasted away on whatever leftovers they were tossing us for the job.

Still, my cheeks were warm as I walked to my car and pulled out of the multi-million-dollar drive-way. I couldn't get Kai's dark eyes and his self-satis-fied smirk out of my mind. Had he known I was in the bathroom? It wasn't like he'd stopped to use the toilet or blow his nose or anything. He had simply straightened his already straight tie and left like it was business as usual.

Was he always so strange? So self-assured? And how did he know my name? I'd hardly spoken a word to him since I started at Emerson Academy this fall. Add that to the fact that everyone called me a 'ship (short for scholarship student), it was a wonder he remembered my name at all.

When I got to school, I still hadn't solved the mystery of the morning's encounter. I parked in my designated spot and turned off my car, the engine squealing and sputtering to a halt.

I kept my eyes down as I grabbed my backpack and stepped out of the car.

"Nice ride, 'ship," a guy called.

I ignored him and walked inside to my locker.

Attention only fueled antagonists, and I had no intention of giving them extra material.

Farther down the hall, I saw my friends congregated around Ginger's locker.

They were clearly mid-conversation, but Rory smiled at me as I approached them. "I was just saying how thankful I am for you guys!" She pulled me in a one-armed hug. "Last night was so sweet!"

I grinned. "No problem." I loved making the people I cared about happy, and setting up a surprise make-up "homecoming dance" for her and her boyfriend definitely fell under that category. "How'd it go with Beckett's dad?"

I knew things had been a little awkward for them since the homecoming game when he found out, along with the rest of the school, that Rory had bet Merritt she could get Beckett to fall in love with her.

"It was fine," Rory said. "A little awkward, but things eased up, I think."

"Good," I replied, then lowered my voice. "You guys won't believe this."

They leaned in, curious. I never had juicy gossip.

I took a deep breath. "My mom's new cleaning client is Kai Rush's family."

Zara rolled her eyes. "My condolences."

"Right?" Ginger said, shaking her head. "He's such a snob. He hardly speaks to anyone."

Callie frowned, but left it at that. I knew she didn't like trash-talking, but some people deserved it.

"And you had to help with the job?" Rory asked with a pout.

"Yep," I answered. "And get this. My mom told me not to date him."

Ginger snorted. "As if."

"Right?" I said.

Ginger shut her locker. "Doesn't she know you don't date high school guys?"

I shook my head. "She would be more than happy if I didn't date again after what happened with Martín." I glanced around the hallway at all the guys who were *not* interested in dating a plus-sized 'ship like me. "She might just get her wish."

Callie rubbed my arm. "You'll find someone who treats you right."

My heart swelled at the genuine way she spoke the words. Like she really believed them. I was starting to lose hope myself.

The bell rang, signaling the end of our conversation. Ginger and I usually walked together to videography class, but I had to get my books.

"Go ahead," I told her. "I'll catch up."

She waved and started down the hall, her red curls bouncing. I turned the opposite way, stopping at locker 334. After dialing my combination, I caught sight of something unusual out of the corner of my eye.

I did a double-take and saw Kai walking toward me, shaggy black hair falling across his forehead.

Instinctively, I folded my arms across my chest, like I could retroactively cover up from being exposed this morning. "Yes?"

He lifted a folded piece of paper. "You forgot something at my house this morning."

"What's that?" I asked.

With a crooked smile, he said, "My number." He handed me the paper and took a few steps backward then turned and disappeared in the sea of students.

My mouth gaped open, still in disbelief. I opened the paper to see if I'd had a momentary lapse in my grasp of reality, but no such luck.

Inside the note, there was a phone number and two words: Call me.

FOUR

I MET the girls at our usual table in the AV storage room and slapped the paper on the table.

Zara picked it up and eyed it. "Whose number is this?"

I glanced at the note, hardly believing what I was about to say. "Kai's."

A collective gasp rippled through my friends.

"No way!" Ginger cried, taking the paper and looking at it up close like someone might examine a counterfeit bill. "When did he give you this?"

"On my way to first period." I told them how he'd given it to me, and Zara rolled her eyes.

"What a line," she said.

"I know." I scoffed. "It's ridiculous. Why would he want me to call him anyway?"

All four of them stared at me.

"Um," Rory said, "should I take this one?"

The others nodded.

She cleared her throat and looked me straight in the eyes. "Because you're hot?"

I snorted. "He *did* see me half naked this morning."

The ruckus that ensued was enough to make Mr. Davis, the AV teacher, turn his head toward us. I made a mental note to talk a little more quietly. We all knew his noise-cancelling headphones weren't as soundproof as we'd once assumed.

I whispered the humiliating story to them, covering my face the entire time. The only reason I believed it was real was because it happened to me. It was so embarrassing, and I had an uncanny knack for personal mortification.

Zara grinned, waggling her eyebrows. "Looks like he wants more than the preview."

Ginger nodded. "But there's no way you're calling him, right?"

"Nope," I said. "I would need all my fingers and toes to count the reasons that would be a terrible idea."

"Good," Rory said. "I had him as a partner for our final project in computer class last year. He did the whole assignment before I got the chance to even talk to him about it! He thinks he knows everything because he helped his dad code *Rush+*."

So not only was he rich, he was chauvinistic. Of course. "Not exactly what I'm looking for in a boyfriend."

Callie smiled at me as I sat down. "You can do better," she said. "Imagine all the guys you'll meet in college."

I gave her a grateful smile. "Thanks. Now, can we talk about something else so I can stop thinking about Kai Rush?"

Zara grinned. "Why didn't you ask sooner?"

For the rest of the day, I kept myself busy with classes, Kai Rush long forgotten. I was at Emerson Academy on scholarship, but Headmaster Bradford made it clear in the initial meeting with my mom that this wasn't a handout. I'd be expected to keep my grades up and behave well if I wanted to stay at the Academy. There had been plenty of times I wanted to call people out on their crap, like Merritt when she said plus-size girls couldn't date hot guys, but I had to keep my mouth shut. My future meant more to me than putting people in their place.

When I got home that afternoon, I took out my homework, making sure it was done before I worried about anything else. I had to stay focused so I could help Mom with the business and achieve the way I needed to at school. Once I graduated, I could relax. Now was not that time.

With my homework completed, I set to work in the kitchen. Cooking didn't come as naturally for me as it did for Mom, but I tried. She deserved a good meal at the end of the day, especially with how hard she worked.

I started with the beans that had been soaking and threw them into a pan, along with a few scoops from the massive bag of rice Mom had snagged on a discount. Once I had the rice boiling, I began chopping a sausage into chunks, along with an onion and tomato. All of the main ingredients, plus some seasonings—cilantro, saffron, garlic, salt and pepper.

Soon, our entire apartment smelled of the dish, and I breathed it in deeply. So much better than the sandwiches I packed for lunch every day at school.

I got out an old butter tub and spooned some of the meal into it. Using masking tape and a Sharpie, I wrote what I'd made and the date on top. Bringing my keys with me, I walked out of our apartment and down the dimly lit hallway with fraying carpet and black scuffs all over the lime-green walls.

At the end of the path, I went down the bowing stairs and then headed to apartment 112. The sound of a blaring television came from underneath the door. I rapped on the door as loud as I could because I knew the Gutiérrezes were hard of hearing.

The television muted, and suddenly, the quiet practically echoed off the walls. Glancing side to side, I waited several long moments for them to reach the door.

It swung open, and Mrs. Gutiérrez smiled at me through thick glasses. "*Hola, mi dulce!*"

She'd been calling me her "sweet" since Mom and I had moved in ten years ago. I still remembered sitting amidst what few boxes we owned at that time when Mrs. Gutierrez walked in with a plate full of *polvorones de canela*. Usually we only had the cinnamon cookies at weddings or holidays, but when Mom asked her what the special occasion was, she said, "*Una familia nueva siempre es ocasión para celebrar.*" A new family is always reason to celebrate.

From that day on, they had brought us under their wing, and we cared for each other like family.

Aside from Mom's parents in Mexico, they were the only grandparents I knew.

I grinned at Mrs. Gutiérrez and held out the dish. *"Traigo frijoles y arroz para ustedes."*

Her smile grew wider, showing her straight, white dentures. *"Muchas gracias. Pasale."*

She always told me to come inside, but ever since becoming a student at the Academy, my free time was less and less. Plus, my mom would be coming home soon, and I needed to get my homework done. *"Lo siento. Tengo que hacer los deberes y hablar con mi mama. Pero espero que disfruten la comida."*

With a smile, she nodded. *"Por su puesto."* She held up the butter tub. Of course they would enjoy the food, she told me. *"Gracias."*

The door shut, and I heard two heavy locks slide into place, as well as a security chain. We had to be careful around here—especially those of us who couldn't defend ourselves.

As I walked back to the apartment, I glanced at the clock. It was almost eight. Mom would be home in a few minutes.

After unlocking my own door, I dished two bowls, got out a bag of tortilla chips, and sat at the counter to eat. Usually supper was the time Mom and I debriefed each other on our day and caught up. Without her here to distract me, my mind drifted to dangerous topics. Like Martín and the other man who had left me: my dad. I wondered what my father was doing, where he was. He'd been gone so long, my memories of him were fuzzy. All except one.

One night when I was about six years old, I heard my bedroom door crack open. At that time, I had a canopy over my bed, and I could see the shape of my dad's body through the sheer fabric.

"Daddy?" I'd asked in a confused, groggy voice.

"Hi, honey," he'd said softly, pushing the curtain aside and sitting on the edge of my bed. His large hand had rubbed my forehead and tucked messy curls out of the way.

I'd blinked up at him, tired. "What's going on?"

Wordlessly, he'd kissed my forehead, holding his lips there and scratching my skin with his mustache for a good thirty seconds.

I remembered being confused. Why was Daddy in my room? Why was he kissing me so long when our bedtime kisses only lasted a second? Then, he'd stood up abruptly and left me alone.

I'd called for him, but he didn't come back. No matter how much I cried, he never came back.

The door opened, and I jerked upright, being

forced out of my memory despite distinctly feeling his scratchy kiss. Mom came in looking exhausted and dropped her purse on the counter. Still, she put on a smile and came to kiss me on the forehead, replacing the bad memory with a good one. "How was your day, sweetie?"

You mean besides my humiliation this morning and the confusing advance from a billionaire? "It was fine."

After washing her hands at the sink, she poured herself a glass of water and sat beside me, taking a bite of her meal. She closed her eyes and moaned. "Perfect, *mija*."

"Thanks," I said, even though we both knew the dish didn't even hold a candle to her cooking. *Mi abuela* had taught Mom lessons in cooking and flavor I couldn't grasp no matter how hard I tried.

"How was school?" she asked.

"Uneventful, except..." I debated whether or not to tell her about Kai. We usually talked about everything, but...

"What?" she asked.

I winced. "Kai Rush gave me his number."

She nearly choked on her water, sending half a gulp back into the plastic Waldo's Diner cup. "He did what?"

"Relax," I said. "I didn't call him."

"You better not," she snapped.

I bristled against her tone. She never talked to me like this. It was like she didn't trust me at all. "Amá, I won't."

"Good," she said. "I want to stop living like this." She gestured at our apartment, at the living room where she slept on a fold-out couch because she insisted I take the lone bedroom. "I want furniture I don't have to cover with blankets and shoes that don't have holes. I want to finally take you to Walden Island like you've always wanted. It's half an hour away by ferry, and we've never had the money to go."

"We will have all of those things and more," I argued. "What do you think I've been working so hard at school for?"

"Not when you graduate college," she said. "You shouldn't have the weight of me on your shoulders for eight years of med school."

"But I already do!" I cried. "I have to help work all the time. I'm constantly reminded how much you're sacrificing so I can go to Emerson. I should just be in a public school—"

"Don't you start with me, *mija*," she snapped, her eyes blazing. "You are going to that school, and you are having the opportunities I didn't have. The opportunities you *deserve*. And you will *not* blow it on some boy."

"I won't!" I cried. "Why won't you believe me?"

"I told you Martín was no good, and you didn't listen!"

Her words twisted the knife already in my heart. I didn't want to fight. I didn't want to think. I picked up my bowl and backpack and went back to the room without another word.

Once inside, I grabbed the paper with Kai's phone number out of my backpack and ripped it to shreds.

FIVE

TENSION BLANKETED our apartment the next morning as we got ready for work. I finished showering, turned off the handle, and reached for a towel on the towel bar. It was just a little too far away, and Mom slid it over so I could get it.

"Thanks," I muttered.

"Mm," was all she said in response.

She kept her gaze in the mirror as I left the bathroom and didn't exchange two words with me as we grabbed breakfast from Seaton Bakery, but when we got to the Rushes' mansion and began unloading cleaning supplies, she said, "Remember to keep it professional in there."

I had half a mind to tell her what happened yesterday and let her know just how unprofessional

I'd already been. The other, smarter half of my mind forced me to nod.

I grabbed the handle and began pulling the cart, but Mom stopped it. "*Mija*, I know you probably think I'm being hard on you, but I just want what's best for you."

The funny thing was, so did I. I let out a sigh. "I know, Mom."

She picked up a five-gallon bucket and put her arm around me as we started toward the house, the cart's wheels rattling loudly behind us in the quiet morning air.

The air outside of Kai's house smelled fresh, not like the manufacturing smoke that permeated Seaton. Robert held the entryway door open for us, and I breathed in the freshness one last time before stepping inside.

"Today's the living areas," Robert reminded us.

That was easy because we could start on the living room right off the foyer. Just a few feet away, I could see Mr. Rush working in his office, not giving us a second thought.

"Why don't you start with the dust mop again?" Mom asked, drawing my attention away from the throne room.

I took it from her, put in my earbuds, and got to

work. Around five, we had the entire room cleaned, and I paused my music to see where Mom wanted us to go next.

"Apparently, there's another living space upstairs," she said.

With a nod, I loaded the cart and walked behind her to the main staircase off the living room. She lifted one end, and I grabbed the other, going behind her up the steps.

At the top, she let out a little groan with her hand on her lower back and stretched.

My eyebrows creased. "Have you been doing the stretches I found for you?"

She shook her head and gave me a tight-lipped smile. "I'll get to them tonight. But ibuprofen works just fine for now."

Grabbing the cart handle, she continued down the spacious hallway, leaving me and my concerned look behind. With a sigh, I followed behind her, looking around. This area was different from where I'd been the day before.

I let my gaze wander until we passed a glass-walled home gym that looked bigger than the one at school. Kai and his dad were lifting weights inside the room with the same personal trainer I'd seen from the day before.

I watched through the long, windowed walls as Kai securely held dumbbells and lifted them in a mesmerizing pattern. Under his school uniform, I'd always thought of him as just thin. Lanky even. But dressed in his shorts and nothing else, I could see Kai's strong muscles rippling with each move.

As if sensing me, he glanced in my direction, his gaze colliding with my own.

I froze, caught in his stare until he turned his head, said something to the trainer, and released me.

I quickly shifted my gaze down, catching up with Mom. My heart still beat quickly as I followed her. How many times could I embarrass myself in front of Kai Rush and still show my face?

"This is it," Mom said, opening a door.

As I followed her inside, my jaw fell open. The "living area" up here was more like a full-blown, in-home theater three times the size of our apartment. Stepping into this colossal waste of money did nothing for my distaste of Kai and his father.

I grabbed a rag and began wiping down the leather chairs, growing angrier by the second. Did they think they were too good to grab a ticket and go to La La Pictures like everyone else? I bet the amount it cost to build this room could have knocked out Juana's medical bills in one fell swoop. Half a fell swoop.

"Whoa, whoa," Mom said. "What did that chair do to you?"

I eased up on the chair and finished wiping down the leather. "Sorry." The word barely passed my clogged throat, and I swallowed, fighting the heat building in my eyes.

"Jordan..." She came to me, pausing for the first time since we'd been working on this job. It was too big for just the two of us, but she couldn't afford help yet. "Honey, are you okay?"

I kept my eyes closed as I nodded, gathering myself. How could I tell her I was mad at the Rushes for living such an exorbitant lifestyle without making her feel worse about ours?

She sat on an unwiped leather chair and tugged me down beside her. "You've been working hard. Don't you think I haven't noticed that."

"I'm happy to help," I said. And it was true. I may not have been thrilled about the early mornings or her choice in clients, but I owed Mom for all she did for me.

Her arms encircled me, and she squeezed just like she used to when I was a little girl. I leaned into her warmth.

"I'm sorry for what I said about you dating yesterday," she admitted, head down. "Lord knows I have no room to talk. Look at your father."

"We all make mistakes." I knew that already. Martín had been a mistake, especially judging by the happy photos of him and his new girlfriend he kept posting online. Still, that didn't make the breakup any easier to bear.

She squeezed me tighter before releasing me. "We'll get through this," she said, rubbing my back. "A few more months of this, and I should be able to hire someone else."

A few months? I could do that. Especially with the holiday breaks coming up that would give me opportunities for midday naps.

We worked our way through the media room, and I began helping Mom gather the rags and cleaning supplies so we could move on.

"Go ahead, Jordan," she said. "I can get this."

I nodded and left the room. Walking through the Rushes' home by myself felt like being on the moon without a spacesuit. It was hard to breathe in the air Mr. Wallace had told me ran through a million-dollar filtration system. Even though it probably smelled like the rest of the air in the world, it seemed too clean to me. Too perfect. And I wanted no part of it.

My chest ached by the time I made it to the kitchen and grabbed my drawstring bag from the cart.

This time, I walked to the servants' bathroom, which was still a million times nicer than the one in our apartment. I made sure to quickly change clothes, leaving little time for naked interruptions. As I got out my makeup, I heard male voices above me.

Glancing toward the ceiling, I saw a well-camouflaged ceiling vent. Who would be upstairs other than Kai and his father?

The voices sounded clearer now, almost like they were right next to me.

"Dad, I told you I don't want to apply to MIT."

"I still don't understand why. Until I can make sense of why a bright, talented young man such as yourself wouldn't want to attend a top-tier school, I expect you to submit an application or hire someone to do so."

They fell silent for a moment, and Kai said, "Yes sir."

"Be sure to list that you're a violinist and to mention Rush+ on your essay."

"I will," Kai said.

"Where else have you applied?"

"Berkeley, Cal State—"

"State schools?" his dad asked. "Why would you bother?"

"I want more than a degree, Dad, I want—"

"To spend time goofing off and getting drunk with a bunch of college kids set on not living up to their potential? Because that's what you'll get there."

My lips pressed together tightly. I had half a mind to get a broom and pound on the ceiling above me like someone would have done in the apartments. Not only was Mr. Rush rude, he was *wrong*. Students at state schools often out-performed private school students, and I was pretty sure they had just as much access to beer as anyone at a public college.

"Fine," Kai said quietly. "I'll apply to Stanford."

"And Harvard, and Yale, and MIT."

The voices stopped, and I realized I'd been listening in instead of getting ready. I hurried to finish my makeup and walked as fast as I could back to the kitchen. Mom saw me and said, "Everything okay?"

"Yeah, great." Other than learning we were

working for a complete elitist. But then again, I could have guessed that. I tugged the straps of my bag over my shoulders.

"Jordan?" a low, clear voice said from behind me. I'd only heard it once, but I immediately recognized it as Kai.

I spun to see him and his father, both dressed for the day.

I wished I had another word to describe Kai's eyes other than dark, but they were. So dark. They blocked anything I might have been able to read in them as they scanned my body—from my JJ Cleaning polo to the grungy white sneakers Mom got me as a gift when she decided to start her own maid service. (They'd been pristine then.) I didn't see a hint of disdain most kids from our school would have had, though. Maybe curiosity?

But then I realized I was staring at them, just as he was staring at me, and I cleared my throat. "Hi, Mr. Rush, Kai."

Mr. Rush extended his hand, and I shook it with my own, even though mine was wrinkled from working with a wet rag all morning.

If he noticed, he didn't let on. "You and your mom have been doing great work for us."

Every part of me wanted to spout off about not

living up to our potential, but I had to stay quiet for Mom.

Kai tilted his head, not quite nodding, as he studied me further. I felt just as naked as I had been yesterday morning, even fully clothed. I doubted adding a winter coat to my ensemble would make me feel any different.

My mom thanked him and nudged me with her arm around me as if to *say something*.

"Thank you," I said. "My mom is the hardest worker I know. Always working to reach her full potential."

His smile seemed to wane as he nodded. "I can see that." He picked up two stainless-steel travel mugs filled with coffee made from the thousand-dollar espresso machine and turned to his son. "We better get going."

Kai nodded and took his cup. "See you at school, Jordan."

I was so stunned at the smooth way my name rolled off his lips that I barely managed a nod. I watched as they left the kitchen. Kai stood straight, tall, and I pictured his muscles working underneath the cover of his school uniform.

I tried to ignore how or why the image came to mind as I gave my mom a hug goodbye.

SIX

I WANTED to spend time with my friends after school, but we all had mid-terms to study for. Emerson Academy was designed to prepare us for the most rigorous colleges, and that meant cumulative exams on top of extracurriculars. I was barely keeping up with our school's chapter of FMP—Future Medical Professionals. This quarter alone, we were supposed to have a blood drive, along with the major fall fundraiser to help raise money for a local health-related charity. As the vice president, I had a lot to do.

But now wasn't the time to worry about that. When I reached our apartment, I got out my trig notes and textbook and started there, working through the practice problems at the end of the chapters we'd covered so far. Trig was simple in comparison to my other classes, like psychology. Anyone could remember an equation and plug in the numbers. Understanding why people did the things they did? That was an entirely different story.

My phone chimed with a new text message, and I reached to check it.

Mom: Picked up an extra job. Working late tonight. Don't wait up.

I gave my phone a worried look my mom would never see. Cleaning was hard work on your body. For her sake, I hoped this Rush job was as big as she said it was. She needed to hire help before her back kept her from continuing at this breakneck pace.

Jordan: Sure. Leftovers are in the fridge. Ly
Mom: Ly

In an attempt to drown my worries, I dove into my studies headfirst. School was always the place I could lose myself when the feelings got too big. It was my exit strategy and my escape.

That was until my phone rang from a number I couldn't ignore. Although the name wasn't attached to it anymore, I'd recognize those digits for the rest of my life. A memory of my old contact photo of us flashed through my mind. I had been smiling, my teeth flashing exactly how happy I was. He never smiled with his full mouth, but his eyes were bright as they stared back at me.

I blinked to clear the image, realizing my phone was still going off. This was the first time he'd called since the breakup... Did I answer?

My head said no, but my heart had other plans. It guided my fingers to accept the call and hold the phone to my ear.

"Hello?"

"*Mi cielo.*" His voice was a balm and an acid, soothing and stinging my heart in ways I didn't understand. All the healing I'd managed in the past two weeks was ripped away in that one greeting. In the way he called me his world.

The patchwork wall I'd put in place over my heart kept me from falling completely. "Why are you calling, Martín?"

"I miss you, baby." Now I noticed something I hadn't in his greeting: his words were slurred.

"Are you drinking?" I asked. I'd been to a few parties with him and his college friends before, and I never liked the way he got when he'd had more than one drink. He became handsy. Sloppy. I held on to those parts I didn't like about him and steeled myself against the words that were sure to come next.

"Just had a few," he slurred. "I miss you."

"Where's your new girlfriend?" I demanded.

"We're done. I want *you*, *mi cielo*."

The words were exactly what I'd hoped to hear two weeks ago when he'd first broken up with me, but now they hurt. They made me angry. "Don't you '*mi cielo*' me," I said. "I want no part in your world." And then I hung up and did what I hadn't been brave enough to do before: I blocked his number.

The last words I'd spoken to him weren't wholly true. I did want a part in his world. I missed him. But I had to make them true so this deep, persistent ache in my chest would ease.

Emotionally spent, I leaned over the counter and pressed the heels of my hands into my eyes. I didn't want to cry any more tears over him than I already had.

A knock sounded on the door, giving me just the shock I needed. I took a deep breath and checked through the peephole. A man in a brown delivery uniform stood with a small package.

I opened the door, and he said, "Delivery for Jordan Junco." He said it in the whitest way possible, like Junk-O.

"It's Hoon-co," I said reflexively.

"Sure." He extended the signing pad, and I rolled my eyes. Of course he wouldn't correct himself.

Without another word, I signed and took the package. After shutting and locking the door, I examined every inch of the box. There wasn't a return address on it, and I had no idea who would have sent me something. I certainly hadn't ordered anything online. Maybe an item for one of my classes or FMP had been delivered?

I took my keys off the counter and began ripping through the packing tape. But not before something began to ring inside the box.

"What?" I muttered.

Hurriedly, I ripped the rest of the paper off and took out the latest version of the iPhone with a flawless screen. It made my practically obsolete version with fractures across the screen look that much shabbier.

The flashing number seemed familiar, but I couldn't place who it was. I swiped my thumb to answer and held it to my ear, waiting.

"Hello?" The smooth voice was impossible to mistake.

"Kai? Why are you calling me?"

His words poured over the speaker, soft as

butterfly's wings and as enticing as an adventure. "If you wouldn't call me, I figured I'd call you."

I folded my free arm across my chest. "Usually, if someone doesn't initiate a call, the other person takes a hint."

"I'm not a usual kind of person."

I let out a snort. "I'll say."

The smile in his voice was impossible to miss. "Neither are you."

I knew that already. "Okay, I'll play along," I said. "What's it going to take for you to give up?"

This time, his tone was playful. "Me, give up?"

"Everyone has a price." I winced, thinking what that figure might be for an actual billionaire.

"Go on a date with me."

"I think you'll have to find another girl." I hung up and put the phone back in the box.

Just like I'd assumed, what Kai wanted would cost me too much.

SEVEN

I WAS BURSTING to talk about what had happened the night before, but if Mom knew Kai had sent me an iPhone and asked me out, she would have lost it. Heck, we got in an argument just because he gave me his number. It was easier this way, especially since nothing was going to happen. So, I kept it to myself as we got ready for the morning. She used makeup to cover the dark circles under her eyes from staying out and working the night before. It seemed like we both had parts of ourselves we wanted to hide.

We took our separate vehicles to the bakery, and this time Mom wrote *You are worthy of everything good* on my cup. As I turned it in my hand, examining her neat cursive, my chest tightened. Why did I have such a visceral reaction to that message?

I couldn't find an answer even as we drove to the Rushes' and brought our cleaning supplies inside. We worked our way through their guest rooms, dusting and mopping already spotless floors.

It struck me that it had clearly been some time since anyone stayed in these rooms. I knew why none of Mom's family from Mexico visited us—we lived in a one-bedroom and they had a country to cross—but why were Kai and his father so isolated behind their layer of help? And where was his mom? Why didn't his dad date if she wasn't in the picture? My mom didn't want to become reliant on a man after what Dad had done to us, but that wasn't an excuse for Kai's father, who had all the resources in the world.

The bigger mystery, though, was why had Kai taken an interest in me. He had seen my body, and while I did have a nice chest, I had extra cushion elsewhere as well. He could have taken his pick of any number of girls with small waists, decent bra sizes, and even bigger bank accounts. Why would he want to go on a date with the hired hand? This called for expert advice.

Jordan: SOS

Jordan: Can we hang out tonight?

Zara: It's too early to be awake.

Zara: Besides, you know my house is your house whenever you need it — micassa's sucassa. Right?

I laughed at her garbled Spanish and sent back a text.

Jordan: Close enough. See you in school.

My shoulders lightened now that I knew I'd at least have Zara in my corner. We'd see what the other girls said as they woke up.

Mom leaned on her broom, watching me. "You have friends awake this early?"

I laughed. "Kind of. I was going to ask—is it okay if I stay with Zara tonight?"

"Of course. She's the one with the rich dad, right?"

"I mean, to be fair, they all have rich dads." I chuckled.

"True." She shook her head. "Just be safe. I can take care of the job tomorrow."

I put my palm to my forehead. "I'm sorry, Mom, I completely forgot. I can call her and cancel."

"No, no, no. You be a kid, enjoy your Saturday. I've got it." She took my rag and spray bottle from me. "Now, go change for school."

"I can help a little more."

She held the bottle out with her hand on the nozzle. "Don't make me spray you."

Laughing, I raised my hands in defense and started walking away.

She misted the air behind me. "And don't come back, ya hear?"

I still had a smile on my face as I walked down the hallway toward the stairwell at the far end of the house.

"You're in a good mood this morning," Kai said.

I nearly jumped out of my skin as my head jerked to the left. He stood in a doorway, a towel hanging over his neck and down his bare chest.

Now my heart was beating fast for completely different reasons. "You scared the crap out of me!" I accused.

His mouth quirked in a slight smile. "Do you like your phone?"

"Actually..." I reached in my drawstring bag and extended the box to him. "I need to give it back to you."

He pushed it back. "No way. It's yours."

"I already have a phone," I said, pushing it back

in a weird game of tug of war. "I don't need handouts."

"Whoa." He lifted his hands. "Who said anything about handouts?"

"Hmm." I tapped my chin. "Maybe the delivery guy with the thousand-dollar phone?"

He shook his head. "You know, it's not a crime to accept a gift."

"It is when there are strings attached."

"What strings?"

I mimicked his voice. "Go on a date with me, Jordan."

Instead of looking annoyed, he seemed conflicted. "I just needed a way to ask you out. Mission accomplished."

"So you could just blow a thousand dollars instead of asking me here?" I shook my head, set the phone on the ground in front of him, and continued toward the stairs. I didn't have time for games.

"I'm not giving up," he called after me.

"Look up the definition of insanity," I replied and continued down the stairs. I needed to stay as far away from Kai as possible.

EIGHT

I WALKED into the school's conference room for our FMP meeting. Pixie Adler, the president of the club, sat at the head of the table next to Tinsley, our secretary, and Poppy, the social chair. The four of us made a strange group, but with only eleven people in the club and half of them underclassmen, we didn't have much of a choice.

As the vice president, I took the chair next to Pixie. She called the meeting to order, and everyone straightened up and began paying attention.

"Today we are discussing the blood drive and deciding who gets to be in charge of what," Pixie said. "Jordan, will you begin dividing responsibilities?"

I looked down at my notebook where I had

taken notes from the meeting before. (Tinsley definitely wasn't the best secretary the school had ever seen.) "The first thing I have written down is that we need someone to meet the Emerson Blood Institute reps at the loading dock when they arrive. There will be a lot of equipment to bring in, and we want to make it as simple as possible.

Pixie raised the pencil she held with the feather topper. "I can do that."

"Great." I checked it off the list. "We'll also need someone to set up the gym—get chairs for the sign-up area, a waiting area, and a recovery area."

A couple of sophomores down the table agreed to take care of that.

"Thanks," I said, "and then we need to make sure there's food for donors to eat afterward. I can pass around a signup sheet if everyone wants to say what they'll bring." I began ripping out a page from my spiral notebook.

Poppy shrugged. "I can have my mom order in catering."

I stifled my reaction to the fact that she could volunteer her parents and their money so quickly for catering and crossed it off my list. At my old school, we would have each brought a dish or a pan of brownies made out of a box. Emerson Academy was a whole new world.

Tinsley lifted her phone in its diamond-studded case. "I can work on promotion and making sure that each of the slots is filled."

That wasn't something I had on my list, but I went ahead and pretended to cross it off anyway. "Check."

A couple of seniors agreed to do teardown afterward, and we were almost to the end. "Great, that means that Pixie and I can take turns running the check-in desk. Does that sound good?"

Pixie nodded emphatically. "I think we should all agree to wear our blood drop pins that we got at the last blood drive."

"I'm sure they'll have some there," I said.

"Either way," Pixie replied, "we need to show solidarity with Emerson Blood Institute. They do so much good work for the area."

I nodded. "Should we move on to the fundraiser?"

"Yes." She folded her hand and leaned forward. "Last year we raised money for the hospital, but I'm open to ideas."

"Ooh!" Poppy raised her hand. "We should

support some kind of weight loss cause. Jordan can be, like, our figurehead!"

I glared at her. "Are you kidding me?"

"What?" Tinsley defended her friend. "She's not wrong."

The force it took to keep my mouth shut should have won me a medal, because I was seconds from telling them that we should support a proctologist so they could figurehead as butt holes.

All business, Pixie said, "We did a weight loss program last year when Mrs. H. sponsored us. Now that Mrs. Bardot has to sign off on it, we should probably have something related to mental health."

My ears perked. "Why don't we do Invisible Mountains? They're a nonprofit and they support local mental health efforts, even in Seaton. Plus, Callie's dad is the CEO, so we'll have an easy time communicating with them."

With an appreciative nod, Pixie said, "I think it will be a great option for our school's image. It will help us show that we aren't discriminating against people based on their socioeconomic status or anything like that."

Never mind the fact that we could actually help people...

"Besides," Pixie continued, "if we give it to something like the local hospital, there's no telling where the money will go, or that it will be fairly distributed."

At least she had that one right. Historically, people of color had higher infant mortality rates and didn't receive the same quality health care. I couldn't imagine what it must have been like for my mom when my sister was suffering from cancer. Especially when they brushed her off at first, saying that she was just overly worried.

"What do you think as far as a fundraiser?" I asked.

Poppy clapped her hands together. "A gala sounds fun. We could have a big party."

I shook my head. "A gala is a lot of work. Do we really have time to plan that?"

Tinsley frowned "Well, if you're not that interested in raising money for people with mental health issues, then I guess we can just do another car wash."

"Yeah," Poppy said. "Besides, we can have my family's party planner handle it."

I closed my eyes and checked myself. If I didn't, I would lose it.

"It's settled then," Pixie said. "We'll have a gala for the fall fundraiser. There are a few details we need to iron out..." She began divvying out tasks well outside of my comfort zone. I couldn't believe these people making plans to rent buildings for thousands of dollars and order catering and planning for extravagant silent auction items. It made me realize just how small my world had been before, how small it was now.

The fact of the matter was that a goal like this could really help people. I tried to keep that in mind as I listened, but it just made me feel smaller. I wished I could do it on my own.

"Anything else before we close the meeting?" Pixie asked me.

I shook my head.

She nodded. "Meeting adjourned."

Everyone else hurried out of the room, but I took my time, trying to calm down. I hated that people like Poppy, who didn't really care about anyone else, could be more helpful than me, who had a heart full of love but nothing of substance to give.

The door handle twisted, and our school janitor, Phil, poked his head in. "Oh, sorry, I didn't realize you were in here. I was just going to lock up, but I can circle back."

"No." I shook my head. "That's okay." I gathered my things and stood to leave. As I passed him, I gave him a grin and said, "Thanks for your work around here. It looks great."

"Thanks for saying that." His smile crinkled the corners of his eyes. "I don't hear that too often."

I knew the feeling too well, of being unappreciated. Of feeling like your work didn't matter to anyone. When I replied, I was speaking as much to him as to myself. "The world needs all kinds of people. Especially ones who work as hard as you."

His eyes seemed to shine as he clapped my shoulder. I passed by him and entered an empty hallway. My footsteps echoed off the wall as I went to my locker to retrieve my books for the weekend. They strained against the worn canvas of my backpack, and I made a mental note to ask Mom to sew on the ripping strap again before it came off all the way.

From my pocket, my phone made its notification sound. I withdrew it, reading the new message in my *Sermo* chat app.

Zara: We're going to the diner. Meet us there?

Jordan: About to leave the school. See you soon!

My locker door clanged noisily against the metal, and I cringed. During the school day it didn't seem this loud. As the echo faded, a new sound hit my ears.

Soft violin notes floated through the hallway, enchanting and haunting at the same time.

I followed the sound, not completely sure why. Deep down, I knew it had to be Kai playing. I'd heard him once before and this song was every bit as beautiful as that time. As I reached the music room, my suspicion was confirmed.

He stood in the middle of the floor, his angular chin pressed against the cherry wood of his instrument. The song must have been one he knew by heart, as his eyes were closed, his black lashes fanned against his pale skin.

The sight was mesmerizing. I didn't have anything I got lost in, heart and soul, quite like that. The song filtered through the door and swirled around me, taking my heart for a ride I hadn't expected. Classical music wasn't my jam, but I'd never heard it performed quite like this...

The final notes of the song played, bringing tears to my eyes I didn't quite understand.

Kai opened his eyes. They flashed on me, and my heart stuttered.

NINE

FOR A MOMENT, we examined each other. Him, curious. Me, frozen.

He set down his violin to put it in the case, and I realized this was my chance to move. I dodged out of sight of the window and hurried down the hallway toward the parking lot. I'd been stupid to linger for so long, especially with my friends waiting on me.

My shoulders didn't relax until I'd reached the doors to the parking lot without hearing footsteps behind me. Now, there were only a few cars left in the student lot. A flashy Tesla and my decade-and-a-half-year-old vehicle stood in stark contrast, the perfect reminder of how Kai and I belonged in different worlds. Even without my mom's rule, I never would have dated him. I couldn't love someone who sat on so much wealth—lived in such excess—without using it for good.

"Jordan!" Kai called.

I got into my car and turned the key. The engine sputtered, and I gassed it—just as the mechanic had taught me to do—to no avail.

I let off the gas and took my hand off the ignition for a moment. I didn't know much about cars, but I knew gassing it too long could flood the engine.

Kai's long legs carried him quickly over the pavement.

My heart sped up as I reached for the keys again and said a quick prayer that my car would start.

It did—but only for a moment. The engine died just as quickly as it had come to life. I tried again, but it was useless. Kai was drawing nearer now, and I was no closer to getting out of the parking lot than I had been without the pressure of his proximity.

Frustrated, I dropped my hands to my lap, then reached for my phone. I hesitated over the screen. This was the last thing my mom needed. One mechanic issue could set us back months. She was so close to paying off Juana's bill. I couldn't take that from her.

A soft knock came on the window, and I glanced over.

I didn't know why. I knew it was Kai, and I also knew I didn't want to see him.

He was bent over, his face near the crack in my window, and he spun his hand like he wanted me to roll it down . He'd probably never used a hand-operated window in his life.

That was beside the point. I couldn't open it even if I wanted to.

I shook my head and held up my phone. "I'm fine."

"I can take you to your house," he offered. "You don't have to wait for a tow."

I barely held back a laugh. Mom and I couldn't afford a tow. And I'd never let Kai see the shabby apartment building Mom and I called home, with the jacked-up cars in the craggy parking lot and patchy grass covered in dog excrement. Shaking my head, I said, "I've got it."

He glanced over the parking lot. "I'll wait to make sure you get out of here safely."

Now he was just messing with me. I glared at

him, but he missed it as he went to his Tesla. It easily, and almost silently, came to life.

I hit the back of my head against the headrest. What now? It was already getting dark outside, and I was hungry.

I lifted my phone and went to the *Sermo* app to find a few new chats waiting for me.

Callie: Beckett says there's a DP stunt near La La Pictures tonight!

My mouth fell open. I'd been so jealous of my friend Rory when her boyfriend took her to see one of *Dulce Periculum's* stunts. The group was an urban legend around Emerson. I didn't want to miss my chance to see them.

Jordan: Can you guys swing by the school and pick me up? Car troubles.

Callie: We just ordered. But one of us can leave and get you. Or send you an Uber?

The worst part about having rich friends was knowing that, no matter what, you'd never be able to return the favor. Feeling like a burden, I typed a quick response.

Jordan: No worries. I'll see you there.

Of course, I had no idea how I would actually get to the diner. And Kai's perfectly running car was just sitting there, mocking me.

A year ago, I could have texted one of my friends from Seaton High, but after I transferred, they thought of me as a traitor. Called me stuck-up. If only they knew I was going somewhere the majority of the student body would treat me like old bubblegum stuck to the sole of a perfect Prada shoe.

I let out a frustrated groan.

Now I had the choice of two evils: interrupt Mom on her job to let her know we would have yet another unplanned expense, or...

I glanced over to the shining Tesla.

Kai it was.

TEN

KAI PUSHED the passenger door open from inside the car with a satisfied smirk.

I got in without speaking a word.

"Where to?" he asked.

"Waldo's," I answered and closed the door.

He sped out of the parking lot, his car taking each bump softly, unlike my car, which practically rattled my teeth out every time I hit so much as a crack. Actually, every part of his car was better than mine, from the touchscreen on the dash between us to the flawless leather interior that smelled as if it had just been driven off the lot. Apparently, his car hadn't been pre-owned by multiple families with messy, cracker-eating children.

The windows were tinted so dark, I felt removed

from the rest of the world, except out the windshield, where I could see him easily guiding us down city roads.

"You seem uncomfortable," he observed.

"No, I'm perfectly at ease." I shifted, trying to relax my shoulders, to no avail.

His long fingers went to the touchscreen. "I can change the temperature."

"It's not that," I said, my voice tight.

His hand fell to the center armrest, and he took me in for a moment before turning his eyes back toward the windshield. They glittered in headlights from oncoming traffic. "What is it?"

I wondered whether I should say it, really, but I couldn't help myself. I gestured at his car. "It's *this*."

He seemed confused. "What? I think you can adjust the seat back—it's supposed to be ergonomic."

Exasperated, I sighed. "This car is ridiculous. I could buy a house bigger than the postage stamp my mom and I live in with the amount you paid for this car, but you drive it around like it's nothing."

His black eyebrows came together, but he didn't speak, which just made me angrier.

"You and your dad live in this fancy castle, and you have your personal trainers and chefs and a butler, but you never think of what it's like for regular people or that people out there have rent to pay. Which my mom and I could do for *years* with the money from a car like this."

I glared at the dash for good measure, hating everything the car stood for. And hating myself even more for wanting it.

"I didn't choose to have money," he said quietly, keeping his stare ahead now.

"Just like me and ninety-nine percent of the world didn't choose to be poor," I returned, my voice hard. "But here we are. Just surviving, while people like you and your dad live like kings."

His voice reflected my anger. "My dad works hard for what he has."

"And my mom doesn't? The people picking fruit for two dollars an hour just miles from here don't work hard?"

That silenced him.

"It isn't about hard work," I said. "It's about luck. And opportunities." If Emerson Academy taught me anything, it was that rich people got to be that way on a combination of luck and connections. People like my mom could slave away every day of their lives and wind up with nothing but arthritis and just enough government help to get by. All while being judged by the lucky ones for taking what little leg up they could get.

"There's nothing I can do about how much money my dad has," he said.

I shook my head and looked out the dark window, at what muted view I had of the passing buildings.

"So, what?" he pressed. "That means I'm a terrible person?"

A harsh laugh escaped my lips. "It means we exist in different worlds."

He pulled into the Waldo's Diner parking lot and turned toward me. "What does that mean?"

I grabbed my backpack and opened the door. "It means you make the messes, and I'll worry about cleaning them up."

I slammed the door behind me and walked into the restaurant without another look back.

ELEVEN

MY BREATH WAS STILL COMING HARD as I approached the table where my friends sat with Carson and Beckett. Their eyes were wide.

"Who drove you up in a Tesla?" Carson asked in awe.

Beckett furrowed his brows. "That looked like..."

"Kai's car?" I blew out another angry breath and sat down in the long circular booth. "It was his car, and can we talk about something else? Please?"

Zara nodded sarcastically. "Yes, there are so many more interesting topics than you riding to the diner with a billionaire. Callie, tell us about your dog's diabetes shot again."

Callie straightened. "Oh, well, it's just in his—"

"I was kidding!" Zara cried, giving Callie a good-natured smile, which she returned with a blush.

I shook my head at them. "My car wouldn't start, so he gave me a ride." I rubbed my arms. "I need to get the smell of thousand-dollar cologne off me."

Beckett's eyes widened. "His cologne cost a thousand dollars?"

"Are you and Callie having a gullible contest?" I teased. "It was a figure of speech."

As if sensing my frustration, Rory changed the subject like the true goddess she was. "We were just talking about the *Dulce Periculum* stunt." She lowered her voice. "Beckett said it should happen around nine."

I squinted at Beckett. "Who's your connection?"

"Give up," Rory said. "He's a steel vault."

As if to prove his point, he lifted his shirt and hit his rock-solid abs.

Okay, Jordan, insert tongue back in mouth. That's Rory's guy.

Ginger put down her burger. "We should probably head that way, right?"

"Yeah," Carson said and stood up from the booth so everyone else could follow suit.

Even though I hadn't eaten since lunch, I got up too.

"Did you want to get something to go?" Callie asked.

I shrugged. "I can wait 'til we get to Zara's."

"Here," Ginger said. "Do you want the rest of my sandwich?"

"Sure," I answered. Beggars couldn't be choosers. Besides, free was my favorite flavor.

While they went to pay, I picked up the uneaten half of the sandwich and followed behind them. As we walked toward the register, Chester, the old guy who always hung out in the restaurant, perked up.

"Tough last game, huh, boys?" he said to Carson and Beckett.

"Yeah," Beckett answered. "Rough break."

Chester leaned forward conspiratorially. "And you heard about that girl who got dessert thrown at her? That was so sad. Kids these days are cruel."

Beckett shifted awkwardly, and Rory made herself invisible behind the group. I swore I could feel how uncomfortable she was from here.

"Hey, Chester," I said and slid into the booth across from him so I could eat my food.

He broke out into a toothy grin, the lines in his face deepening to dark wrinkles. "How are you doing, girl?"

I would have been offended at the diminutive, but he called everyone girl. He couldn't remember anyone's name long enough to call them anything else.

"I'm good," I said. "My mom's been keeping me busy with our cleaning business."

His eyes lit up. "I used to work as a custodian in the hotel down the street."

"Yeah? What was the weirdest thing you ever found?"

Leaning in, he whispered, "I'll tell you mine if you tell me yours."

I paused for a moment, chewing over my food, even though the item was already coming to mind. He was eating this up, the anticipation. Finally, I said it. "This one kid in a house we cleaned had an old applesauce jar full of spiders."

I shivered just thinking of it. There had to be at least a hundred in there.

"I can do you one better," he said, lifting his finger.

Callie approached our table. "Ready, Jor?"

Chester gave a sly smile. "Guess you'll have to wait."

"Come on," I said, actually curious. "Don't leave me hanging."

He pinched his lips together and shook his head. "A little mystery does the soul good. Come back and see me sometime."

I gave him a two-finger salute and stood to follow Callie out. As we reached the swinging glass door, she whispered, "That was nice of you."

I shrugged, because really it wasn't. I was just talking to someone. Most people who went to Emerson Academy didn't understand how sheltered their lives were. Kind people like Chester or the Gutiérrezes were everywhere, and I'd sooner ride home in a car with them than someone like Kai— bad eyesight and all.

The drive to the theater took about ten minutes, but finding a good spot to watch DP was more of a challenge. La La Pictures was on the outside of Emerson Shoppes, and across from it was an office park. With all the rocky landscaping, it was hard to find a decent hiding spot to watch from.

After walking along the sidewalk for a while, we decided one of the huge ornamental rocks at the office park would do. Using blankets from Ginger's car, we hunkered down behind the rough stone and waited.

I sat between Rory and Beckett and Carson and Callie, and honestly, I just felt lonely. Even if Callie and Carson were just friends, their bond couldn't be denied. Rory had her head resting on Beckett's shoulder, and he held her close to his side. The love between them hit me like a sack of bricks. I used to feel like that about Martín, but our breakup had erased months of intimacy and left me feeling like a wound barely scabbed over.

"Look!" Ginger said in a hushed whisper.

I followed her finger—her white, freckled skin practically glowed in the moonlight—and caught sight of black figures moving across the theater's roof. The people flipped, cartwheeled and spun over the surface, getting closer and closer to the edge.

My mouth fell open in a silent scream, worried they were going to get hurt. What the hell were they doing? I hadn't quite believed DP was real until Rory told me she'd seen them, but now I knew they wouldn't be real much longer. They'd be dead on the sidewalk in seconds.

One cartwheeled over the side of the building. I gasped, and Callie flat-out shrieked.

For a sickening second, he silently soared through the air as if he had not a care in the world, but then my eyes discovered what he already knew. A blue inflatable of some type absorbed his fall, and he rolled away, moving toward the next building, shouting, "*Audentes fortuna iuvat!*"

I remembered those words from Latin class: *Fortune favors the bold.*

They were bold alright, and apparently the phrase was true, because I didn't know how they'd survived this long.

My eyes followed the others—four, five, six guys—tricking off the roof and leaping effortlessly through the air. They scaled the next building and moved over the next few roofs with ease. If my guess was right, they were going toward the manufacturing plants. Toward more adventure.

"That was amazing," Zara breathed.

Feeling a little sick to my stomach, I whispered, "My nerves can't take it."

Still, I wished I were that brave—that I could go from this life, where I was constantly afraid of a car breaking down or having a medical issue, to a better reality. A life of freedom like I saw the DP guys living right before my eyes.

Beckett grinned at us. "Worth the frostbite?"

I nodded, but now I just felt sad. Kai had wealth. DP had freedom. Beckett and Rory had each other. What did that leave me?

TWELVE

I WOKE up to bright light pouring through the window of a guest room in Zara's house. I'd slept on one side of the king-sized bed, and Ginger still snored softly on the other end.

Rolling to my feet, I grabbed my phone from the nightstand and walked to the bathroom, closing the door behind me. I felt like I'd been sleeping forever.

My screen came to life. Six in the morning.

I let out a quiet groan and set my phone on the counter. It would be hours before the others woke.

After I used the bathroom and washed my hands, I went to the upstairs living room. Through the floor-to-ceiling windows, Brentwood and Seaton sprawled before me, shifting from thick trees losing their leaves to tightly packed buildings and eventually the ocean. It was gray out today.

I turned away from the view and spread out on one of four white couches. There was so much room here, and it was nice to have space, even if it wasn't my own.

Being at Zara's house didn't feel like being in Kai's. Here, I was a guest, welcomed. Mr. Rush treated us like we were untrustworthy, never allowing us to clean without the supervision of him or Robert. He made sure my mother and I knew we didn't belong.

An ache grew in the pit of my stomach from thoughts of the Rushes and seeing DP the night before. I was unsettled, restless, but I couldn't run out and jump off a roof—at least, not with as positive of an ending as those guys.

I rolled my shoulders, hoping to ease the tension, and began scrolling through social media. A notification slid down my screen, from my mother.

Mom: Staying with Camilla tonight. Isa's sick and she can't call off work. Want to come over?

I smiled at the phone. My mom would do anything for her friends. I admired that about her.

Jordan: I'll stay at the house. Give Isa a hug for me. :)

Mom: I will. Call me if you need anything. Ly

Jordan: Lym

Even though I loved my mom, I looked forward to a night to myself. I needed a break sometimes too. Like now, sitting in the sparse living room with just myself and the scent of rose petals diffused throughout the house, I could just relax.

I lay back on the couch and looked at my phone. My notifications showed I had several unopened messages—mostly promotional items or automated texts sent from the school, so I opened my messenger app and began clearing them out.

An unknown number topped the list with a text from around two in the morning. I squinted at it. The preview had my name...

I tapped it, and the messages I'd missed filled the screen.

Unknown number: Jordan, I miss you, baby.

Unknown number: Why did you block my number?

Unknown number: I need you. Talk to me.

Unknown number: I thought you loved me.

Unknown number: I know you're up. Call me.

Unknown number: When can I see you?

Hair rose on the back of my neck as I read to the bottom, where the messages stopped at four in the morning. My fingers flew over the screen with a response.

Jordan: Leave me alone, Martín.

And then I blocked this number too.

My stomach turned uneasily. I shifted in my seat and chewed on the crook of my index finger. Martín's new girl had probably left him, and now he was feeling bad. He wasn't dangerous, I told myself; he was heartbroken.

Well, good. Maybe he would understand how I'd been feeling the last several weeks knowing he'd chosen someone else over me. The fact that he wanted me now that I wanted nothing to do with him felt satisfying somehow. I had no other guy waiting for me, no other options, and I'd still said no.

"You look happy," Rory said, walking into the living room.

Adrenaline flooded my body, and I gasped. "Rory! You scared me!"

"Sorry!" she said with a yawn as she sat on one of the couches. "Why are you so jumpy?"

I blushed a little. "Just blocked Martín's number." For the second time, I didn't add.

She grinned. "Good for you. You'll find a good guy—even better than Martín or Kai."

"Easy for you to say," I countered. "You landed Mr. Perfect."

Her smile grew even wider. "I can't really argue."

"Exactly," I said. "So, what's the plan for the day?"

She shrugged. "Homework?"

I shrugged too. "Not like I have anything better to do." We went back to the room and grabbed our backpacks. For the next few hours, we worked in silence on our assignments, waiting for the other girls to wake up.

When they did, we spent most of the afternoon baking cookies in Zara's gourmet kitchen—well, eating cookies that Callie baked based on her mom's recipes. Romcoms played on the TV embedded in the refrigerator, and between shows and taste tests, we talked about life. I knew this was one of those days that I'd always cherish and was sad when it came time to go. Zara had a blind date to get ready for, Ginger had curfew, and the rest of us had no reason to hang around.

"Can someone give me a ride?" I asked.

"I can," Ginger offered.

We got in her car, and after I buckled in, I

asked, "Are you sure your parents will be okay with it?"

"Oh yeah," she said. "They would never want one of my friends walking outside at night."

I raised my eyebrows. "Your parents would be horrified at some of the dates I'd had with Martín, then." We'd been to college parties that lasted well past six in the morning.

"Just call me Rapunzel, locked away in my tower." She frowned, giving away the hurt behind her joking words.

"Only until graduation," I reminded her.

"Nope." Her red hair shook around her as she turned onto the main highway that led to Seaton. "They want me to go to UCLA. Close enough to commute. Where's your house again?"

The image of my crummy apartment building on trash pickup day with litter strewn over the parking lot made me cringe. As bad as I felt knowing I lived there, it would be worse if Ginger knew as well.

"Drop me off at Seaton Bakery?" I said. "My mom texted me." It wasn't technically a lie, but I still felt bad. I'd seen each of their homes at least once, even if it was just from the outside. They had houses they could be proud of, with white picket fences and landscaped lawns. If they lived some-where like I did, I had no doubt they'd want to keep it secret too.

"I can't believe I hadn't been there before we set up Rory and Beckett. Their cupcakes are *so* good," she gushed.

"The best," I agreed.

She pulled into the parking lot and said, "Mind if I come in and grab one with you?"

I hesitated, worried she might guess my mom wasn't actually meeting me, but eventually shrugged. "Sure." It was a free country after all.

We walked inside and scanned the shelves of treats.

She ordered one of my favorites—a cookies and cream cupcake—and then waited. "Aren't you going to get something?"

I shook my head. "I'll grab one with my mom...Tradition," I added for good measure.

She scanned the room. "Where is she?"

"Probably running late." I shrugged. This lying was getting old, but I couldn't give this away without explaining why I'd lied in the first place. "You can head out if you want."

"Are you sure? I can call my parents and see if I can wait with you?"

"Nah." I started walking toward the exit so she'd get the hint. "I'll see you Monday?"

She nodded with her hand on the door. "Call me tomorrow if you want. I won't be doing anything exciting."

I told her I would text her and waved goodbye as she backed out of the parking lot. When I saw her tail lights instead of headlights, I couldn't help the relaxed sigh I let out. I loved the girl, but I wanted to get home too.

"What was that about?" Gayle asked.

I spun at the sound of the bakery owner's voice, not seeing her before. She shooed away the kid behind the register and leaned over the counter.

I let out a sigh and walked toward her. At this point, she was like a second mom to me. "I just wanted to get home."

Gayle looked through the painted windows at the parking lot. "I don't see your car?"

"She drove me."

"So...you wanted to get home so you had your friend drive you here?" Her eyebrows drew together. "Something's not measuring up, kid."

A tall, slim man passed through the swinging doors to the kitchen. "I told you I'd get new measuring cups!"

Gayle batted her hand at her husband. "We're not talking about that...but it's about time," she added.

Shaking his head, Chris came to the counter and leaned beside his wife. "What's up, Jordo?"

I shook my head at his nickname. He was definitely the only one allowed to call me that. "I just didn't want my friend driving me home is all. Is it a crime to want some fresh air?"

Gayle raised her eyebrows. "When it's fifty degrees outside? Maybe."

"You need a ride?" Chris asked. "I can drop you off real quick."

I shook my head. "No, no, no. I just—it's one of my friends from the Academy, and I didn't want her seeing..." My sentence hung between us.

Gayle and Chris were Seaton natives, like me, and they had built their life and business here. They understood as much as anyone how hard it had been for me to leave public school and switch to the Academy.

Chris lifted a corner of his mouth. "You know, Beckett's been great to have around. Kind with the customers...if that's what your friends are like, I'd say they probably don't care where you live."

"But I do," I said. The second they saw my run-down apartment, they'd feel sorry for me, start giving me things they wouldn't normally. As a 'ship, I already didn't fit in. I didn't need any help.

Gayle frowned. "Are you sure you don't want a ride?"

I shook my head. "I can walk."

"You have your pepper spray, right?" Chris asked.

Actually, it was in the glovebox of my car, but I nodded anyway. They were just being overprotective. "I'll be fine."

They nodded, and Gayle said, "Be safe, honey."

"I will." I smiled and walked toward the door. "See you tomorrow."

"Bright and early," Chris said.

With a wave, I walked outside and started down the sidewalk.

I'd taken this path many times before, mostly with Martín. He loved that I could get free desserts here, so half of our dates consisted of us hanging out at the bakery. Now sitting inside didn't seem as sweet.

The walk from the bakery to my apartment wasn't the safest to make by myself at night, but I'd hurry. Hitching my backpack over my shoulder, I clenched my phone in my hand and picked up the pace. In the distance, I could hear car engines gunning—a street race. I'd been in a few of those with Martín, against all my wishes.

The more I thought of him, the angrier I got. The nerve of that guy, treating me like he did and then calling me after I'd blocked him, requesting— no, ordering—a meeting.

I sneered at his memory, but no one could see. The streets were mostly empty and dark, without regular streetlamps. If I saw Martín face to face, I'd tell him. He'd see the disgust on my face. The contempt in my voice.

I was so deep in my plotting that I missed the dark car with tinted windows driving around the apartment complex's parking lot. Didn't see it slow and stop.

But I heard the door open and then slam shut.

I froze, seeing Martín's frame silhouetted by the lot's floodlights. What was he doing here?

"Jordan, why are you out here by yourself?" he barked, but his voice was fuzzy.

I gripped my phone tighter. "I was with my friends."

His footsteps were heavy on the ground as he wobbled toward me. "Friends? You don't have any *amigas* since you switched to that rich school."

I narrowed my eyes at him. "Get out of here, Martín."

"You don't tell me what to do," he spat, literally, on the ground. "*Puta.*"

My lip curled in disgust at the swear word. "You're drunk. Go home."

He stepped closer, and I backed up. His meaty fingers clenched around my wrist, and I opened my mouth to yell for help, ask him to stop, but nothing came out. Why couldn't I yell? I felt powerless, help-less, and his grip was tight. Too tight.

"Let her go!" a voice yelled, controlled but ready to snap.

Martín turned his big dumb head away, and I tried to use the distraction to jerk out of his grasp, but he doubled down, squeezing even tighter.

I finally found my voice as I cried out with pain. "Ouch! You're hurting me!"

"Good," he growled.

"I said, let her go!" The voice was just as loud but twice as deadly.

Hope swelled in me so strongly it almost hurt. I had no idea who was here, but I loved them.

As a thin figure approached us, all hope fled my chest. What was Kai doing here? He had no busi-ness being at my house and absolutely no chance against Martín. What I used to see as big and secure was now suffocating, terrifying. Especially since it outweighed my only defender by at least a hundred pounds.

If Kai noticed how outmatched he was, he ignored it, running right up to us. "Back off of her!" He shoved Martín's shoulder, barely causing him to move despite the inebriation.

Finally, Martín released my wrist, and I cradled it with my other hand. The returning blood pumped painfully through my veins.

Now Martín spun on Kai, reaching his beefy arms out to shove him. I screamed, fearing Kai would be hurt, but he ducked easily out of the way.

"Go home," Kai warned.

"You screwing my girl?" Martín roared.

"Go *home*," Kai said through clenched teeth.

Martín stalled, his chest heaving, and then turned like he was going toward his car, but he swiveled at the last second and slung a fist at Kai.

Kai was ready. He ducked out of the way and jabbed quickly at Martín's throat. A strangled cry came out his fleshy lips, and he grabbed at the spot Kai had hit.

Sirens sounded in the distance, and Martín's

eyes got wide. He stumbled toward his car, letting out a string of curse words on the way.

The door slammed, and his tires squealed against the pavement.

"He's so drunk," I managed, worrying he might hurt someone else in his escape.

Kai reached into his pockets, grabbed his phone, and held it to his ear. "Did you hear that?" His deadly, glittering eyes followed Martín's car. "He's intoxicated. Heading south on Bixby...I can't see him anymore." He hung up and shoved the phone into his pocket.

I stared at him, unable to find words. What just happened?

His fingers went to my wrist, gingerly turning it so he could examine it. "Are you okay?"

I was still stuck in stunned silence, though. How had he just taken down a guy twice his size? And how was he here? At my apartment complex?

He could give me an answer to one of those questions at least. "What are you doing here?"

He glanced up at me, meeting my eyes for a second before looking back at my arm. "I had your car brought here. Wanted to make sure you got the keys." His touch was soft on my arm as he turned it again. "It's going to bruise pretty badly, Jordan."

"My car?"

His lips softened into a smile. "Your wrist. Can you wiggle your fingers?"

Carefully, I moved each of them. It hurt, but I was fine. Thanks to Kai. I shuddered to think of what might have happened if he hadn't been here. But that part—his presence—still didn't make sense.

"I don't think it's broken," Kai said, releasing my hand a few seconds after he could have.

"My car was broken down. How did you get it here?"

"Your lips are blue," he answered. "You're cold. Let me get you inside."

My knees locked, keeping us from moving. "You can't come inside."

He looked like he wanted to argue, but finally he said, "My car?"

Not having enough energy to argue, I nodded.

He led me across the parking lot to a silver Honda sedan. It was a newer model, but it didn't look brand new. There was a dent in the hood.

When he opened the door, I said, "Who's car is this?"

"Mine."

"Did you borrow it from your butler?"

"Damn it, Jordan, get in the car before you freeze to death."

My eyes snapped harshly to his, but I followed the order. He shut the door behind me and walked purposefully to his side. After getting in, he said, "You weren't comfortable in my Tesla, so I got this one instead."

"You got a new car because I didn't like your last one?" My eyebrows came together, this news competing with everything else from the evening.

He turned in his seat, his eyes shining in the floodlights. "You were right. I have no idea what it's like to live your life." His gaze went to the parking lot where broken glass from shattered beer bottles glinted in the moonlight. "But I want to understand. I don't want to be your enemy."

My heart had lodged itself in my throat, making speaking difficult. I swallowed. "Rule number one: most regular people can't just go out and get a new car at the drop of a hat."

"I'll write that down." He reached for his glove compartment. "I think there are some napkins and a pen in—"

I shoved his arm, finally smiling.

The smile he turned back on me warmed me

better than the used-car heater he had cranked the second he got inside.

"So, friends?" he asked. The hope in his voice tore me in two.

Behind him, I caught sight of my car, rusted paint and all. "Did you have my car towed here?"

"After I had it repaired. My mechanic says you need to release the parking brake before driving."

My cheeks heated. "One time..."

He extended a set of keys my way. "Some extras we had made."

"How much was it?"

His gaze was sharp. "Don't insult me."

"I just want to pay you back. Is there an issue with that?"

"What kind of jerk would sign off on a multi-thousand-dollar repair without your permission, then stick you with the bill?"

I raised my eyebrows. "I'm not used to this side of you."

"There's a lot you don't know about me," he said evenly. "But you will."

The fighter in me that had been painfully absent around Martín rose up now. "Oh really?"

"Yeah." A smile lit his eyes that didn't touch his

lips. "I'll see you tomorrow. At that bakery over there." He jerked his head in the direction I had just come from. "Now get out. You need to get some rest...unless you would like me to walk you to your door?"

Feeling shell-shocked, I shook my head and reached for the handle.

"Wait," he said, "pass me your phone."

"Why?"

Extending his hand, he said, "You're texting me when you get inside. I want you safe."

Bubbles lifted from my stomach and rose to my chest as I unlocked my phone and handed it to him. His fingers swiftly typed in his number and sent a text. His phone dinged before he gave mine back to me. "Ten in the morning," he said.

"And why should I?" I asked, finally coming to my senses.

He stared forward for a moment, but finally he shrugged. "You owe me."

For once, I couldn't argue.

THIRTEEN

AT FIVE BEFORE TEN, I got in my car, and it started more easily than it ever had before. No gassing it, no trying more than once, nothing.

I sat back and stared at the tachometer resting around fifteen hundred RPMs. Part of me wanted to check under the hood and see what space gear he'd had installed to make it run so smoothly. The other part was too terrified to try.

So, I shifted it into gear, and it purred as I took off. I never thought I'd describe my car as purring. Screeching like a cat in a bathtub, maybe, but purring? No way.

Every second of the short drive to the bakery just proved that he had fixed my car—completely. When I pulled into the parking lot and saw Kai's

Honda already parked, I felt something between disbelief and frustration. I was thankful, but I didn't like owing him something I couldn't dream of paying back.

As I got out of my car, I was intensely aware of how I looked, knowing Kai would be watching. I'd worn a long-sleeved shirt—partly because of the cold, but mostly because of the handprint bruise blooming on my wrist. I wanted to forget all about it, that I'd ever been stupid enough to love such a monster.

I folded my arms across my chest and walked toward his Honda. Before I reached him, the door opened, and he stood. The wind swept his black hair across his forehead, and his eyes shined golden brown under the streaming sunshine.

Why the sight of him made my heart beat faster was cause for concern. I attempted to stuff the feeling as I approached him and his curving lips.

"Hey," I said, "I'll go in and grab us something and meet you out here."

He furrowed his eyebrows. "Why?"

"They know me here. People talk. And my mom would kill me if she caught me here with you."

His lips had set into a line, any hint of the smile

from before completely gone. "Where are we going then?"

"The pier?" I suggested.

If he had an adverse reaction to the place that smelled of rotten fish and saltwater, he didn't let on. He reached into his pocket and began opening his wallet.

"I don't have to pay here," I said.

"Then a tip," he countered, retrieving a bill and pressing it into my hand. The brush of our skin crackled across my mind, clearing all other thoughts. Maybe it was the power that lay within him, unknown unless needed. He'd *protected* me the night before. I'd lain awake for hours thinking of it —how easy he'd made it look to defend me.

I curled my fingers around the bill and went inside. As I waited in line, I glanced at the hundred in my hand. So much for flying under the radar.

When I reached the front, Chris greeted me.

"Working on a Sunday?" I asked. Usually he and Gayle had someone to cover the weekend shifts.

He shrugged. "Sam called in, so here I am." He grinned at me, deepening the happy smile lines around his mouth. "Good to see the weekend crowd, though."

I smiled back. "Good to see you too." I wondered what would have happened if I'd just accepted his offer for the ride last night? Would Martín have advanced on me? Would Kai have tracked me down?

"What can we get you?" Chris asked. "A mocha and..."

My smile grew. "Yes to the mocha. Two actually. And then two coffee cake muffins?"

His smile faltered. "You're not with Martín, are you?"

I couldn't help the shudder that came with his name or the painful throb that shot through my wrist. "No, a friend from school."

That answer seemed to please him. "Coming right up."

As his back turned, I slipped the hundred in the tip jar and walked to the counter where they placed completed orders.

Within minutes, he had two cups and a white paper bag ready for me. "Have a good day, kiddo," he said.

"You know you're the only person I let call me kiddo, right?"

He chuckled. "I consider it a privilege."

"See you tomorrow," I said.

"Bright and early," he agreed.

I was still smiling from the exchange as I walked outside to Kai's car. He got out and opened my door before taking the food and drinks from me.

His chivalry left me so stunned, I barely had words as I settled into the gray fabric interior. As he handed me a drink and the bag of food, his eyes held mine. What was it about his eyes that captivated me so? Maybe the spark of fire I now knew hid behind the black irises.

In the time it took him to walk around the car, I took a breath and gave myself a pep talk. I needed to remember this was Kai Rush. Just because he was here didn't mean I needed to fall apart. He was still a billionaire. I was still the poor, curvy girl who cleaned his house. In no equation did that equal happily ever after.

"How do we get to the pier?" he asked, shutting the door behind him.

I stared at him, not bothering to hide my shock.

"What?" he asked. "I've never been there."

My jaw practically rested on his dash at this point. "You've *never* been to Seaton Pier?"

He shook his head.

"You've never gone fishing?"

"Not there."

I raised my eyebrows. "Never threw rocks into the water or had a corn dog off a street cart?"

"No?" he said like he was confused by my shock.

"Where have you been living all your life?"

"Here." His lips turned down at the corners, and it struck me that I was starting to pick up on his subtle expressions. Kai wasn't like most people who wore their emotions like statement necklaces. No, he was guarded. And I wanted to know why.

FOURTEEN

I GAVE Kai directions to the pier, and his eyes were hungry as he drank in our surroundings. On weekends, the spot bustled with life. Little kids fished off the edge of the pier while their parents and grandparents made sure they didn't fall through the wooden railing into the ocean. Couples walked over the weathered planks hand in hand. A couple of food carts even popped up here on weekends too. The corn dogs were the best, but I also liked the funnel cakes and roasted peanuts.

He put the car in park and scanned our surroundings. "What now?"

"Nothing." I opened my door. "And everything."

With a small smile, he got out of the car and

walked with me to the grubby sidewalk. I wondered what it looked like to him—seeing it for the first time.

"Where do you and your dad go when you want to see a beach?" I asked.

"A friend of ours has a private beach, down the coast."

Of course. Rich people knew other rich people.

"You seem upset," he said.

I held my disposable mug to my chest and shrugged. "You just live in a different world is all."

He pressed his lips together, hardly seeming satisfied with my answer.

"Have you tried your drink yet?" I asked, nodding toward the styrofoam cup in his hand. If we kept talking about all the ways we were different, we'd never discover ways we were the same.

With a shake of his head, he lifted it to his lips and sampled the foamy liquid. His dark eyes brightened. "This is amazing."

"Right?" I said. "Wait until you try the muffin." Still walking, I reached into the bag and handed him the pastry crusted with cinnamon and brown sugar. He promptly bit into it and moaned.

I laughed. "Get a room."

He shook his head and swallowed. "I might have to."

A giggle escaped my lips—foreign and familiar. Wholly welcome.

We walked down the wooden planks of the pier with about a foot separating us all the way to the end. While Kai looked over the water, I sat down, dangling my feet over the edge and my arms over the middle railing. I liked the way the air circled my legs. How freeing it felt to be right up against the edge of forever.

So much of my life had been tethered to California, to Seaton. Here I could imagine sailing to the horizon and discovering what was possible beyond what I could see.

"You're thinking about something," Kai observed and took a sip of his mocha.

"I am," I admitted, but I wasn't quite ready to trust him enough to tell him the truth. Out here, I didn't need to be anything but honest. Anything but myself.

For a moment, he watched me, but then he turned his gaze over the gray waves rolling in. "I can see why you like it here."

"It's not pretty. Not in the traditional sense."

"No, but it's real."

My lips turned up. He got it. Maybe I didn't have to explain it after all.

"Can I ask you something?"

I smiled at him. "You just did."

He pressed his lips together in an exasperated smile, shaking his head. It made him look silly, teasing, completely at odds with his usual serious demeanor.

"Go ahead," I said.

He rolled his cup around his long fingers. "Who was that guy last night? Did you know him?"

My wrist throbbed again at the memory. "My ex. Martín."

A thunderous look crossed Kai's expression. "He wasn't always..." His voice shook like he couldn't manage to say the word.

"Abusive?" I finished for him. "No."

He nodded, but something in me wanted him to understand that I wasn't the kind of girl Martín had made me appear to be. Like a victim who couldn't protect herself.

"He used to be sweet," I said. "On our first date, he took me dancing at one of the college bars. Got his friend to let me in. And he made me feel beautiful. Special." I scoffed at the word now. Special was the last thing I felt now.

"What happened?" Kai asked gently.

"He left me for someone else." I looked down, realizing for the first time that thinking of Martín breaking up with me didn't leave a huge gash in my psyche. "But now that I look back, I could see it was a long time coming."

"What do you mean?" He seemed genuinely curious.

I shrugged, picking at the edge of my coffee lid. "One day, things start to feel off. You have an argument that never completely resolves. You start to wonder if they actually like you. Start to do extra to make the distance go away, but it just gets worse. And even though things look good on the surface, they don't feel good. Not as good as it used to be. Not as good as you dreamed."

His hand was soft on my wrist, sending tingles through the sensitive skin over my bruise. "You deserve better."

The strength of his words pulled the threads of my heartstrings apart. I swallowed to keep the jagged lump in my throat from growing.

I deserved better. I just couldn't tell what better was. Didn't know if better was sitting next to me.

FIFTEEN

KAI STOOD and extended his hand to me.

My heart sank. He was ready to leave, and I'd been enjoying his quiet companionship—even though I'd never admit that to him. Maybe it was better that we left now, before I let ideas that shouldn't exist take on a life of their own. I tugged my feet back over the edge and let him wrap his fingers around mine.

In an easy motion, he pulled me to my feet. He was sure, steady. For a moment, his hand lingered on mine, and the crash of the waves had nothing on the swell of blood rushing through my ears. My breath hitched in shock, and I took my hand away.

Why had I reacted that way? Had Kai noticed the way the ground shifted beneath us or was it only me? I had to find a way to change the subject—to regain some semblance of normalcy.

"Do you have to head home?" I stuttered.

"No way." His eyes sparked. "I'm not leaving here without trying one of those corn dogs."

I felt so light I smiled. "If you don't love it, I'll know there's something wrong with you."

"Are you saying you think I'm perfect?" he teased. There was a lightness in his voice, too, like he could be himself out here, let his controlled demeanor slip away to reveal the real Kai.

It scared me. Because if Kai wasn't the brooding billionaire who stole away to his tower to lord over everyone else, what was there left to hate? He said he didn't want to be my enemy, but what if I needed him to be?

We walked over the creaking boards, his shoulder brushing mine occasionally. Everything in me told me I should pull away, but for some reason, I didn't. We were just friends, hanging out on the pier. How did that happen? And more importantly, why did I like it so much?

We reached the dingy white stand selling corn dogs, and I grinned at the guy standing behind the burners in his oversized white apron. "Hey, Carl."

He smiled back at us, revealing his missing front

tooth—which he said was from a fight with a seag-ull, but I bet the real story was much less interesting. "Two dogs?" he asked.

"I'm good," I said. "Just one."

"Nonsense," Kai said. "Two, and two waters?" As Carl bent to reach into the cooler, he said, "It's a part of the experience, right?"

I cringed, not wanting to tell him the truth. But hey, maybe if he knew my real reasoning, he'd remember who I was. "It's not really a good idea for a girl my size to have a muffin, a coffee, and a corn dog in one day."

"You deserve to splurge just as much as the next person," he said, then his eyes flitted down my body. "And for the record, your size is perfect."

I got that exposed feeling again, like Kai was seeing me with my bra on and loving every second of it. It excited and embarrassed me at the same time, making my cheeks feel warm despite the chill.

Carl held out a couple of white paper bags and frosty waters with the labels peeling off from the moisture. They crinkled as we took them.

Kai extended a hundred Carl's way, and Carl's bushy eyebrows rose up his forehead. He pushed the bill back Kai's direction. "I can't break this."

"Keep the change."

Before Carl could argue—because I knew he would; people out here didn't accept money they didn't earn—Kai turned and picked up some mustard packets.

I just shook my head at Carl like *don't bother*, then I followed Kai as he stepped to one of the nearby weathered wooden benches.

He sat down near the middle, meaning I'd have to sit near him no matter what. I left a little space between us, not wanting to give him—or me—the wrong idea.

"For the record," he said, "I don't think your size should keep you from enjoying a perfectly good corn dog."

I glanced down at the paper bag in my hand, already soaking through with oil. "You don't understand. It's different when you're a big girl."

"What do you mean?" he asked like he was genuinely curious.

I turned my eyes toward the overcast sky and sighed before turning back to the perfectly fit person next to me. "When you're overweight, that's all anyone sees about you. If you eat unhealthy food ever, even if it's just a splurge, they have all the evidence they need to write you off as just another person who can't control their cravings. Never mind the fact that you can only afford beans and rice to eat and you look forward to getting vegetables from other people's gardens every year just for a change of pace."

His eyelashes fanned over his cheeks as he looked down at his untouched corn dog, then he turned his creased eyes to me. "I'm sorry you have to go through that."

My throat felt tight, because even though I hadn't wanted his sympathy, it meant more to me than I wanted it to. "It's fine."

"It's not," he said. "But that doesn't change the way things are, does it?"

I shook my head. Nothing would—except, iron-ically, him and his dad. Their job meant the world to my mom, and therefore, to me. I didn't want to think about it.

"Will you just eat the corn dog already?" I asked. "I'm dying to see if you'll like it or if we'll get to feed the gulls."

He shook his head and peeled back a small corner of a mustard packet. The yellow sauce spurted onto his corn dog and dripped dangerously down. My hand shot out to catch it—which I did—

but I also got a good feel of his tight stomach and the ridges of his abs.

I gulped as I pulled my hand away. "Sorry, I—" I held up my hand with the mustard spot.

"Thanks," he said, his eyes following my hand as I drew it to my mouth and licked off the sour liquid.

Slowly, he brought the corn dog to his lips and took a bite, chewing thoughtfully. I watched him like a gift giver on a birthday, waiting to see if the person liked the present I'd worked so hard to find.

Again, he moaned, and I laughed. "Please tell me you don't always do that when you eat."

"Apparently only when there are trans fats involved." He laughed.

The carefree sound warmed my heart. "Good point."

We sat and ate our corn dogs, talking about nothing and everything—having the kind of conversation you'd never remember but always long for the way it made you feel.

When we reached the base of our corn dogs, I said, "This is the best part. I like to chew off the crunchies at the bottom."

"Crunchies?" he asked with an amused smile. "Is that a technical term?"

I slapped his shoulder, laughing. "Just be quiet and eat it."

He seemed unsure as his white teeth pressed down around the round brown spot and crunched. I did the same, and when he met my eyes, I giggled. This was the most carefree I'd felt in a long time, and it was happening with Kai Rush.

"You were right," he said. "The crunchies are the best part."

"Told you," I said with a pleased smile.

He stood and took my trash from me, then tossed it. Martín had always made me do that.

"Are you okay?" Kai asked. "You seem upset."

I shook my head, trying to wipe the frown from my face. "No, I just need to get home."

He frowned too now. "Oh. Okay." He extended his hand to mine, and I only held his for a fraction of a second before letting it go. We walked to his Honda, and I stared at the dent in the hood. Maybe that's what I was to him—a flaw in an otherwise unblemished existence. I hated the thought of being something that stood out in a bad way—that took value away from something.

We rode in silence to the bakery where my car waited, but when I reached for the handle, Kai put his hand softly on my arm.

"Hey," he said, his tone gentle. "I just wanted you to know, I had a good time today." A corner of his lips quirked as he looked down. "The best time I've had since I don't know when."

My heart stuttered at his words, because the truth was, I had too.

SIXTEEN

MOM CAME home that evening looking every bit of exhausted. She hung her purse over the door handle and slowly snapped the deadbolt shut.

"Hey, *mija*," she said.

"Hey." My stomach tightened with guilt, and I shifted on my seat at the counter. My mom had been working and caring for her friends while I'd been out with Kai, something she'd forbidden me from doing. Still, I couldn't stop thinking about Kai and the moment he said goodbye. How he'd smiled at me, genuinely smiled, and made me feel like maybe I'd misjudged him.

Even if I didn't need to hate him, why did I want him to brush his fingers over my skin again? My wrist was tender from the bruises, but still tingled from his gentle touch. Everything he did was careful, measured, and I wanted to know where he'd gained such control. I needed control now more than ever.

"How was your weekend?" Mom asked.

"Better than yours," I hedged. "Is Isa feeling better?"

"Definitely," Mom said, coming to give me a hug. "She slept and cuddled mostly. Remember when you used to sleep in my bed with me and snuggle? I miss that."

I managed a smile and nodded. What Mom didn't realize was that I'd done it to comfort her. That when she thought I was asleep, I could feel her clinging to me and quietly sobbing over the daughter she wished had been there.

I was so happy when Lucinda had gotten a new couch for herself and gave us the one with a fold-out mattress. I had missed having my mom so close, but I needed my freedom from the sadness that followed her everywhere. I could sense it in the way she looked at me, in the way her lips drew down at the end of a long day, how her smiles were just a little too big.

Thankfully, Mom had turned to the fridge and

was digging through storage containers of leftovers, so I had a few seconds to gather myself.

"So, back at the Rushes' tomorrow?" I asked, trying to keep my voice even. Except talking about Kai was not helping with that right now.

"Bright and early," she said obliviously. After popping some cilantro lime rice and a chicken leg quarter in the microwave, she turned to me. "I know it's been hard on you to get up so early and keep up with your studies and your friends. I'm so proud of you and *so* thankful. Especially for you keeping your distance from his son. I remember what it was like to be a teenager, and if I'd been around a boy that cute—well, let's just say I wouldn't have stayed away for long."

The microwave dinged as if punctuating her point. Or alerting her to my secret.

"Of course," I said shakily. Spending one day with Kai was fine. I owed him. But I owed my mom more, and I needed to remember that.

Our routine went back to normal the next day. Mom nudged me out of bed, and I got dressed, packed a bag with my uniform, and left the house.

Except when Mom came out of the bakery with my breakfast, she said, "You didn't tell me you were with a *boy* yesterday!"

I nearly choked, and I hadn't even taken my first drink yet. "Who told you?"

"Gayle, of course." She narrowed her eyes with a pleased smile. "Who was it?"

"Some guy from school," I replied, ripping open my bag. If she saw my eyes, she would know that it wasn't just *some* guy. He was *the* guy.

"A high schooler?" She bent over the car. "Intrigue! Tell me more!"

"Did you just say 'intrigue'?" I laughed.

Her fingers gripped the door of my car as she looked down at me. "Was it that cute blonde you and your friends always hang out with?"

"No!" I cried. "Carson is Callie's guy."

"I thought they were just friends?" she said suspiciously.

"I mean, that's what they tell everyone, but you can tell it's just a love story waiting to happen."

She tapped her chin. "So it's not Carson... Who is it? Is he ugly? Is that why you don't want to tell me?"

Actually, there were plenty of reasons I didn't want to tell her. Not to mention the fact of how painfully (literally) right she had been about Martín. Thank goodness it was winter and I didn't look weird by wearing a long-sleeved shirt under my polo. But Mom was still waiting, so I just said, "He's a friend, Mom. We went to the pier to study. No big deal."

"How neat. Is he a scholarship student too?"

"No," I answered too quickly. "The opposite." Well, it looked like my foot and my mouth were getting up close and personal. I needed to step up my game.

Mom's eyebrows rose like she clearly didn't believe me, but she simply shrugged and said, "Can't wait to meet this high school guy—a rich one, no less—who's stolen your heart."

As she walked away, I shut my door and let out a breath, easing the tension in my shoulders. Coffee. I needed coffee.

I reached for my mocha and saw Mom's writing. Gracias por ser me mejor amiga With a heart for a period.

Thanks for being my best friend.

My gut sank. As hard as it was to admit, my mom was my best friend too. We'd been with each other through everything, and this was no different.

I didn't want to keep secrets from her, whether I had a reason to or not.

Mom pulled out onto the road, and I followed her, deciding once and for all that was the end of it—I couldn't have any more "hangouts" with Kai. No more corn dog outings or giggling laughter or compliments. Even if a small part of me longed for more.

I easily maneuvered my functioning car into the garage and walked with Mom toward the tall front door. Despite my earlier decision, nerves skittered through me, making my heart beat faster. What would it be like to see Kai this morning, to go back to pretending like we were just classmates, barely acquaintances?

Robert let us in, and we walked toward the dumb waiter we'd discovered in the back of the house. Mom loaded her cart on, and then we took the stairs to the rooms. We were on the final portion of the house—the bedrooms.

My phone said it was just barely four in the morning. Would Kai be awake? Would we be working on his room? What would it look like on the inside? I reminded myself I had no business to know. No business to be curious.

"We're starting with Mr. Rush's room," Mom

said, leading me to the dumb waiter. "Then we'll do Robert's, his son's, and the rest of the guest rooms."

"We've already done three of the guest rooms. How many more are there?" I asked, trying to add up how much time it would take us, how much we could knock out before I went to school.

"Five," she answered simply.

My mouth hung open. "Five? There are eight *guest* rooms in this house?"

She nodded. If she was as stunned as I was, she didn't let on.

"So, you're telling me——"

"Shh."

I lowered my voice to a whisper. "Two people need *ten* bedrooms?"

"We're not here to judge," she said. "We're here to clean."

The dumb waiter opened, and she pressed a dust mop into my hands.

I glared at her, but she wouldn't meet my eyes.

"Just because we're poor doesn't mean everyone else needs to live that way," she said.

Her words hit me like a slap in the face. Couldn't she see how excessive and unnecessary it was? How wasteful? And why was I the one being chided here? They were the ones wasting money, not me. With anger fueling me, I went to the room farthest from where she was and began cleaning. As I scrubbed down floors and surfaces, my frustration with my mom subsided. She and I were in this together.

I made it through two guest rooms in relatively quick fashion, then knocked on the next door, just as nondescript as the others. When no one answered, I pushed inside, but quickly froze. This was Kai's room. It had to be.

There was a computer with three screens on a broad, light wooden desk. A poster with the *Rush+* logo hung over the screen, and a music stand stood in the corner of the room, his violin in an open case next to it. And there was the bed—perfectly made with white sheets and a comforter. A few framed photos hung on the walls, one of him and his dad, one of just him perfectly posed in front of a studio backdrop, and another of him and his dad in front of a *Rush+* Banner. I wondered if that was from the launch of their app a couple years ago.

I didn't know him then, but word flew through Seaton High about how a kid from the Academy created this app everyone had on their phones. For a while, kids tried creating apps of their own, always to much lower levels of recognition and success.

In this picture, he looked younger. Less jagged around the edges.

I didn't see any photos of his mom, though. Or cousins. Or anything that indicated he had a life outside of the app, violin, and school. It left me curious, hungry to know more. Who was Kai? I could already tell there was more to him than the carefully controlled self he showed everyone else.

The en suite bathroom door opened, and I jumped back, the dust mop handle clattering on the marble floor.

Kai took me in, alert even in cotton joggers and a loose-fitting white T-shirt.

"I—" I began, but then realized I had no plan for what to say. Sorry? For cleaning his room?

Wordlessly, he stepped forward and picked up the handle, but he didn't give it to me. Instead, he examined it in his hands. Apparently, he didn't have anything to say either.

For a moment, we stood in silence, but it grew too uncomfortable for me.

"I need to get back to work."

"You shouldn't have to clean my room." His

eyes hit mine then, full of an emotion I couldn't place. The force of it overwhelmed me.

And then I realized what it was: guilt. Pity's ugly first cousin.

"It's my job," I said roughly.

"It shouldn't be. Why should you have to work before school every day just because you have a different parent than I do?"

Now I was really getting frustrated. "You might have just realized that, but that's the way the world works." I reached for the broom, but he stepped back, too quick for me.

Gritting my teeth, I stepped forward to take it, but again, he dodged me.

There was an edge in his voice as he said, "Stop."

"And what?" I asked. "Get my mom fired? She needs this. *We* need this."

His jaw ticked off each long second that passed. "It feels wrong."

The fire spread in my chest, breeding anger and even worse—embarrassment. "Then I suggest you go."

Mom gasped behind me. "Jordan! We *never* talk to our clients like that." She took my shoulders and guided me out of the room. As I walked through the doorway, I could hear her offer profuse apologies to Kai, along with his futile attempts to defend me.

I was in trouble, and I knew it. But that just made me angrier. Kai was right. I didn't choose to be here, to have a poor family with an absent father and a dead sister whose medical bills hung over us.

I grabbed a spray bottle and a dingy rag from the cart and went to the guest room farthest away from Kai's. My fury carried me as I dusted surfaces, scrubbing harder than necessary.

I didn't know how long my mom watched me, but when I turned and saw her studying me, it had clearly been a while. I braced myself for her fury, for the guilt trip she was so good at placing on me—and herself. But it never came.

"Do you need help in here?" she asked.

Silently, I shook my head.

She nodded swiftly. "I'll clean the Rushes' rooms from now on."

I nodded as well, keeping my eyes peeled open to prevent the tears that were coming.

Another nod, and she left, leaving me with all the emotions I didn't understand and even more I didn't want to face.

SEVENTEEN

WHEN THE FINAL BELL RANG, I was beyond ready to go home, knock out my homework, and go to sleep. I said goodbye to the girls and went to my locker to grab my books.

My eyes caught the smooth, swift movements of Kai walking toward me. It was like they were trained to notice the purposeful placement of his feet, the controlled way he held himself. I wondered how I'd gone so long simply dismissing him, never really seeing him.

He seemed to stand out from everyone—apart from everyone. Kind of like me. Except he didn't have friends. He had classmates, project partners, teachers, but no one who seemed to really *know* him. He was an enigma. One I'd humiliated myself in front of far too many times.

His eyes landed on me, and he lifted a hand in a wave. He wanted to talk to me.

My heart jolted into action, along with the rest of my body. I hurried to shut my locker door and began walking away. I glanced over my shoulder to see Kai still walking purposefully toward me and sped up.

My shoulder rammed into someone stepping back from their locker, and then my feet stumbled over her heeled ankles, and I crashed to the floor, heavy books thudding in front of me.

"Ouch!" Merritt cried so loudly it echoed off the walls. "You nearly took me out, you 'ship!"

My wrist had hit the ground, and hard. I twisted on the ground, holding my wrist to my chest, and saw her examining herself like my fat or poverty might have somehow rubbed off on her. "I didn't see you," I said, my voice coming out in a groan.

Tinsley rolled her eyes. "Pay attention, then."

Poppy laughed. "She probably just can't afford glasses."

With a scowl, Merritt said, "I might need my insurance policy to donate some. For public safety."

My eyes were watering now from shame and

pain. I tried to capture my books from between everyone's feet, hurrying to get out of the building.

"That's enough," Kai said, and I felt his hand underneath my arm, helping me up.

Merritt studied him, her eyes stalling where his hand still rested on my elbow. She had met her match with Kai, the one person whose bank account could outweigh her family's. Zara came close, but not close enough to make a difference.

After a moment, she sniffed. "I wonder what your dad would think of you fraternizing with a 'ship."

Ignoring her, Kai bent to pick up my books.

"Interesting choice, Rush," Merritt said, slamming her locker shut before storming away, her friends in tow.

I took a book from him and muttered, "I can take care of it."

His eyes turned on me. "I know." But he didn't change his actions, helping me gather every last paper clip and pen that had scattered from my busted pencil case. When he handed them to me, his skin brushed mine, and the contact fired through me. Not like electricity, but like weight. I fully understood the heaviness of what standing up to Merritt meant. I worried what would happen when she leaked the news to his dad that he was hanging around someone like me.

I owed him for helping me, and I was already more in his debt than I cared to be. The crowd had thinned now, leaving only a few stragglers in the hall to hear what he said next.

"Come with me," he said.

"Where?" I asked, when I should have been asking why or simply saying no. I'd had the strength to run away, but now, with him up close? My willpower was waning.

"You showed me a day in your life. I want to show you part of mine." He slipped his hand into mine to hold it, a first that felt more like a thousandth.

A new weight settled over me. The kind that made sure I was aware of the cost. This was off limits. There was no doubt about it. But if I was being honest, I was tired of living with less, of restricting myself on every level possible. Today, I wanted to say yes.

My nod was cautious, but Kai picked up on every subtlety there was. Keeping my hand in his, he walked to his car—the Honda he was still driving, like he was afraid I would change my mind about not being his enemy.

There was no going back now. Kai was a mystery, one I wanted to solve, even if the hunt only lasted a day.

This time, we drove down a path familiar to both of us for different reasons. The one that led to his house.

"Will your dad be okay with this?" I asked.

"No."

I waited for him to elaborate, but I could have waited forever. He was done speaking.

He drove to the garage my mom and I weren't allowed to park in and then led me through a back entrance. We walked up stair after stair until my breath was short. Kai was in shape, but he moved slowly for me without my ever having to ask.

We crested at the roof and stepped into brilliant afternoon sunshine and crisp fall chill. But I could only focus on one thing: the black helicopter in front of us.

"Is that..."

"Our plans?" Kai finished for me. "Yes."

My body hummed in tune with the quiet excitement that laced his voice. He stepped ahead, and the closer we got, the better I could see the pilot in the front window.

Kai easily stepped up to the chopper, and he

extended his hand for me. I followed behind him, impossibly aware of the swish of my uniform skirt across my thighs and the breeze catching my thick ponytail. But nothing came close to the strength leaching through every bit of his skin that touched mine.

I'd never felt small or dainty. My mom and I were large women, built with curves and extra of everything. Extra-large eyes, extra-large cheeks and curls and smiles. But Kai made me feel light as he lifted me.

He moved to one of the seats, seemingly unaffected by the heat moving through my body. Did he not have the same reaction when we came in contact with each other? Was he aware of the questions that flew through my mind about him, begging to be answered?

His eyes caught mine, and I was convinced he saw everything. So much so, I turned my gaze to his hand and the headset extended there.

I took it and lifted it over my ears, adjusting the microphone to be positioned over my mouth. Kai's fingers brushed my shoulder, and I jerked, still unprepared. Would I ever get used to that?

He smiled at me, sweeping my hair out from where it had been tucked under the earpiece.

"Headphones on?" the pilot's voice came through my earpiece.

Kai's voice came next, muffled by the speaker system. "Yes, sir."

I found myself disappointed, missing the clear notes and inflections I was now robbed of.

Kai moved the mouthpiece and mouthed, "Can you hear us?"

I cleared my throat. "Yes." I needed to pay attention. Kai would think I'd somehow conned my way into an EA scholarship if I kept this up.

The pilot ran though some safety information and then asked if we were ready. Kai looked at me, waiting, like he was wanting to know the same thing.

I took a deep breath. "Yes."

EIGHTEEN

THE BLADES WHIRRED and the helicopter lifted from the rooftop of Kai's home, making my stomach drop. Like I was outside of my body, I saw us, sitting in the leather seats, gazing out the windows, because this couldn't be me.

How was I sitting with a *billionaire* in a helicopter, lifting into the air? Keeping secrets from my mom? She could never know about this, no matter how much I ached to tell her every thought passing through my mind with each revolution of the chopper blades.

Within minutes, we were high in the air, the Rushes' mansion like a tiny square below us. My eyes were glued to the window, but I could feel Kai's eyes on me. Every bit of me ached to turn and see while he spent them improving himself. Why I clung to every glimmer of opportunity when he had them delivered on a silver platter.

"We've sacrificed everything to pay off Juana's bills, and until we do..."

"You have it hanging over your heads."

"Exactly."

"And until then...I'm just a reminder of everything you can't have."

I couldn't even nod, because for the first time, he understood the truth. At least, as much as he could living the life he did.

Carefully, cautiously, he reached for my hand. And even knowing exactly the distance that lay between us, I let him.

"I'm sorry," he said.

I didn't even bother with the lies that people usually said when responding to an apology about tragedy—that it was a long time ago or that it wasn't his fault. Because that wasn't true. Her sickness had affected every second of my life that followed her diagnosis. Of my mother's. And people like the Rushes had all the power to take away the extra burden. But we weren't their responsibility, and they didn't want us to be. There was always the weight of grief on me, but now it was so big I couldn't shove it down. It was as much a part of me as my curves or the birthmark on my shoulder.

We finished sipping our mochas, and Kai helped me back over the rocks and to the helicopter. Hank flew us back to Kai's house and out of the bubble of our evening away.

We drove in mostly silence to the school, but when I reached for my door handle, Kai said, "Wait."

I turned to him, my hand still on the smooth grip.

He rested his fingers on my forearm, just over the bruise he'd kept from being so much worse. "You and your mom—you deserve everything my dad and I have."

I immediately recognized the guilt on his face, but instead of frustrating me, it made me sad. Was it worse to know what life could be like or to live in darkness without seeing the light? I didn't know. I simply did my best to smile at him. "Thank you for today. It was...incredible."

With a small curve of his lips, he said, "It was better—seeing it through your eyes."

His words warmed my stomach, but that was all there could be between us: words. A deep well of regret pooled within me as I nodded and left the car. How long he watched me after I got in my car and drove out of the parking lot, I didn't know. I just knew he did watch. I could feel it just as surely as I felt the ghost of his touch on my arm.

When I got home, Mom was curled in the mattress of the fold-out couch. Instead of walking to my room, I slipped off my backpack and climbed under the covers with her like I had when I was six years old. But now, I held her from behind and clung to her for dear life. In this big world with never-ending skies and islands and caves and boys with deep black eyes, she was all I had.

NINETEEN

FOR THE NEXT FEW WEEKS, life went on. My bruised wrist completely healed. We cleaned the Rushes' mansion in the mornings. I went home and did homework before making dinner and going to bed. On the weekends, the girls and I hung out when we could. And Kai and me? We went back to exactly how we should have been. Acquaintances passing in the hallways of school and his home.

Until one night I was sitting at the counter, eating a bowl of potato soup. My mom opened the door, carrying a cake half her size.

I furrowed my eyebrows. "What is that?" I would have worried that I'd forgotten her birthday if it weren't in June.

"We"—she set the cake on the counter—"are celebrating."

"Celebrating what? A sugar coma?" I stared at the fresh raspberries topping the cake. It had to be *tres leches*, my favorite. My mouth was salivating already.

She laced her fingers together, practically dancing. "My medical payment was returned today."

Now I was confused. Really confused. "You didn't have enough money?"

"No." She placed her fingers on the counter, steadying herself. "Honey, our debt is paid."

"What?" I asked. "You had thousands—"

"Some local charity called Invisible Mountains covered it all!"

My eyebrows came together. "Invisible Mountains?" The nonprofit for our FMP fundraiser was known for their mental health advocacy, not medical bills. But maybe they did more than I realized. "I don't understand."

She took my face in her hands. "Don't question it, sweetie. Stop second-guessing. I called the collection agency, and we are done. We're done!"

My heart soared, taking in what that meant, and I grabbed her wrists as her hands still rested on my cheeks. "We're done?" My throat was tight, but the words were clear.

"We're done, baby," she breathed, wiping my tears with her thumb. "We're done."

I sobbed into her chest, and she cried into my shoulder, and we held each other tightly, rocking and swaying and silently thanking whatever light had finally shone upon us after years in the darkness.

We ate our way through nearly half of the *tres leches* cake before falling asleep in a sugar-induced coma. Mom even did something she never did and called in sick the next morning. I heard each word as she told Mr. Rush she was ill and would not be coming in for the day. She used her phone to email the school and let them know I was sick and wouldn't be coming in either.

"What are we going to do?" she asked me. "I know we've been wanting to go to Walden Island, but since the ferries aren't running, maybe we can do something else? Massages? Mani-pedis?"

My eyes lit up. If anyone deserved a spa day, it was my mom. "Let's do it."

She dressed in one of the few pairs of jeans she had, and I convinced her to borrow a blouse from my closet. We wore the same size, and even though she was older, she looked just as good in it.

I fanned her and sang, "Jordan's mom has got it going on."

She held up a pretend mic and sang, "Jordan, can't you see? You're just not the girl for me."

We burst out in a fit of giddy giggles, and she wiped at her eyes. "Let's get out of here, eh, *mija?*"

I nodded emphatically and grabbed the whipped cream container off the counter that had extra cake for the Gutiérrezes. We stopped by their apartment, and Mr. Gutiérrez opened the door.

"Hola, bonitas."

Mom grinned at the compliment, and I extended the cake. *"Para usted y su esposa bonita."*

He took it with a chuckle. *"Estoy rodeado."*

I laughed at his joke about being surrounded by beautiful women. We waved goodbye and went down to Mom's car. Hers was a little nicer than mine, but I pictured her driving something even better in the future. One she didn't have to add oil to every couple thousand miles.

Having the debt paid off was like someone had taken the sun guard out of our windshield and we could finally look ahead instead of only seeing our current situation.

"Where should we go?" Mom asked.

I realized I was stumped. We'd never gone and gotten pedicures before. The best we'd done was a walk on the beach with a bottle of fingernail polish. "Let me text the girls. They probably know someone."

I sent a quick message asking for recommendations. Zara quickly replied with a list of her favorite people, then texted, *what? Did the doctor prescribe a spa day?*

I laughed out loud and turned the phone so Mom could read what Zara said.

Jordan: No, but we got some good news that deserves celebrating. Want to meet up tonight so I can tell you what happened?

A few dots popped up on the screen.

Zara: We'll meet you at Waldo's after school, you delinquent.

I laughed and exited out of the messaging app so I could type in the address. The navigation took us all the way across town to this boutique spa on the edge of Emerson. We checked in with the front desk and scheduled ourselves for the next available appointment, which was for a couple's massage.

Mom waggled her eyebrows at me. "I didn't even get a couple's massage on my honeymoon."

This was the first time Mom had mentioned her relationship with Dad to me, even if it was in a roundabout way like talking about their honeymoon. When he left, I'd been too young to get all the stories about how they fell in love, but now so much time had passed it felt weird to ask.

"That was weird, huh?" she said quietly.

I shrugged. "I just don't know much about your life with him."

"What do you want to know?"

I glanced around the waiting room, at the receptionist pretending not to listen to us. "Now?"

"Why not?"

I'd take what I could get. Who knew when Mom would be ready for this again? "Where did you go on your honeymoon?"

"Walden Island."

My eyebrows rose. "What?" A feeling much too close to betrayal rose in my chest. We had been wishing and planning for a trip there as long as I could remember. "You never told me you'd been there."

She nodded, looking down at her cracked fingernails. "We eloped, and since he was just starting a new job, we couldn't take a longer trip to Playa del Carmen like we'd wanted to. We caught the ferry and explored Walden Island all day. I remember there were these caves there. When no one was looking, we carved our initials into a stone." Her smile was bittersweet. "Part of me wishes I could go carve something over it." She shrugged. "Maybe someone already has."

My stomach felt cold. I'd been there, in the caves, with Kai. I'd seen the carvings and graffiti. Without knowing it, I'd taken part in my parents' legacy and created memories of my own with Kai. Even if it didn't last, it was there. My parents' was written in stone, while mine was written in my heart.

What did it mean now that the Rush job didn't have such a huge bearing on our financial future? Would Mom lighten up on her rule? Did I dare hope?

When the massage therapists came out to get us, I still wasn't sure, but I knew my heart felt lighter than it had in months.

TWENTY

MOM DROVE me to the diner and parked in one of the spaces up front. Through the windows, I could see Chester talking to the waitress as she poured him another cup of coffee. My friends were farther down, the four of them around a booth, huddled together. So much love swelled in my heart. I had everything I needed—a mom who loved me, great friends who showed up when I needed them to, and a means to getting an education that would let me provide for us.

I grinned over at my mom. "Thanks for today. I needed it."

She smiled and scratched my shoulder with her bright pink fingernails. "It was good to see you so happy, *mija*. It's been a long time since I've seen you smile like this."

"What do you mean?" I asked. As far as I could tell, I've always just been me.

Her eyes creased regretfully at the corners. "I started noticing it about a year ago. You stopped laughing as much. You went to bed earlier. It was like you had the weight of the world on your shoulders with no means to rest."

My eyes felt hot. A year ago, I was applying to study at the Academy, having heard it would help prepare me for medical school. Then I started dating Martín, and the time that belonged to my mom and me became his. But it was more than that. It was constantly feeling like I was the one who had to dig us out of the Grand-Canyon-sized hole we were in using only a toy-sized shovel.

She took my face in her hands and brushed her thumbs over the crest of my cheekbones. "Even though you're my best friend, I hope you know you can count on me as your mom."

I blinked quickly and nodded. I leaned across the console and wrapped my arms around her. "I love you, Amá."

"I love you more."

I pulled back and smiled through the tears that had fallen.

"It's been a crazy twenty-four hours," she said.

"It has."

"Enjoy your time with your friends." She grabbed her dollar-store sunglasses from where they hung over the visor and put them on. "I'm feeling a little beachy relaxation."

The thought of Mom laying out on the beach and just relaxing made me smile. "Have fun."

"You too."

I got out of the car and walked up the ramp to the restaurant. The second I swung the heavy door open, I was enveloped in warmth. They must have begun using the heater. It was always a big deal in our part of California who could hold out on using their furnace the longest.

The smell of grease and the sound of fries crackling in the fryer assailed my senses. For what seemed like the first time, I was taking everything in —the scuffs on the black and white checkered floor, the fall-themed window clings, the feeling of vitality that seemed to fill each vinyl booth.

"Hey, girl," Chester said.

I grinned at him. "Hi, Chester. How are you?"

He lifted his cup of coffee. "Can't complain. You?"

"Amazing," I said with a smile and waved goodbye so I could continue to my friends.

They sat in our usual booth—the big circular one that we could all scoot into and fit around, even with boyfriends tagging along. Callie caught sight of me coming and waved. The others followed her eyes and grinned at me.

Instead of getting into the open seat they'd left for me on the edge, I wrapped Callie in a big hug.

"I love you too," she giggled.

I stepped back. "I could kiss you right now."

She was blushing. Actually blushing. "Um, can I ask why?"

My other friends looked just as curious as they stared at me from around the booth.

Zara lifted her eyebrows suggestively. "Is there something you're trying to tell us?"

Laughing, I said, "Yes! Invisible Mountains paid off my sister's medical bills!" My voice echoed off the tiled floors. I didn't even care who heard me saying we'd accepted charity. As the CEO, Callie's dad had a major role in completely changing our lives. Mom and I wouldn't be rich. Not on our income, but we would be able to afford groceries.

More than beans and rice and potatoes and the occasional on-sale meat. She wouldn't have her wages garnished each month. If she kept her business going, we would make it and maybe have a little extra to spare.

"What do you mean?" Callie asked. "Dad didn't tell me that!"

Rory reached across Callie to grab my hand. "That's huge! I'm so happy for you."

"Me too," Ginger said emphatically. "This is awesome!"

I slid into the seat next to Zara. "My mom just came home last night with a huge cake and told me the rest of the bill was paid by Invisible Mountains. We took a spa day—at one of the places Zara suggested—and got our nails done." I flashed my French-tip nails with palm trees painted on my ring fingers.

"Nice," Zara said approvingly as she inspected my manicure.

Callie frowned. "I still don't get it, though. Usually Dad has a big press conference when they do something like this."

With a shrug, Zara said, "Maybe it was a silent donor?"

"What do you mean?" I asked.

Callie finished sipping from her soda, then set it down on a napkin. "Sometimes people who give to a specific cause don't want to be named."

In the back of my mind, I saw Kai telling me that my mom and I deserved better. My blood ran cold. It couldn't be. "Callie, we have to find out who it was."

I watched the battle war on her open-book face, but finally she nodded. "I'll see what I can do."

Zara leaned forward. "Who do you think it was?"

I shook my head and told them a lie because seeing their reactions and answering their questions would be scarier than the truth. "I don't know."

Callie reached across the table and put her hand on mine. "We'll find out."

TWENTY-ONE

I WOKE up with a *Sermo* chat staring at me from my phone.

Callie: Silent donor. No idea who, and Dad can't tell me.

I blinked my eyes against the screen. Her dad didn't need to tell her, because I already knew who it was.

Instead of the tired way I usually got out of bed, I rolled to my feet and got ready, already shaking with energy. Ideas of what I could say to Kai flooded my mind, but none of them seemed good enough. How did you thank someone who broke you from the chains that bound you, especially when they weren't responsible for placing them there? He had the resources to drive the most expensive cars on the market, to have the best in technology, to live the carefree life of every other student at Emerson Academy. He could have kept it to himself, never paying my mom or me any mind, but instead, he'd laid it at my feet.

We couldn't get to his house fast enough.

Just like every other morning, we drove to Seaton Bakery for breakfast. The message on this morning's cup?

Take every chance.

I felt like I was in the helicopter again, flying over the city ang going to an incredible, unknown destination. The view from this perspective was amazing. We drove down the suburban streets to Kai's home, and brown leaves swirled through the air in front of my windshield, giving way to a new season of life.

We parked in the garage, and I couldn't get the cart loaded fast enough.

"You are perky this morning," Mom said. "Maybe we should have spa days more often."

"Definitely," I agreed, even though that had little to do with my hustle.

I got the last of the supplies in the cart and began wheeling it toward the house.

"I will say, my back feels better than it has in ages."

The light way my mom said it tore at my heart and lifted it at the same time. This was the beginning, I promised myself. She would get the care she deserved, not have to strain so hard each day of her life just to get by.

Robert greeted us at the door and told us we could begin dusting the wine cellar. He led us to a basement near the kitchen lined with bottles and bottles of the stuff. One of the labels I passed by said it was from the early 1700s.

Mom got out rags and solution for both of us, and we got started, but I was antsy. I wanted to see Kai. To thank him.

"I need to use the bathroom," I said, and my voice echoed off the stone walls.

She nodded her chin toward the stairs. "I got this."

Trying not to go too quickly, I went up the steps and passed both Robert and Mr. Wallace in the kitchen. I stalled by the servants' bathroom and twisted the lock so Mom would think I was in there if she came to check. I could always use my thumbnail to twist it open later.

The stairway seemed both impossibly long and incredibly short. I was simply feet away from the room I knew was Kai's. Light wood and slightly darker lines stared back at me. I'd been waiting for this moment all morning, and now that it was here... I shook out my hands and attempted a deep breath before gently turning the knob and pressing the door open.

An alarm clock glared red numbers at me through the darkness. It wasn't yet half past four. My eyes took a second adjusting to the dark, but when they did, I could see Kai's form, shifting under the covers. His hair lay in a messy pile atop his head, and he squinted at me.

"Jordan?" he asked, his voice rough from just waking up, saying my name for the first time in what felt like forever.

My heart surged. This was the guy who'd fought for a chance with me. The one who gave my mom and me a fighting chance. I went to his bed and knelt at the side. He turned to me, his eyes questioning.

"You did it," I breathed.

He knew what. And he didn't deny it.

His eyes slowly blinked open, and a soft smile

touched his lips as he reached his hand to my cheek. "You're not on your own. Not anymore."

My heart moved my body for me before my brain could react, and I was leaning to him, pressing my lips to his in a kiss that transformed every bit of me. His fingers worked through my hair, pulling me closer to him, like this, us, was just as natural as the changing leaves outside.

He tugged the covers back and pulled me next to him so we could lie beside each other in the warmth of his nest. Our lips separated, and he held my stare. I didn't know how I'd never seen the softness of his eyes before—the depths of kindness that lay there.

"Thank you," I breathed.

A smile made his lips that much better. "For you? Anything."

My heart swelled as I leaned my cheek into his hand. I wanted to stay here forever, never leaving for work or caving to expectations. But my mom needed me, and I had a job to do.

"Meet me after my FMP meeting?" I asked.

"Where?"

"Anywhere."

"Under the bleachers. Five o'clock."

I nodded and dropped a kiss on his palm before leaving his room.

As I walked down the hallway, my entire body alight with excitement, all I could think was maybe our hearts weren't as far apart as I had always suspected.

TWENTY-TWO

MY CHEEKS WERE hot as I approached my friends in the hallway. Even though I looked the same on the outside, I was different, thanks to Kai. To the kiss we shared that turned my world—and my heart—upside down.

Ginger narrowed her eyes at me. "You've been keeping a secret from us."

My stomach bottomed out. "Wh-what?"

She held up a piece of cardstock with scripted writing on it. Leaning closer, I could make out the fancy font inviting her to a gala for Invisible Mountains. Poppy's event planner must have gotten the invites out, as promised. Still, I cringed to think of how much the cardstock and gold inlaid lettering must have cost.

Ginger twisted and tucked the invite in her backpack. "You didn't tell us there was going to be a gala."

"Yeah," Rory said, "I thought FMP just did a blood drive every year."

I rolled my eyes toward the ceiling, glad for a sense of normalcy. "You know how Poppy and Tinsley are."

"True," Zara said. "I bet they had Pixie's full sign-off."

Callie shrugged. "Dad's really excited about it. He said it will be great press for the organization."

I nodded. It would be. It was just the last thing on my radar. "I need to get through the blood drive first." I lowered my voice. "Honestly, Poppy's parents are basically paying to put the whole thing together. FMP hardly has anything to do with it."

"Ah," Ginger said. "Well, here's to hoping my parents actually let me go."

Callie frowned. "They won't let you go to a school event?"

My eyebrows came together. "Do you have to work or something?" That was the only reason I could imagine for my mom to straight up forbid me from something, considering I was eighteen and months from starting college.

Ginger's voice lowered as she scrunched up her face. "Galas are a drunken fest for people to brag about who's richer while little is done for actual charity." Her voice went back to normal as she shot Callie a quick, "Sorry, that's what my dad said about the last school gala," and went back to her impression. "No one mans the open bars, and you, *young lady*, have no business drinking."

"Ugh," Zara said. "Doesn't he know we could just sneak from the liquor cabinet like every single sleepover if we really wanted to?"

"Um, no," she said. "Because he always thinks I'm staying the night at Rory's, and he trusts her mom."

Rory rolled her eyes. "All we would have to do is ask my mom for a glass of wine, and she'd start pouring. She says one glass of red wine with dinner is good for your heart."

"Can't you just tell him you're staying at Rory's that night?" Zara asked. "If he's so against the gala, there's no way he'll show."

"I can stay in with you," I offered. "I don't really have anything to wear." Plus, it wouldn't be as much fun without everyone there.

"Come on, girl," Zara said. "You're the VP of

the organization that's putting on the event. And you know you can raid my closet any time."

"No," Ginger said. "You shouldn't have to suffer with me. Have fun. Save yourself. Meet yourself a man and have a nice life. I'll be busy serving my sentence. Eighteen to life."

I chuckled. "They'll ease up."

"Easy for you to say," she muttered. "What are you guys doing tonight? I have about half an hour before I need to get home."

Rory readjusted her backpack. "It's dinner night with Beckett's dad."

"Blind date," Zara said. "Another one of my dad's setups."

Ginger kissed three fingers and held them out, and Callie did *The Hunger Games* whistle in return.

I giggled at them.

"What about you?" Ginger asked.

"Oh, I—" Something stopped me from telling them about Kai. "Nothing much. Homework. I can hang out for a little bit."

I couldn't even justify my answer not being a lie. Seeing Kai, the guy who had single-handedly lifted the biggest burden of my life...there weren't words to describe how big of a deal it was.

The bell rang, and Ginger saluted us. "Back to the chain gang. Pray for me."

With smiles and varied condolences, Ginger and I left for videography. Even though her parents treated her like a criminal, she was a model student. She loved the subject, and in class, Ginger paid attention and asked all the right questions.

After we finished videography and the bell rang, she and I parted ways. Next up, health class with Rory and Zara. Unfortunately, Merritt, Tinsley, and Poppy were in that class too.

We began our lesson on diabetes and the different types when Mrs. Bardot stepped into the classroom and asked for Mrs. Hutton.

Rory leaned over so she could talk to Zara and me. "I think we should all get ready for the gala together. It could be super fun."

"Yes!" Zara agreed. "And if Ginger's dad won't let her go to the party, maybe they'd at least let her get all dressed up and take pictures with us."

While they continued with all their plans— including snacks we could have and movies we could watch while getting ready—my mind wandered to Kai. But thinking of him and the gala hurt. We couldn't exist in public together, and I didn't know how to explain that without losing what small chance I had with him. For the brief moments we'd spent together, I'd felt something real. But maybe that was all it was supposed to be—a momentary feeling, not a lasting reality.

Merritt's voice trilled from the row ahead of us. "Who's your dad going to pay to take you, Zara?"

Zara rolled her eyes. "Your mom."

Despite myself, I laughed out loud. I'd thought we were way past 'your mom' jokes, but here came Zara, bringing them back to life.

Merritt's blue eyes narrowed to slits. "What's funny, 'ship? It's black tie. Your hood-rat boyfriend won't be able to meet the dress code."

My nostrils flared, and I clenched my fists under the desk. Merritt knew how to get under my skin, and the worst part was that I couldn't defend myself. If we were ever on an even playing field, I'd clobber her.

Rory shook her head. "Jordan's done with him, which you'd know if you spent any time looking past your own nose."

With an acutely false sympathetic look, Merritt said, "Aw, he finally realized he could do better than all *that*? I did not see that coming."

My face became a steel vault, devoid of emotion. Bullies like Merritt fed off of pain and heartbreak. Show one crack, and they'd come with a sledgehammer to dismantle the rest of your composure. I couldn't risk that, not with my scholarship on the line, and she knew it.

"How dare you," Zara began, "you bi—"

The classroom door opened, and Mrs. H came in, carrying a stack of papers. Walking to the first row of desks, she separated a small stack. "Mrs. Bardot has a new handout for all students on what to do if you're feeling bullied by another student. Please take one and pass it back."

Rory, Zara, and I gave each other a look. Regardless of what the paper said, we knew people like Merritt always got a pass. We'd seen it with Rory at homecoming and every other day in class.

I still couldn't believe some of the things Merritt and her crew had said when Mrs. Hutton left the room. They really believed curvy girls didn't deserve happily ever afters—that no guy would want to be with someone who looked like one of us.

I hated to inform them that the only billionaire in our school was more than willing to date a girl with a little more cushion. Except I couldn't. He wasn't mine, even if my heart was beginning to think it belonged to him.

TWENTY-THREE

NOW THAT FOOTBALL season was over, the path to the field was deserted. Still, I checked around to make sure no one was watching me from the school's parking lot. Jordan Junco and Kai Rush hiding under the bleachers? That would make headlines. We'd never live it down.

With the coast appearing clear, I headed to the back side of the bleachers. The tall metal stands cast a long shadow behind them, and the second I stepped into the shade, the cold became that much more intense. I pulled my coat tighter around me and pushed my hands deeper into my pockets. All of that was completely unnecessary. As my eyes found a long, lean figure leaning against one of the support posts, heat spread through me, starting in my stomach and reaching my cheeks.

"Kai," I breathed. My breath came out in a puff of steam.

"Jordan." His features changed, brightening at the sight of me. I couldn't quite comprehend the way it made my chest rise.

I didn't waste time getting to the question I'd wanted to know all day. We were past beating around the bush. "Why did you do it?" I had to know before my heart got too involved.

He glanced down, his hair falling over his fore-head as he did. "You and your mom deserved better." His gaze met mine, his dark eyes holding entire universes within. "I *wanted* you to have better."

My heart stuttered along with my mind. The emotion behind his words was every bit as strong as the steel holding up the bleachers, as ironclad as the circumstances keeping us apart.

"Does your mom know it was me?" he asked.

I shook my head. "Does your dad know?"

He shook his head.

"He's not going to notice the money missing?"

"It's from my account."

The casual way he said it made me take a step back. I couldn't imagine having my own pool of money to draw from—much less one that could accommodate such a large bill. And then giving it so freely? The depth of his gift touched me, put me forever in his debt. My heart sank. We could never be more as long as I was less.

"I'll pay you back," I promised. "Once I graduate med school, I'll—"

"That's not the point," he snapped, taking my shoulders in his hands. "Don't you get it, Jordan? I like you. I want to help you. You not being crushed under debt before you even have the chance to spread your wings is enough for me. That's all I want."

"Why?" I demanded. It didn't make sense.

His jaw ticked. "Why what?"

"Why all of it!" I cried. "I've been awful to you from the second we met. There's no reason for you to like me."

Then he did the craziest thing. He smiled.

It lifted my entire soul. Overjoyed and annoyed me as only he could do. "You're a masochist," I finished.

He chuckled softly. "I'm not a masochist."

"Then what is it?" I had to know.

His hands were firm on my shoulders and held me in place for the message I had to hear. "My whole life has been decided for me. What I do when I wake up, what I eat for breakfast, where I go to school...No one cares what I have to say, much less asked. And then I met you, and I realized, it mattered to you. Not what my dad did, not what he chose for me, but what I chose for myself. For the first time, someone hated me for my inaction, just as much as I was beginning to hate myself."

Guilt whipped through me. I'd never wanted him to hate himself. "Kai, I—"

His hand moved from my shoulder to my chin as he stopped my words. "I've never met someone so selfless, and I *know* if you were in my position, you'd help me however you could, even if it meant getting up at four in the morning to work on a cleaning job to pay the bills." With a soft smile, he sighed and ran his fingers down my cheek, sending tingles in their wake. "Somewhere between seeing you in my house for the first time and sitting on the pier with you, I started basing my actions on what you would think of them, because I know you always do what's right."

But it still didn't make sense. "If you like me, why are we here?" I gestured at the grungy underside of the bleachers where we stood with abandoned gum and ages of dust. "Are you ashamed of me?" I barely choked out the last words, hating myself for thinking them and preemptively hating Kai for feeling them.

"No." He took my hands and pulled me toward him until we were inches apart. His eyes traveled from my shoulders to the spot where my olive skin met his pale flesh. "Has anyone told you about my mom?"

"No." My answer was barely a whisper in the wind. I shook my head.

"She was my dad's maid. Well, his parents' maid." He looked up at me. "And he fell for her."

An uncomfortable laugh rose in my chest. "Like father, like son."

But there was no humor in his eyes. "She wasn't like you. She immigrated illegally from Korea, and she used him. He fell in love with her, married her, had a child with her. After I was born and she had her permanent citizenship papers, she left."

The impassive way he said it made my chest tighten. There had to be pain under his composure. "That's awful."

"It was," Kai agreed. "And ever since, my dad

has said we should only date our equals. Power imbalances only lead to heartbreak."

A small part of me agreed with his dad, but I stifled it. "But if she only cared about gaining power, why wouldn't she stay with him? He's a literal billionaire."

"We weren't always this rich. We were well-off, but *Rush+* launched us to the next level—and that much further away from anyone who would ever be good enough for me in my father's eyes."

Finally, he met my gaze, examining me. I felt almost as naked as the hopelessness on his face.

I dared myself to hold his stare. "What does that mean for us?"

"It means as long as there is an 'us,' he can never know." The layer of composure was gone now, and a blend of desperation and disappointment took its place. "I like you, Jordan, but you deserve someone who can love you out in the open." He gestured around us. "Not hide you under the bleachers."

My mind wanted to listen to his logic, but my heart was stuck on one fact: he liked me. He had access to a caliber of girls I could never dream to compete with in real life, but in this fantasy, he'd chosen me. Through all my judgement of him.

Through the cold treatment. He'd seen something in me, and he liked it.

Picking up an arsenal of reason, my head warred with my heart. There were countless reasons Kai and I shouldn't date, but one that we should: I liked him too. I couldn't hold it back, couldn't argue myself away from seeing the truth of how incredible he was. Bravery welled up inside my heart, and it fought back, cajoled my brain into understanding. This could work. In secret. His dad wouldn't find out, and neither would my mom. "I won't tell if you don't," I whispered.

His breath was warm on my lips as he spoke. "It's our secret."

"What do we do now?" I asked.

"I could try..." He was so close now. Less than an inch away. Close enough for me to reach up and feel his arms, the muscles underneath his winter coat. Every millimeter he came closer to me, closer to my lips, the shallower my breath became, like I needed his kiss as much as I needed the air around me.

The second our skin touched, everything inside me came undone, exploding into brilliant, clear colors of possibility and hope and desire and need and murky shades of fear and danger and forbid-denness.

I ran my hands over his chest, inside his coat and uniform jacket, feeling each bump and ridge, all the sensations colliding in my nerves and making every inch of me more sensitive than before.

His hand found my waist, and he held me against him, so close I could feel his planes and edges through his clothes.

I'd never imagined kissing Kai before this morning, and maybe it was good that I hadn't, because I never could have imagined *this*.

This was not allowed. And maybe that was what made it so dangerously, unbearably, addictingly sweet.

He pulled back, and I slowly blinked my eyes open. I didn't want to exist outside of the world of his tantalizing touch and purposeful movements.

He rubbed his thumb over the raw skin of my lower lip, but his eyes sizzled every other part of my skin.

"I have to go to my violin practice," he breathed, an almost imperceptible note of disappointment in his voice. "When will I see you next?"

My heart leapt to attention. He wanted more, just like I did. "What are you doing Saturday?"

His fingers swept over my cheek. "Whatever you want."

Was it just me or was there a teasing hint in his voice? I was so busy wondering, I almost forgot to respond. Almost.

"Meet me at Emerson Trails. Four o'clock?"

"I'll be there."

TWENTY-FOUR

I WIPED AT MY FOREHEAD, leaving a smear of paint behind. "Thanks for helping with this, guys."

"It's kind of fun," Rory replied, easily keeping her own brush within the lines she'd set out for us. This was way better than the signs for the blood drive I could have made on my own. I would have just ended up sitting at home and stressing about my meeting with Kai later while Mom worked on a solo cleaning job.

"Yeah," Callie agreed. "These are so good. They will definitely draw some attention!"

I hoped so. Rory had helped me get a massive banner and carefully lettered a sign to advertise the blood drive coming up. While we painted the letters, she worked on filling in the other smaller posters she'd gotten and outlined.

Tinsley and Poppy probably would have bought something or hired a graphic designer, but I wanted to do this on my own. All the events at Seaton High had gone on just fine with hand-painted signs and posters stuck to a cluttered bulletin board.

"Hey," Rory said, "How's cleaning at the Rushes' going, by the way? You've hardly said anything about it. Has Kai been bugging you?"

"It's been fine," I said, even though that was the understatement of the century. Just the thought of Kai had goosebumps rising on my arms. There was something about him that was such a strong contrast to any other guy I'd ever dated. He was kind and generous and actually listened to me. He'd traded in a brand-new car for a used Honda, for crying out loud. And he looked just as good in his beater car as he did in the morning when he still wore a groggy look or in the late evening when his eyes glittered in the darkness.

"No falling in love?" Rory asked, a teasing smile.

My hand stilled but finally, I shook my head. "Honestly, me getting a boyfriend right now is about as likely as Merritt signing up for seminary."

Ginger snorted, then frowned. "At least you have guys interested. I'm never going to fall in love the way high school's going."

"Come on," Rory said. "You know you will."

Ginger tilted her head to the side. "Not with my parents around. The guy would see how they treat me and get worried about taking out a child."

"If they know about it," I said. "They don't need to know."

"What do you mean?"

"I mean, if they're going to treat you like a delinquent, maybe you should act like one."

Her eyes sparked for a moment, and then she shrugged. "I'd have to find a guy worth risking it for first."

"How will you know?" Callie asked, chewing her lip. "If he's worth it, I mean?"

With a dreamy look, Ginger turned her paintbrush in her fingers. "He'd have to be generous, kind, giving...strong."

It struck me that I already found a guy like that. Each of those words applied to Kai.

Zara raised her eyebrows. "If you find one of those, let me know if he has a brother."

A burst of giggles sounded down the hall, and we each craned our necks to hear.

"What was that?" Ginger asked.

Rory shook her head. "Aiden and Casey. I swear they get cuter by the day."

A small frown found my lips. Maybe it was in Rory's DNA to be in a good relationship. Her parents seemed so close, her brother and Casey were the perfect candidates for the high school sweethearts who made it all the way, and she and Beckett? They were practically the picture in the dictionary next to happily ever after.

My mom hadn't dated since Dad left, and my relationships? I shuddered thinking of Martín and the man he'd revealed himself to be. How could I be with a guy for nearly a year and not know all that anger was lying underneath the surface?

No matter how excited I was to see Kai, I had to admit I was still fearful. Could I really trust that I knew the real Kai? Was I ready to risk everything to find out?

"You seem deep in thought, Jordan," Callie said.

I kept my gaze down on the letter I was painting. "It's been a busy couple weeks."

"Yeah," she said. "How have you been getting enough sleep with all the early mornings at the Rushes'?"

I could feel the others' eyes on me as I shrugged. "You get used to it, but something happened a little while back..." There was so much I wanted to tell them, but couldn't yet. Not until I knew it was real.

My hand shook on the paintbrush. I couldn't tell them about Kai without telling them about Martín without telling them that I'd lied to Ginger and my mom hadn't actually met me. And then I'd have to explain why I hadn't let her drive me home. Shame flooded me, and it was a wonder they couldn't see it seeping through every one of my pores.

Ginger put a gentle hand on my free arm. "Is it about Martín?"

The bruise on my arm had healed, but the feeling of betrayal and helplessness was still strong. Taking in a deep breath, I nodded. "He...attacked me."

Rory's peaceful studio erupted into a chorus of gasps and cries and questions.

"How did you get away?" Zara asked.

I slowly looked up and met their wide, sympathetic eyes. I didn't feel judged for ever having liked him or for putting myself in a vulnerable position.

There was just concern and care. It expanded the moisture in my eyes.

I sniffed and answered. "Kai saved me."

"WHAT?" Rory cried. "Kai Rush?"

"The Kai Rush who plays video games all the time?" Zara asked.

Ginger looked equally as shocked. "Wasn't Martín a big guy?"

"Was he hurt too?" Callie asked.

I shook my head. "Martín didn't even stand a chance. He was bigger, but Kai was trained. It was crazy."

"I never would have guessed," Zara said.

"Me neither," I admitted.

Ginger pulled at one of her bouncy curls, twirling it around her finger. "So Martín followed you to Kai's house? That's so creepy. Are you worried about him doing it again?"

"No, I—"

The studio door opened, and Rory's mom came in carrying a tray of veggies and cheeses, along with a clear pitcher of fizzing liquid with mint sprigs, cucumbers, and lemons. "How about some refreshments, painter bees?"

I flipped my expression to a pleasant one and said, "Of course. Thank you, Mrs. H."

I wanted this raw, pounding sensation to leave and the excited one about seeing Kai later to return. Like he could protect me from the painful memory just as well as he had an agonizing reality. Now, more than ever, I couldn't wait to meet him later that afternoon and see what our future had in store.

TWENTY-FIVE

I GOT in my car and drove from Rory's pristine suburban neighborhood to Emerson Trails. One day, when I was an oncologist, I wanted to live somewhere like this. Somewhere I could have a yard and a house with some space to just relax. Not so big, though, that it ate up precious resources I could use to help others.

Kai's face popped into my daydream, welcoming me into my—our home—and I slammed my eyelids shut, quickly blinking away the fantasy. Why had I pictured Kai? It was way too soon. And it couldn't happen. No matter how long we dated, there wasn't a public future for us even after we graduated. Mr. Rush had power in this town, which meant he could ruin my mom's reputation, before or after I moved out.

There it was, that heavy blanket weaved from guilt and shame. That should be plenty to keep daydreams I shouldn't be having from entering my vision. For good measure, I took a deep breath as I parked a few spots away from Kai and quietly said, "This is just for now. Not forever."

Kai appeared at my car door, a genuine smile on his face. One that shined through his carefully controlled exterior, and suddenly my willpower was gone. He opened the car door for me, and I stepped out, aware of his eyes on me and the tight leggings I wore.

I pushed the lock down on the driver's side door and shoved my hands and keys into my pockets.

"Ready?" he asked.

Not knowing if I was, I nodded. "Let's go."

For several minutes, we walked down the open trail. The cold weather had cleared it out for us, but he kept his cap low over his eyes.

We were so close to each other, and all I wanted to do was reach out and touch his hand, feel his long fingers and the need they had as they explored my body.

"Want to step off the trail?" I suggested.

His eyes sizzled on me. "Just a little way longer. I have a plan."

I'd suggested Emerson Trails, simply hoping for some privacy amongst the canopy of trees, but he'd gone above and beyond, planning something for us instead.

"How far are we walking?" I asked.

"Not much farther."

With a nod, I continued on with him, taking in the nature around us. All the leaves had changed to shades of orange and red and brown, bathing us in a flood of color. Even though I had nothing to compare it to, I loved California in the fall.

"Do you come here often?" Kai asked.

I giggled. "Are you using a line on me?"

The corners of his lips twitched. "It would be kind of redundant, since I already have you on a date."

A date? It had taken Martín months to say we were doing more than hanging out.

"Is everything okay?" he asked.

I nodded.

"Are you sure?"

I looked at him under my lashes. "Can I tell you something?"

"Anything."

Steeling myself, I began, "With Martín, we were out in the open, but it never felt this...honest?" Kai nodded, and that simple gesture had the next words flowing out of me. "I like that you don't play games."

"I don't play games," he said evenly. "I create them."

Before I had a chance to dissect and examine his words, he stepped off the trail. Reaching a fallen tree, he effortlessly climbed over and extended his hand to me. My fingers slipped easily into his, and even after I stepped over, he kept a hold of my hand. I liked the warmth that passed silently between us. It seemed like that was how most of our relationship was—a connection I couldn't pair with words.

The trees opened into a grassy clearing lined with paper lanterns and a blanket with a picnic basket. If I was wordless before...

Kai stepped to the blanket and turned to me. "What do you think?"

I covered my mouth, shaking my head. "It's amazing."

His smile melted me even more completely. "It seemed like your style."

"My style?"

He sat and began opening the basket. "You seem to value time over money, substance over show."

I blinked, my eyes stinging.

When he realized I wasn't joining him, he looked up at me. "Everything okay?"

My throat was raw, so I swallowed. "You just...see me."

Within seconds, he was standing, taking my hand again. "Of course I see you. Who wouldn't?"

"No one sees me," I said. "They see a Latina or a fat girl or a cleaning worker or a 'ship. Never Jordan. Sometimes I wonder if there even is a *me* under all of that."

"I don't know who made you believe that you don't deserve to be seen, if it was Martín or some other guy, but that's over. Today. As long as you're with me, my eyes are on you. Not the tough show you put on for everyone else. But the Jordan who's kind and loyal to her mother, even when taking on the burden of her sister's loss. Or the Jordan who looks at me and sees through the money that doesn't matter. Sees into me."

I reached with my free hand and brushed my thumb over the smooth skin of his cheek, wanting to see every inch of his heart. "There's still so much I don't know."

"For you, I'm an open book."

My lips quirked, and the stinging in my eyes slowly subsided. Quietly, I said, "I can't wait to start 'reading,' but first, coffee?" If he knew me like I hoped he did, it would be here.

He scoffed. "Coffee? Only the best for my girl." He reached into the picnic basket and withdrew two cups from Seaton Bakery. "Mochas."

I let out a dreamy sigh as he handed me one of the cups. He seemed perfect. I needed to level the playing field. "Now that we have that covered...I want to hear about your most embarrassing moment."

He shot me a look over his own drink. "Book closed."

"Come on," I said. "It's not fair. You know I'm a maid and that I'm poor and that I'm on scholarship. You're just some perfect billionaire who's weirdly good at martial arts."

He chuckled. "Well, first of all, I'm not a billionaire until I'm a college graduate."

I raised my eyebrows. "What do you mean?"

"It's a clause in my trust fund."

I found it hard to swallow my coffee. Kai was a

trust fund baby. And me? I didn't want to think about it. "Move on to the embarrassing moment."

"Okay, okay." He gave me a pained smile. "If you must know, it was during the Thanksgiving Day recital. I was so excited because I got to be the chief—which now that I think of it might have been for entirely racist reasons—but when I got up in front of everyone to say my lines, I completely choked. And instead of saying 'Welcome to our table,' I said, 'Welcome to the turkey party!'"

Giggling, I said, "What were you? A fourth grader?"

"I'll have you know I was well into my fifth-grade year."

I rolled my eyes. "So your most embarrassing moment ever was forgetting your lines in fifth grade and coming up with a way better name for Thanksgiving? That just makes me look pathetic."

He shook his head, smiling. "I said that was my most embarrassing moment. Not my *only* one."

"Fess up," I said.

He looked over his shoulder and the rustling leaves around us. "How about seeing a new, beautiful girl and being too afraid to talk to her?" He turned to me, his black eyes intense. "Being too afraid to ask for her number and giving her mine instead?"

My cheeks warmed. "How about being half-naked in front of a bill—"

He gave me a look.

"An *almost* billionaire?"

He scooted closer to me on the blanket. "That wasn't embarrassing."

"Oh really?" I asked, my eyes on his lips. I was having trouble catching my breath.

"No," he said. "It was sexy."

Those lips touched mine for a second before moving to my jaw.

A soft moan escaped my lips, and he responded by nipping my neck.

I ran my fingers through the smooth strands of his hair and pulled. When his eyes met mine, they were blazing, heating me all the way to my core. Need welled within me, and I moved to my knees, getting closer to him until he leaned back and I hovered over him, wanting to devour his lips and feel his skin against mine. If we weren't in the trails, in the cold air, I'd be in trouble of losing my mind —and maybe my clothes.

He held my face in his hands and pulled me down so our lips were tasting, feeling, exploring this new connection that felt more intense than I knew it could.

He took my bottom lip between his teeth, and my stomach swooped. How he had such a strong effect on me, I didn't know. He left me breathless and wanting more as he pulled back, all of him composed except for the hazy hunger in his eyes.

My cheeks were pink, thinking about how easily I dove into his kiss and how much more I wanted to do.

I sat back and redid my ponytail, desperate for something to keep my hands busy. You know, aside from exploring Kai's hard muscles under his coat.

When I finished tightening it and looked back to Kai, he had a spread of snack food out, chocolate-drizzled popcorn and mini cupcakes. It looked like heaven. I took a bite of popcorn, savoring the salty sweetness. "So good."

He nodded and moved to lie on his back. One hand was behind his head, but his other arm was out. It was clear what he wanted me to do.

This seemed so much more intimate than giving into the flames in my stomach. This looked like closeness. Tentatively, I turned over and rested my head on his shoulder. I'd worried about it being bony, but it simply felt strong, like where I belonged.

I turned my head, my face only inches from his, and he smiled at me.

Softly, he pressed his lips to my forehead, dousing the fire and transforming it to a comforting warmth.

"I like spending time with you," he said.

My tender heart swelled against the cracks Martín had left. Kai was becoming more than an off-limits guy who set my body burning with his kisses. He was becoming a fire, consuming me completely. I knew I could handle burning. But what about falling?

TWENTY-SIX

ON SUNDAY EVENING, I sat at the counter working on homework while Mom flipped through channels on our boxy television. We'd never had cable before—only DVDs or VHS tapes found at garage sales, but now that our debt was gone, Mom wanted to give me the "comforts" other kids had. Never mind the fact that she was sleeping in the living room or that her sneakers were sprouting holes.

"Come sit with me and watch...*Family Feud?* Or we could watch *Sex and the City?*" She lifted her eyebrows suggestively. "Looks like they're playing it all day!"

I put my hand on the assigned reading to mark my spot. "Sorry, but homework calls."

She stood up from the couch and came to the counter. "What are you working on?"

"Reading some Emerson essays. And then I have an essay to write on them. Not to mention trig or advanced accounting."

She frowned. "You *could* do that. Or you could take a fifteen-minute break and hang out with your amá and Steve Harvey?"

"When you put it that way." I laughed and aligned my pen so I would know where I left off and then got off the stool.

On the couch, Mom opened her arms to me, and I curled against her. For the next ten minutes, we made guesses, shouted at the contestants, and talked about how amazing we would be instead.

As the credits rolled, she patted my head. "Thank you, *mija*."

"Anytime. It was kind of nice just to relax."

A sad smile crossed her face. "I know you've had to work hard, but a few referrals from the Rushes, and I'll be able to hire someone. Maybe I'll be taking care of you by the time you're in college instead of the other way around."

My lips faltered. It was more than I'd hoped for, but Kai was starting to show me how much I *should* have been hoping for. And what I couldn't have as long as my mom needed me.

"Love you, Amá," I whispered.

She kissed my forehead. "Love you more. Now get to work on your homework. *Baggage* is coming on at ten."

"I'm in," I said with a laugh. "Anything that makes me feel better about my love life."

She chuckled and turned back to the TV like it was no big deal, but my eyes were wide. I'd almost let too much slip. I needed to be more careful. I didn't like hiding things from my mom. It had been just her and me ever since Dad left, but she wouldn't always be here.

Great. Now I was sad. I took a break and picked up my pen from the spot I'd saved. Ralph had better do a good job of distracting me.

And he did. For about an hour until my phone vibrated.

My eyes widened at the name on the screen. Kai.

I'd removed the setting that showed a message preview while dating Martín because he liked to send pictures that would make my grandma roll over in her grave.

I hurried to open the screen.

Kai: I can't stop thinking about you.

My stomach swooped, and I couldn't help the smile that touched my lips. Truth be told, I couldn't stop thinking about him either. But I couldn't lay all my cards on the table. When someone had your whole heart, they could also break it.

Jordan: Is that so?

I set my phone down and tried to focus on my homework, but with my eyes bouncing between the phone and the assigned reading, Ralph didn't stand a chance.

The phone lit again, and I took it in my hands.

Kai: I was thinking that I haven't heard your most embarrassing moment. And it's hardly fair that you know my epic fail as chief of Turkey Party.

A quiet laugh escaped my lips. Thankfully, Mom was so absorbed in a show she didn't hear.

Jordan: I can't tell you.

I hardly had to wait, as his message came back almost instantly. I liked it, because then I wouldn't have to pretend to be busy or wait before texting him back.

Kai: And why is that?

Jordan: You're assuming I have only one most embarrassing moment.

Kai: And?

Jordan: I have a collage, a smorgasbord if you will.

Kai: I hardly believe that.

Jordan: Sounds like a personal problem.

Kai: Top three?

Jordan: What's in it for me?

Kai: I'll make it worth your while.

Just the words sent a burst of excitement through me.

Jordan: How?

Kai: Some of my plans for you might not be appropriate to send over text message.

My cheeks heated, along with other parts of me. I looked over my shoulder to make sure my mom hadn't snuck up on me while I'd been distracted texting, but found her completely absorbed in something on the television—four women sitting in a café talking about blow jobs.

Well, they weren't too far off.

Jordan: And when do you intend to show me these plans?

Kai: As soon as you tell me.

Jordan: I plead the fifth.

Kai: Okay, I suppose I can dispose of said plans in File 13.

Jordan: That seems like overkill...

Kai: I'm waiting.

I shook my head at the phone, smiling. This boy

was more than I'd ever imagined under his designer clothes-clad surface.

Jordan: You're impossible.

Kai: And you're stalling.

Jordan: Top three?

Kai: And then the plans.

I cringed at the phone.

Jordan: Here we go.

Jordan: Okay, number one.

Jordan: I can't believe I'm saying this...

Kai: Go on...

Jordan: One time I was giving a presentation in class, at my old school, and I farted. Like, loud. And for the next six months, my nickname was Gassy J.

Kai: You're kidding.

Jordan: I wish.

Kai: Ouch. How did you get them to stop?

Jordan: I switched schools.

Kai: So EA got lucky enough to have Gassy J?

Jordan: I hate you.

Kai: No you don't.

Jordan: I don't.

Kai: Number two?

Jordan: Um, what if I told you I got gum in Merritt's hair my first day at EA?

Kai: What?! And she didn't have you expelled?

Jordan: Well, she didn't know it was me. I was laughing on the second floor, and my gum fell and landed on her head.

Kai: Are you a cartoon villain?

Jordan: I wish.

Kai: Okay, number three has to be good.

I glanced at the ceiling, debating on whether or not to send the message I wanted to. Could I lay myself barer to Kai than I already had? But then I realized a deep part of me wanted to be seen and known. At my last school, I was just a nerd, one with a nickname I couldn't live down. I got picked on for not being Mexican enough or for being "too white." Whatever that meant. At Emerson, I was a quiet scholarship kid with a crummy car. But with Kai, I was just Jordan.

Jordan: I judged an incredible guy based on his money before getting to know the wonderful soul underneath.

I stared at my phone, holding my breath as I waited for his response. What would he say? And what did it mean that I cared so much?

Kai: Would you believe it if I said the mornings are now my favorite part of the day?

I chewed my lip, hoping my mind had gone the same place as his.

Jordan: I might. Why is that?

Kai: I love being able to see you before everyone else. It's like I get two sunrises every day.

I swore my heart could burst, just from those words. And my lips had to be permanently trans-fixed into a smile.

Jordan: I like seeing you too.

It was a simple sentiment, but it felt like laying myself bare.

Kai: I'll see you in the morning?

Jordan: I'm looking forward to it.

Kai: Not as much as I am. Goodnight, beautiful.

I closed my eyes and breathed in this moment before typing back my final reply.

Jordan: Goodnight.

TWENTY-SEVEN

I'D NEVER GOTTEN up as easily as I had the next morning. Even after staying up way too late with my mom to watch *Baggage*. How they found such crazy people to air their dirty laundry on TV, I had no idea, but it made me feel way better about my past, Gassy J and all.

Still, I made sure to put on my makeup before work, carefully applying eyeliner and mascara and even some matte lipstick to make my full lips stand out. I wanted Kai to think about kissing them as much as I thought about kissing his.

"You look nice," Mom said on the way to our cars.

I shrugged. "Thought I should start focusing more on making a good impression."

"You're always beautiful, *mija*. With or without makeup."

"Thanks, Amá," I said, going to my car.

This morning my cup from Seaton Bakery said *Anything is possible*.

The words just reminded me of Kai. Since when did possibility look like glittering black eyes and a breath-stopping smile? I knew obsessing about him wasn't productive, but each time I got him shoved out of my mind, a new thought returned. Every sip of my mocha was just another reminder of Kai and the moments we'd shared in the caves or in our secluded spot near Emerson Trails.

Each taste only made me crave more.

When we pulled into the garage, I hurriedly checked my hair and makeup and then got out of my car. Pushing the cart in with Mom was so routine by now, but my heart rate said this was anything but regular. I'd see the guy who thought I was the sunrise. And maybe he was mine too—transforming my world into a new day where anything was possible.

We got to work in their laundry room, where it was clear that little laundry was actually done. The angry part of me welled up, wondering how many

families could be fed for all the state-of-the-art equipment that sat in here, unused. I shoved that thought
down, thinking of how Kai had helped our family.
Money didn't have to mean evil. It could mean
resources to actually make a difference. I had to
believe Kai would use it less frivolously than his father.

We finished the laundry room and then climbed
the stairs to the kitchen. As we neared the top of
the stairs, we could hear Kai and his father.

Mom paused, looking to me. By their tones, it
was clear they were arguing, but we were in the
awkward spot of choosing to break it up or listen
instead.

"I'm done discussing it," Mr. Rush said. "We
donate nearly a quarter of our income to charity
each year. Why up it?"

"Because it's the right thing to do," Kai argued.
"Invisible Mountains does great work in the
community. You can't attend the gala without
donating."

"We will match the donations raised and not a
penny more, do you understand?"

Mom pushed through the door, and my eyes
immediately fell on the stunned expressions of Kai
and his father.

Kai's eyes lit at the sight of me, but his lips stayed in a soft smile. I had to fight to keep my own face from breaking out in a grin. My memories of him didn't hold a candle to the person standing across from me. His heart looked every bit as good as his body still dressed in gym clothes that revealed muscled arms and toned legs.

Mr. Rush nodded at me and my mom. "How are you ladies doing today?"

"Great," my mom answered, doing a great job of pretending we didn't hear their conversation. "We just finished with the laundry room."

He nodded. "And how are you liking the job?"

"It's excellent, sir," she said, all business. My mom was always good at being a professional without kissing up to her clients. I secretly loved seeing her in action.

"No need to call me sir," he replied with an amicable smile, but he didn't give her an alternative. "Any plans for Thanksgiving?"

Kai snorted, then pretended to be coughing.

Mom put her arm around me. "Dinner in with my girl. And you?"

He gripped Kai's shoulder. "Same with my boy."

Kai looked at him. "They should eat with us, Dad."

My mouth fell open.

"Oh, you don't have to do that," Mom said quickly.

Thank God Mom still had her wits about her because I was still staring at Kai, trying to decipher what on earth he was thinking. He knew how his dad felt about women like my mom and me—that we were a different caliber, lower. Why would he want to subject us to an evening of that?

Mr. Rush nodded. Unlike his son, his eyes were a light, clear blue. I could practically see thoughts whirring behind them. "That would be a great idea. Mix things up a little for us."

Was that a chill I felt? Because hell had definitely frozen over.

"So it's settled," Kai said, sounding confident and not at all surprised. "We have Thanksgiving at six on Thursday."

"No need to bring anything," Mr. Rush added. "Mr. Wallace makes the best Thanksgiving dinner."

"Well, that simply won't do," my mom said, sending a smile my way.

I caught her drift, and my mouth practically

watered thinking of her birria. "That's true. My mom makes the best *birria*."

Mr. Rush actually smiled. I didn't even know his face could make that expression. "Well then, we'll have that to look forward to, in addition to the company."

Mr. Wallace handed Kai and Mr. Rush their smoothies, and Kai lifted his to us, a secret in his eyes. "See you in school, Jor," he said.

The nickname made my smile grow a little too wide, and I realized just how bad of an idea this was. An entire meal across the table from Kai would be too hard. My mom was smart—she would know there was something going on, even if Kai's dad didn't. As soon as they walked away, I turned to Mom to convince her not to do this, but she began talking.

"Is that okay with you that we join them? I want them to get to know us, you know? It will make it that much easier to recommend us—and that much harder to find fault."

The shrewdness in her eyes caught me. This business mattered to her more than anything had in a long time. She needed this.

"It's fine," I said. And I resolved that no matter how hard it was to be in the same room with Kai and act like we were no more than classmates, I would make it work.

"Thank you, sweetie," she said.

"Of course." I kissed her on the cheek. "Happy to help."

She smiled at me and held my cheeks in her hands. "Since when did you grow up to be such a beautiful, smart, mature young woman?"

I smiled back. "I learned from the best."

"Oh hush." She kissed my forehead. "Now, go get ready for school. I've got this."

"Are you sure?" I glanced at the time. "I can work for another fifteen minutes or so?"

"Nah," she said and then winked at me. "I can tell you need some extra time to impress some boy."

All the blood drained from my face. "What?"

"The makeup," she said. "There must be some boy at school. Knock him dead."

My stomach sank as I muttered a thank you and escaped to the bathroom. She knew there was a boy.

Let's hope she didn't find out which one.

TWENTY-EIGHT

I GOT to school early enough to hang the posters the girls and I made. When I finished, I went to my locker and spun the combination to open it, expecting to find only my books inside.

Instead, I found a cupcake, clearly from Seaton Bakery, with a note underneath.

To second sunrises. Meet me after your FMP meeting, in the mu room.

I ran my fingers over the handwriting, imagining Kai carefully pressing his pen to the paper. It made electricity sizzle in my fingertips.

"Secret admirer?" Merritt crooned.

I shoved the note in my locker and turned, blocking it from her view. "Hi, Merritt."

Her eyes narrowed, obviously annoyed at my

composed exterior. Of course, she didn't know the panic welling inside me. She'd humiliated Rory, and I didn't put it past her to do the same to me. Or find a way to have me expelled. Her family certainly had enough social capital to make it happen.

A fake sympathetic frown twisted her dainty features. "Is he a toad?"

"Excuse me?"

"He's ugly, right?" She leaned against the locker next to mine. "For him to want all of that, he must be. And you're obviously ashamed of him."

"That's not it, I—"

An arm encircled my shoulders, and I looked up to see Beckett standing beside me, staring hard at Merritt.

"What's up, Jordan?" he asked, keeping his eyes on her.

"Just trying to grab my books." I couldn't quite meet either of their eyes.

But I did hear a frustrated groan and Merritt's heels clack away.

Beckett's arm slipped from my shoulders, and when I was sure Merritt was gone, I muttered, "Thank you."

"No problem," he said. "Saw her going in for the kill."

I rolled my eyes. "No, just toying with me." The hatred in my voice was clear. I couldn't stand people who picked on those with no means of defense. The best thing to happen all year was Rory winning that bet. Especially since she and Beckett had managed to work it out and were clearly happy together.

"Don't worry about her," he said. "She just senses when someone's happier than her and gets jealous."

"I'm happier than her?" I turned and retrieved my things from my locker, including the cupcake. "She has everything."

A corner of Beckett's lips lifted. "Except someone who's putting that kind of a smile on her face." He glanced at my hands. "Or a cupcake in her locker."

With a salute, he continued down the hallway, and I turned toward videography class, my smile back again.

I took a bite of the cupcake, and the only thing sweeter was my anticipation to see Kai again today.

In videography class, Ginger sat next to me and leaned across the aisle. "What's this I hear about a cupcake in your locker?"

I raised my eyebrows. The wrapper had already been disposed of before she walked in. "What?"

"Word travels fast, and I need someone to live vicariously through. Now spill."

I shook my head, half pleased people were talking about me in a positive way and half frustrated that Emerson was such a small school. Everyone knew everything about other peoples' business. That kind of thing never happened with my class of nearly a thousand at Seaton High.

"You know how I've been cleaning Kai's house?" I said.

She nodded, her red curls bouncing.

I had to think fast. "His dad had him get it for me... as a thank you."

"So, there's nothing going on between..."

"Me and Kai?" I shook my head, hoping to look appropriately disturbed by the very idea. As put off as I might have been a month and a half ago. "No way."

She let out a relieved sigh and slumped theatrically in her chair. "Phew, because that would have been crazy! I would have wondered if he'd used some of his billion-dollar technology to addle your brain."

My first thought was that he didn't own billion-dollar technology—yet. My second was that I wished I could tell Ginger. Now that I knew him for who he really was, I thought they would have liked him. But her judgement of him only affirmed my decision to keep my relationship with Kai a secret. My friends wouldn't understand. And besides, Kai and I had agreed to keep this to ourselves. It was the only way our relationship could work.

I tried to listen to what Mr. Davis was saying about filming with DSLR cameras, but thoughts of Kai made it nearly impossible. Which was crazy, because I wasn't that girl—the one who met a guy and forgot about school or made her life about him and not her friends.

But my grades were still good. I had all A's. I could read Mr. Davis's notes online later when my mind wasn't filled with rumors and expectations and my friends' misguided distaste for Kai Rush.

I tried to think back to the time when I hated him, but I realized I hadn't hated him. I'd despised his privilege. If I was scarily honest with myself, I was jealous of it.

That realization stuck with me through the day, as I ate lunch with my friends—reassuring them that I was not, in fact, in love with Kai Rush. As I took my trig midterm. As I sat in the FMP meeting, going over schedules for the next day's blood drive.

"Can we move on to the gala?" Poppy asked. "It's not like the blood drive matters anyway."

I looked up at her over our notes. "You may be more interested in wearing fancy dresses than saving lives, but that's what medical professionals do. Save lives."

"Not without money," Poppy argued.

Rage made my nostrils flare. "Just because you are privileged enough to never worry about health-care doesn't mean the rest of the world feels the same way."

She rolled her eyes at me. "Thought since you were getting laid, you'd simmer down."

Pixie cleared her throat. "I'll let Jordan go through the checklist for the blood drive, and then we can use the rest of the time to discuss the gala."

My jaw clenched and relaxed before I began reading down my list. It was people like Poppy who gave people like Kai a bad name. How could they exist in the same school? On the same planet?

I reached the bottom of the list and Pixie said, "I think we're good to go. Poppy, can you go over plans for the gala? What are our next steps?"

Poppy cleared her throat and got an overly eager look in her eyes. "As you know, the gala is coming up in a matter of weeks." Even though it was a statement, Poppy said it like a question, and it took all of my "simmer" not to roll my eyes. "We expect all representatives, meaning everyone in the club, to wear black tie. We can get that donated if you need, Jordan."

My mouth fell open. "Are you seriously calling me out as poor in front of the group?"

She winked at me. "We can talk more discreetly later." She moved on and continued talking about décor that had nothing to do with serving as a medical professional. After the meeting closed down, I cornered Pixie.

"You cannot let Poppy and Tinsley keep detracting from FMP. They're turning it into a debutante club."

Pixie frowned and pressed her fingers down on the desk. "Look, Jordan. I don't expect you to understand this since you haven't been in this world long, but you have to pick your battles. If everything's a fight, then you'll never get what you want. You let them think they're in charge, and when it really matters, they'll go along with you."

Appalled was the only word to describe my feelings at that point. "So you're saying we can let them make a mockery of our entire profession as a *political* play?"

"That's exactly what I'm saying." She stood and patted my shoulder. "Imagine what you could do with that much power behind you. Is a little bit of pride that high of a price to pay?"

With that, she picked up her books and walked out of the meeting room, leaving me with my jaw still hanging open.

Was this really how the world worked? Did connections and power and political agreements really control life as I knew it? Sure, I expected some people to work that way, but I'd hoped as a doctor, I'd eventually be above that.

With a sour taste in my mouth, I left the meeting room, not sure if even Kai's sweet lips would be enough to kiss it away.

TWENTY-NINE

I STOPPED outside music room near the library and tried to look through the window, but it had been covered with a curtain. Someone walked past me, and I pretended to be digging in my backpack for something until they were well out of eyesight. And then I tried the handle. Locked.

The door cracked open, and Kai tugged me inside, right into a breathtaking kiss that shoved my worries away.

His touch was like a breath of fresh air against the cloudy day of rumors and expectations. Here, all that mattered was him and me and the way our bodies moved against each other. I loved the way his hands explored my body, feeling each curve like he cherished them. He seemed to like them almost as much as I loved the hard tone of his arms and sure grip of his hands.

He pulled back, his smile dazzling me. "Hi."

It was impossible not to smile back. "Hi."

I saw the wires and cords and whirring machines for only moments before he kissed me softly again and pulled back. "How was your day?"

"Insane," I said, sitting in one of the two rolling chairs in the small space. "My mom and I got invited to this rich family's Turkey Party, and there's no way all the outfits in our closets cost as much as one dress we should wear."

"I would imagine your company to be worth more than all the dresses in the world." He moved to the chair opposite me, and his knee brushed mine as he sat.

My cheeks warmed. "That might be a bit of an exaggeration."

"Not even in the slightest." His fingers took mine, his thumb rubbing slow circles on the inside of my palm.

I closed my eyes, soaking in the feeling, wanting to push out everything else and focus on this moment, so sweet in its simplicity. How had I gone so long without feeling his touch? Without understanding the kind heart that lay underneath his composed exterior?

"It's good to see you," he said.

I smiled, looking back at him. "You too."

"I mean, it's not every day you get to sit in the presence of Gassy J." His face was completely impassive, even though his eyes sparked with humor.

I reached forward and hit his shoulder. "You're the worst."

"I know," he said. "But I must have done something right to be sitting here with a girl like you."

I shook my head. "I'm still wondering what you see in me."

Kai turned my chair so both of my knees were locked with both of his, and he looked me dead on, all sense of humor gone. "What I see in you is an amazing, strong, independent woman who's like no one I've ever met. Not on trips abroad, not in the halls of Emerson Academy, and not on any business for *Rush+*."

I couldn't manage to look in his eyes. Not when he was seeing things in me I didn't quite see in myself. I didn't even have the power to help a club dedicated to future medical professionals see the importance in a blood drive.

"You know Emerson Academy's motto?" he asked.

I nodded. "*Ad meliora*. Toward better things."

"I don't think I understood it before." This thumb stroked my knee. "I thought they meant careers and wealth and service and scholarship. I've been at the Academy, hearing *ad meliora*, since kindergarten, and for the first time I feel like I know what it means." His voice became soft. "When they talk about better things, the better thing for me is you."

My throat grew thick, and I looked at him with glassy eyes. "Do you mean that?" My whole life, I'd known people to leave. My dad, my friends, Lucinda, but Kai was telling me he wanted to move toward me, be closer. That I was worth it.

"Come here," he breathed.

I rose from my chair and went to him, settling on his lap. He linked his arms around me, pulling me close to him.

"I've never been more certain of anything in my life," he breathed into my ear.

I'd never felt *less* sure of anything. In a world where boys you hated could turn into men you loved, how could I be? I'd thought Kai was my enemy, but now all I could think of were his lips on mine and his cologne and the way he held me like he never dreamed of letting go.

"I like being in the quiet with you," he said.

A smile tugged at my lips. It was quiet in here, except for the soft humming of the air conditioner. "Me too."

"Are you donating blood tomorrow?" he asked.

"I'll try," I answered. "My iron is usually too low. Are you?"

He sucked in a breath through his teeth. "Needles and me..."

I twisted in his arms to see him shaking his head with a terrified look.

"Kai Rush, are you...*afraid?*" I tried to keep a straight face but couldn't help my smile.

He glanced down at me but didn't answer.

"You took on a guy twice your size in the middle of a dark parking lot, but you're afraid of a little pinprick?"

"Yeah, but that was different."

My eyebrows came together. "How?"

"Because I had something to defend. I had you."

The smile spreading on my face was undeniable. "But what about the three people you could save?"

"Three?" he asked.

I nodded. "That's what they say. Each donation can save three lives, especially if you have a rare blood type."

"Is O- rare?" he asked.

"Oh my gosh. Now I know you're kidding."

"It is?"

I twisted enough so I could put one of my arms around his shoulders. "You have a very rare blood type. They're always in desperate need of more O-."

"Well then," he said. "Sign me up."

And damn, if he wasn't attractive before, he was now. "Are you sure?"

He nodded. "But if I pass out, it's all your fault."

I smiled, my eyes shifting toward his lips. "I wouldn't mind kissing you back to life."

"In that case...do you think we should practice?"

Grinning, I answered, "Definitely."

He closed the gap between us and pressed his lips to mine.

THIRTY

I FELL asleep thinking of Kai and the words he'd said to me about *ad meliora*. My heart felt fuller than it had ever been. And when I woke up, the feeling was still there, mixed with excitement that I would be able to see him in just one short hour.

I checked my phone, squinting against the bright light. There was already a chat from him.

Kai: Good morning, beautiful. I can't wait to see you.

Jordan: I can't wait to see you either.

I smiled, holding the phone to my chest. I'd never felt this... wanted before. Not even when Martín and I had lived our love story in the open, sharing cute pictures online, hanging out with friends and family. What I had with Kai, just the two of us, it topped that, no contest.

Now that I had something to look forward to, getting out of bed and dressing for work was much less painful. I stood beside Mom in the bathroom, brushing my teeth.

She bent over the sink and spit. "You look happy today."

I slowed brushing and then spit as well. "It's the blood drive. I get to skip a couple classes to help."

After rinsing out her mouth, she said. "Who knew I'd have a daughter thrilled at the sight of blood."

"Daughter…or vampire?" I teased, drawing the shower curtain over my face like I was wearing a cape. "The world may never know."

Shaking her head, she left the bathroom to me, and I stared in the mirror. I did look happier. My face didn't look so heavy, serious. Or maybe that was just how I felt? How Kai made me feel?

I grabbed my lipstick and put on an even layer, then pressed my lips together. It was impossible not to remember the sure, adoring way Kai had kissed them. They were his now.

After I finished getting ready, Mom and I went down to our cars and drove to Seaton Bakery. Today I got out, and Mom glanced over at me. "Are you coming in?"

"Yeah," I answered, clearing the front step with her. "Just wanted to get an extra cupcake."

"Hungry?" Mom asked.

"I need a snack for later," I said, thankful for the out.

We walked inside, and Gayle grinned at me from the front counter. "There's my girl!"

I smiled back and sidestepped the counter to give her a hug. She squeezed me tight and then said, "I haven't seen you in a while. School must be brutal."

I lifted my eyebrows. "You have no idea."

Mom jerked her thumb at me. "This nut would rather study than watch *Sex and the City* with me."

Reaching for a couple of muffins, Gayle said, "If you ever need someone to watch TV with, hit me up. My husband is out like a light at seven most nights."

"I will take you up on that," Mom said. "Oh, and can you put an extra in a separate bag? She's studying up an appetite."

Gayle winked at me. "I've got you."

The way she winked made me wonder if she knew something I didn't. I hoped not. She went back to the kitchen and came back with two cups. "The message is from me this time."

I glanced at the cup in my hand and saw Gayle's looping handwriting. *You are BEAUTIFUL.*

Mom looked up from the note on her cup and said, "Aw, you are so sweet."

Gayle grinned back and shrugged. "Can't help but speak the truth. I wish I had a mom like you when I was growing up." She looked at me. "You are so lucky to have your mama."

"I agree." In some ways, I was incredibly blessed with my mom. Zara had lost her mom as a young girl. Rory's mom had just recently eased up on the excessive dieting. And there was Ginger, whose mom treated her like a child, even though she was well into her teens. My mom wasn't like that. She treated me like I was responsible, so I acted that way.

On the way out, Mom rubbed my back. "I'll grab some extra snack food for you this grocery trip."

My mouth parted. Snacks had never been something on our shopping list. Our budget didn't allow for it. Just another way Kai had changed our lives. "Thank you," I said, half to Mom and half to him.

I couldn't wait to see him. To drink in his appearance and maybe sneak a touch or a kiss.

Going all day without one would be beyond difficult. Especially since we didn't have another meeting planned. At least, not yet.

When we got in the house, my entire body hummed with anticipation. "Where are we working today?" I asked Mom.

She pulled a laminated sheet out of her pocket that Robert had given her to keep track of the schedule, scanning it. "Do you want to take the pool locker room or the upstairs sunroom?"

"Sunroom," I said quickly. That would be closer to Kai's room, to the second sunrise of the morning.

She shrugged and handed me the dust mop and window cleaning equipment. "I'll be up there when I'm done."

I nodded and walked toward the stairs. As I passed the second floor, I paused. Kai's room was on this floor, and it was calling to me. Begging me to go inside and see him—touch him.

I steeled myself and continued upstairs. I had a job to do, and of all the safe places in the world to hide away with him, his home was not one of them. The upstairs sunroom was this big, beautiful room encased in glass windows, with comfortable seating and plants spread throughout. It wouldn't be a bad place to spend the morning.

I put in headphones and a Julieta Venegas playlist. Cleaning was so much better when I had something to listen to, especially good music that made me want to dance. Who cared if the broom wasn't a man? Not me.

I shook my hips, spinning the broom in a slow circle, and froze at the sight of Kai. He had his lips pressed together, trying not to laugh, and his eyes were alight with mirth.

"Oh my gosh!" I cried, pulling off my headphones. "What are you doing here?"

"The box office didn't tell you? I bought tickets."

My cheeks were on fire now. "How much of that did you see?"

"Not enough."

I crossed the room and hit his shoulder.

He pretended to be wounded, but his eyes were still dancing. And now that we were this close...the air seemed warmer.

"Hi, sunshine," he whispered, tucking a strand of hair behind my ear that had escaped my ponytail.

I closed my eyes. The sensation was so powerful.

How did he have this effect on me? When I opened them, he was still taking me in.

"My mom's going to be up here," I breathed.

He took my hand. "I'm not done yet." Quickly, he led me across the room and into a closet full of blankets. It was dark in here, but my eyes adjusted to him like they didn't want to waste a minute of seeing him.

"This was your grand idea?" I whispered. "Hiding in a closet?"

He silenced my worries with a kiss. And who was I to argue when his lips were on mine, giving me everything I needed in this moment and more?

Something about the darkness empowered me. I slipped my hands under his shirt and felt the hard muscles of his sides, his stomach.

He didn't make a sound, but his breath sped, giving me all the encouragement I needed.

My hands explored, over the ridges of his abs and up to his pecs. Every part of Kai was on purpose, not soft or round, but hard, present. I loved the way his body felt against mine, under my fingers.

He nipped at my lip, sending a shiver down my spine.

"Jordan?" my mom called.

My eyes flew open. "Oh my god," I whispered.

He shook his head.

"What do we do?" I panicked.

His hand covered my mouth, warm, firm. "She'll leave to look for you, and I'll sneak out behind her."

I wasn't sure his plan would work, but it was the only one we had.

Dropping his hand from my mouth, he slipped his fingers through mine and held on. But my heart was pounding.

What had we been thinking? We'd almost been caught by my mom—could still get caught. What if it had been Mr. Rush up here to look for Kai?

The soft sole of Mom's shoes walked away, and I looked to Kai.

"There's a bathroom over there," he whispered. "Pretend to be in it. I'll creep past your mom."

I nodded, and the second he opened the door, I thundered from the closet to the bathroom, closing the door behind me. As I leaned my back against the wall, my chest heaved with the force of my breaths, and a sense of dread pooled in the pit of my stomach.

Kai and I needed to be more careful if we wanted this to continue. And I did want it to continue. I couldn't imagine ever going without Kai's touch or feeling the way he set me on fire.

Within a few minutes, a knock sounded on the door. "Jordan?"

"Yeah, Amá," I called through the door and then turned on the sink. "Just finishing up."

"Oh, good," she said. "I couldn't find you, and Kai told me there was a bathroom up here."

My heart constricted at the sound of his name on my mother's lips, but I had to cover it. I turned off the sink and walked out. "I wonder how many bathrooms there are in this house."

"Ten," she said, eyeing me. "Are you okay? You look flushed." She poked her head in the bathroom and sniffed like that would reveal if I was, in fact, alright. "Is your stomach upset?"

"Amá! I'm fine. Just needed a bathroom break."

"Okay," she said. "Let's knock this room out and get you to school."

I'd never been more grateful to start cleaning in my life.

THIRTY-ONE

WHEN I GOT TO SCHOOL, I grabbed my backpack and the bag with Kai's cupcake and went
inside to the gym. Grateful for the distraction of the
blood drive, I got to work helping the other FMP
members and the Emerson Blood Institute set up.
We had to have a sign-in table, a recovery space,
and an area to give away the shirts they got upon
donating with the words *multum in parvo* across the
front. Much in little.

One of the sophomores and I unfolded the legs
on a table, and then while he got chairs, I set up a
sign that said *One Donation Saves Three Lives* along
with a picture of the shirt.

When we were all set up, I went to Pixie to get

the tablet we would use to check people in. "How'd it go this morning?" I asked her.

"Good." She pushed some hair out of her face. "They were a little late, but I think we'll be able to get started on time."

I nodded. "And the catering?"

"Poppy came by and confirmed."

"Awesome," I said, even though a part of me would love to see Poppy fail. That probably made me a terrible person.

Pixie reached into her messenger bag and pulled out a tablet in a fancy leather case. "The passwords seven, seven, seven, seven."

I gave her a look.

"What?" She asked. "It's a lucky number."

"Nothing," I said with a smile, shaking my head, and went back to the sign-in table. I pulled up the Emerson Blood Institute app and signed in to see who all had signed up. I raised my eyebrows. We'd filled almost every spot!

The first name on the list? Birdie Bardot, our overly cheery guidance counselor. I needed more coffee for this.

At eight o'clock on the dot, she stepped up to the table, wearing a bright red dress, blood drop earrings, and a bright red headband. "Nice to see you, Jordan."

"Right on time. How's Ralphie?" I asked about the bird she kept in her office.

"Just tweetling his thumbs." She laughed loudly. "Get it?"

The fake laugh I gave her deserved extra credit. "Yes, so I just need you to sign in, and it looks like Nina's ready." I nodded toward the woman in scrubs standing by her pop-up cubicle.

"I sure am," Nina said.

Mrs. Bardot used her finger to swipe her signature and then walked toward Nina, her blood drop earrings swinging. Once I crossed her name off as complete, I looked down at the next spot on the list. My eyes widened. Johnson Rush. And then Kai. Any excitement I would have had about seeing Kai was immediately shadowed by his father's impending presence. So much for encouraging him about donating or giving him the muffin.

I checked the time. There were a few minutes yet before he would get here, but I had to take deep breaths. I still wasn't sure how I felt about Kai's dad. He gained huge points for raising Kai, but the way he felt about poor people definitely tipped the scale against him.

I steeled myself to be polite, like my mom would want me to be, and waited until I saw his narrow frame walking through the door. Followed by his son.

Kai gave me a smile his dad couldn't see, and I returned it. "Hi there."

"Hello, Jordan," Mr. Rush said. "I didn't know you were involved with the blood drive.

I nodded, and Kai said, "She's actually vice president of Future Medical Professionals."

Mr. Rush raised his eyebrows in a way that told me he was equal parts surprised and impressed, like he'd never expect a person like me to lead. I'd show him just how professional I could be.

"You can sign in on this sheet and then wait for one of the phlebotomists to come and get you."

Kai laughed nervously. "As long as it's not a *lo*botomist."

I rolled my eyes. "Ha ha."

Mr. Rush's face took on a moderately amused expression. "Would you believe it if I said he didn't get his sense of humor from me?"

Honestly, yes. I'd never met a more serious man. But I shook my head.

An awkward silence ensued. What did we have to talk about if not the tile grout?

"I'm looking forward to Thursday," Mr. Rush said.

That surprised me. "You are?"

He nodded. "Your mother's dish sounds delicious."

"It is," I agreed. "Well worth the wait."

"We don't have to wait long," Kai said. "Just two more days."

A phlebotomist named Alex came around the corner of his cubicle. "Who's next, J?" he asked.

I nodded toward Mr. Rush.

He stepped forward and extended his hand, which Mr. Rush shook as quickly as humanly possible.

Alex led Mr. Rush back, and Kai leaned against the table. My eyes went to his long fingers. They were like art.

"How's your morning going?" he asked.

"Oh, you know, after being scared to death my mom would catch us, it's turned out alright." I turned to the empty chair next to me and lifted the cupcake. "I got you this."

He smiled as he took it from me. "That almost makes up for seducing me into donating blood."

Why were my cheeks warm? "Seducing? If I remember right, you signed up willingly."

"Whatever you need to tell yourself to sleep at night, sunshine."

The way he called me sunshine made me feel so light I laughed. "I think I'll sleep just fine knowing I 'seduced' you into saving three lives."

"True, but thanks for the cupcake, really."

I shook my head. "It was no big deal."

"It is to me."

Merritt's voice jarred me like nails on a chalkboard. "Well, well, well. If it isn't my gala date and the maid."

My eyebrows drew together. "What?"

Before Kai could answer, Merritt said, "I'm here to donate. I'm only two pounds above the weight requirement." She leaned over the table so her breasts were exposed to Kai, due to her shirt not being buttoned to dress code regulations.

The only comfort was that Kai kept his eyes on me, judging my reaction.

"Gala date?" I asked him.

"Oh," Merritt said. "You didn't know? I thought since you two were so close, Kai would have told you."

An annoyed expression crossed Kai's features. So she wasn't lying?

Kai opened his mouth as if to explain, but

Merritt said, "His father asked my father if Kai could escort me. It only makes sense that those of us with the highest status attend together."

"Of course," I said, my voice shaking. "That makes perfect sense."

Kai's dark eyes pleaded with me, but I turned them away. Even looking at Merritt was preferable to seeing him right now.

"You're on clean-up duty, right, 'ship?" She put her hand on Kai's shoulder. "Maybe we'll see you there."

I didn't know whether Merritt actually believed any of the words she said or if she just knew they would get under my skin. Because they did. Even Kai shrugging out from under her manicured nails that had never come in contact with bleach didn't comfort me.

Nina stepped out from her cubicle and said, "Next!"

The blood drained from his face.

We couldn't talk. Not in front of Merritt, and especially not with his betrayal giving me a bitter taste in my mouth. "Nina is ready for you."

Reluctantly, he walked to her stall, and I forced myself to keep my expression even as I handed Merritt the tablet for sign-in.

She rested it on her dainty forearm and said, "Anything wrong?"

People like Merritt could smell fear, and I wasn't going to give her the satisfaction. Not if I could help it. "Of course not, the blood drive is running right on schedule. Thanks for making your appointment on time!"

As Merritt furrowed her perfectly plucked eyebrows, I pretended to be bored and used my phone to send a quick chat. I wasn't sure if the girls would see it in class or not, but I needed backup.

Jordan: SOS. Come to the blood drive.

Merritt finished and passed the tablet back to me. "You're not upset, are you?" She was digging her nails into my wound, waiting to see me flinch.

"About you donating blood? I'm happy for everyone that's donating!" I said cheerily, even though my stomach felt hollow.

Why was Kai going to the gala with *her* of all people? Hadn't his dad discovered what an evil shrew Merritt was? Hadn't Kai? He could have told his dad he would go alone.

And why hadn't he told me about his date when just hours ago we were kissing in a closet, risking *everything* for stolen moments together?

But thinking I had any real claim on him was

crazy. Kai and I were a secret, kept from the rest of the world. *Of course* he could go to the gala with someone else. *Of course* his dad would set him up with a socially appropriate date when he thought Kai was single.

But was he? The dread in my stomach from this morning returned at full force. Did he have other girls he kept secret? Kai and I had never discussed the exclusivity of our arrangement. Why wouldn't he want a girlfriend he could attend events with, who would win his dad's approval? After all, his dad was all he had. He'd said so himself.

"Don't worry," Merritt said. "There—"

Ginger banged through the gym door, a camera around her neck. "What doesn't she need to worry about?" She flashed a shot of Merritt, then cringed at the screen. "Oof, let's hope that one doesn't end up in the yearbook."

Merritt turned all her hatred on Ginger. "You wouldn't dare."

Ginger shrugged. "That's above my pay grade."

If I loved Ginger before, it didn't come close to how I felt about her now. I grinned at her, watching the easy way she took on Merritt.

"If you don't delete that photo, I swear, I'll—"

"Next!" Alex called.

"This isn't over," Merritt whispered, then turned to Alex with a wide smile. "Hi there, handsome."

Ginger and I gave each other disgusted looks as she sat next to me behind the table.

"Thank you," I said, putting all of my gratitude in my voice.

"No problem," she replied. "Shouldn't have to take on the two-faced monster by yourself."

But I already had. "I guess she and Kai are going to the gala together."

She rolled her eyes. "They deserve each other." She shook her head. "I told Mr. Davis I'd get some pictures for the yearbook, so I better head over."

I nodded. "Go for it."

With a smile, she went to where the people were donating, and I sank back in my chair. The bell had just rung for second period, and I had already burned through the full range of human emotions. And I hadn't even confronted Kai about the gala yet.

"Can someone get me an ice pack?" Nina yelled.

"Got it," I called back since I knew the other phlebotomists were busy with donors. I jogged to the cooler of ice packs, feeling a sense of purpose I looked forward to having as a doctor. I pulled one out, shut the lid, and jogged to the table.

At the sight of Kai, pale, leaned all the way back, my heart stopped. I had to force my legs to carry me farther, and I wordlessly handed Nina the ice packet. His eyes were closed, so maybe he wouldn't even see me.

"Open your eyes," Nina instructed. "I need to know if you pass out."

Great.

Those perfect black orbs landed on me, and his lips parted. "Jordan."

Mr. Rush walked over, holding a cotton ball to his arm. "Son, are you okay?"

Kai looked toward the ceiling and nodded. "Fine."

That was my cue. I left him lying there on the table. He may have been the one who looked ill, but I felt just as sick. He'd given his blood for a good cause, and I'd given my heart for no cause at all.

THIRTY-TWO

I SAT on Zara's bed, staring at her massive closet. She was deep inside the rows of hanging clothes, and I couldn't see her anymore.

"What did you say this was for again?" she called.

"Thanksgiving with some of Mom's rich clients," I replied. "And I need one for the gala too."

"Gotcha. Why did they plan the gala so soon after Thanksgiving?"

"I think that was the only time the venue was free for the next two years."

"Ah," she nodded. "I was kind of surprised you guys got that space at all."

I shrugged. "I have no idea how all of that stuff

works."

"No need," she said, moving a hanger aside. "So you need to look professional but young at the dinner."

"I guess?" I was so bad at this, especially since I apparently had no idea how to leverage social capital.

"What about the gala?" she asked.

And before I could stop myself, I said, "Make me look irresistible."

"Girl, I got you."

She came out of the closet holding up two dresses. One was a pretty purple one made out of what looked like cotton with an asymmetrical hemline and short sleeves. And the other...

"Are you sure there's enough fabric there?" I asked.

She grinned from the dress to me. "Just enough."

My phone dinged in my pocket for the fourth time, and I knew it was another text from Kai.

"You can get that," Zara said.

I shook my head and leaned back on the bed. The more time I had to think about him having a date with Merritt, the more frustrated I became. How long had he known about the date and kept it from me? He knew I was going to the gala. How did he think I'd feel seeing him walk in with Merritt? Dancing with her? Spending the entire evening with her when we barely had time for stolen kisses in hidden spaces?

I knew I had to talk to him about it, but what would I say?

She hung the dresses in a garment bag and then lay next to me on the bed.

"How's the whole arranged marriage thing going?" I asked, just to get my mind off my own problems.

"Dad's still trying to find me an acceptable 'suitor.'" She sighed. "Which probably means one of the actors he wants to sign for another movie."

"It sounds like he's making a business arrangement, not an arranged marriage." The idea hurt. At least my mom wasn't forcing me to date anyone I didn't like.

"It's all a business arrangement," Zara said resignedly. "We attend events because of how it looks, not because they'll be fun. We dress nicely because we may be photographed, not because we like the way we feel. And we date people because of how it will help our reputation, not for love."

I immediately thought of Kai, forced to take

Merritt to an event he probably wanted to attend alone and felt guilty for ignoring him. I rolled my head to the side. "That sucks."

"Yep, but it's life."

Maybe it was for her, but I promised myself it wouldn't be for me. I lifted a corner of my lips. "I'm holding out that your dad sets you up with a mega hottie and you'll fall completely, head over heels in love."

She laughed. "Keep dreaming. I'm just hoping whoever it is still has hair."

I shook my head, smiling. "I better get going," I said. "Thank you for the dresses, really."

"Happy to help." She stood up and handed me the garment bag. "And I can't wait to see you in that sexy dress."

I laughed. "You'll be seeing plenty of me, alright."

When I got down to my car, I skipped past Kai's messages and sent him one of my own.

Jordan: Meet me at the trails? Same place as last time?

He replied within seconds.

Kai: I'll be there.

I drove across town, attempting to imagine all the things I'd say to him, but I kept coming up short. How could I tell him I was hurt without asking him to be exclusive? And how could I ask him to be exclusive when we could never have the type of relationship he deserved?

I pulled into the parking lot, and he wasn't there yet. Somehow relieved, I tugged my coat tighter around me and began walking toward the trailhead. The cold air and dimming sky made each breath seem more purposeful than usual.

I focused on the crunch of fallen leaves under my feet and the sound of my inhalations. Soon, I fell into a peaceful rhythm. Eventually, I reached our spot, and I took it in.

The grassy area looked different now that most of the leaves had fallen off the trees and the grass had completed its transformation to brown.

"Jordan," Kai said from behind me.

I turned and took him in. His face was drawn, concerned.

Seeing him both bolstered and broke me. I was realizing that I wanted more, for me and him.

"I'm sorry I didn't tell you," he began. "It was a plan my dad made in a business meeting with her parents and her brother so he can help promote *Rush+*. I promise I didn't ask for it, and I certainly didn't want to, but my dad said Rush men don't go back on their word—"

I stepped closer and placed my finger on his lips. Just for a moment. Just to stop the nervous flow of words coming from his mouth. "It's okay," I said.

"It is?" He seemed even more confused now.

"Yeah." I looked down at my fingers, at my hands that were so different from Merritt's. Where she had beautifully done nails and supple skin, mine were cracked, my skin worn down from cleaning chemicals and a lack of money for beauty supplies beyond the basics. "You deserve to go with someone like Merritt."

"No." His voice was hard, but his touch was soft as he took my hands. "I deserve to go with you."

I met his eyes, my throat feeling tight. "But you can't."

He let out a swear word, and shock flowed through me at his outburst. Kai was the picture of control. Usually.

When he turned his eyes back on me, they were tortured. "Can't you tell I just want you?" His hand cupped my cheek. "Every *second* I spend with you feels better than hours spent with anyone else."

My fractured heart held on to his words. "But that's all we'll ever have. Seconds. Stolen moments in secret."

"You don't know that," he said. "This dinner

we're having together could change things. Maybe, if my dad knew you and your mom, he wouldn't be so against us. He'd see that you're different from my mom."

"Am I?" I asked. "You dished out money for our medical bills, and what do I have to give you in return? I can't even give you a real relationship."

"I didn't do it to get anything in return. I did it to help."

I couldn't look at him now. Not through the emotion clogging my throat and filling my eyes.

He stepped closer, dipping down until I was forced to look in his eyes. "Jordan, I know you think you don't have anything to give me, but that couldn't be farther from the truth. You give me a new way of looking at the world. You help me see the kind of man I want to be. You make me better, and I'd spend everything for that. To keep working to become the kind of man who deserves your loyalty, your love. Promise me you won't give up on us. Please."

I couldn't speak, so I nodded, sending tears down my cheeks.

He kissed me, hard, and then held me. "We'll get through this."

"Okay," I said. I just didn't know how.

THIRTY-THREE

ON THE AFTERNOON of Thanksgiving Day, Mom and I stood in the bathroom together, doing our hair for our dinner with the Rushes. She was using a curling iron older than me to put soft curls in her hair while I ran a straightener through my waves. Thanks to amazing genetics from my mom, my hair looked glossy, even with basic products. Plus, just wearing it in a ponytail all the time helped to protect it from the heat damage I saw on other girls.

After putting a mist of hairspray on, I worked through each of the makeup products I owned until the person in the mirror looking back at me was unrecognizable. This girl looked nothing like the one who threw her hair up every day and ran to school exhausted and burned out. This girl looked like someone who was confident and could take on the world. Who belonged with someone like Kai.

But which one was I in reality? I identified so much more with the maid than with the millionaire. Could I suddenly belong in a different world? Or at least belong with someone who came from one?

I didn't know, but I did know Kai wanted me to try. The fact that he cared so much kept me going.

"I'm going to get my dress," I said.

"Okay," Mom mumbled through mascara mouth (the weird face we made when putting on eye makeup).

I walked to my bedroom and shoved hanging clothes across the closet rack until I reached the garment bag. I unzipped it, revealing the dress for tonight first.

The fabric was smooth under my fingers, and I was actually excited to put it on. (Unlike the other dress that still scared me a bit.)

I pulled the purple one from the velvet hanger, took off my button-down shirt and shorts, then slipped it over my head. It slid easily over my skin until it fell around my calves. Looking down at myself, I knew it looked nice, but I went to the bathroom to see the effect in our full-length mirror.

I saw myself as soon as Mom did, and we had identical reactions, covering our mouths with our hands and staring.

"You look so grown up, *mija*," she breathed, her eyes shining.

"You think?" I smiled, turning to see how the dress accentuated my every curve. Zara was magic.

"Too bad Kai is off limits, because wow," she said and fluttered her eyebrows.

I laughed awkwardly. "He's not my type."

It wasn't a lie, not really. Rich, tall, and lean had never been on my radar. I'd gone for bulky underdogs, salt-of-the-earth type people who understood hard, physical labor like I did. But maybe I had been looking for comfortable instead of challenging, like Kai.

"I'm sure the right man will show up in due time," she said.

I nodded. "Have you ever thought of dating anyone?"

Her cheeks got hot. This was the one thing we didn't talk about, and I wasn't sure why. It had always been her and me, but I wanted her to know I'd be okay with it. There was no need for me to hold her back, not now that I knew what it felt like to wholeheartedly want a relationship and have to deny yourself for reasons outside your control.

"I don't know," she said at last.

"You'll consider it?" I asked.

She shrugged and capped her lipstick. "Are you about ready?"

I wanted to push, to ask her what kept her from opening up, but it had been just the two of us long enough for me to know that the subject was closed.

"I just need my purse," I said.

"While I finish up, can you grab the *birria*?"

"Sure." I escaped the bathroom that seemed to be getting tighter by the second. But I still had a tightness in my chest. Tonight meant a lot to Kai, and in turn, me.

With shaking fingers, I latched the clips on our slow cooker. It was cool now, but this close, I could still smell the delicious flavors. Excitement blossomed in me to share a bit more of my world with Kai.

Mom joined me, and I took her in. It had been so long since I'd seen her in anything other than a cleaning uniform or the shorts and a shirt she slept in, much less a dress. She was actually wearing heels.

"You have curves, Amá!" I said in admiration.

"Or should I say *mamacita*?" I waggled my eyebrows at her and shimmied my hips.

She swatted at me. "Oh, stop it."

"I didn't even know you had heels!"

Looking a little sheepish, she said, "I borrowed them from Camilla."

So I wasn't the only one who cared about looking good for this meal. I smiled and looped my arm through hers. "Let's go."

We walked down to her car, and I carefully placed the slow cooker in the trunk before sitting in the passenger side. We drove across town, taking every turn as slowly as possible, to the wealthiest part of Emerson. Mom never talked about her clients, but I wondered what she saw when she watched all the big houses pass by. Was she jealous? Resigned? Determined? How did she feel about the people inside?

We parked in the servants' garage and then walked toward the house, *birria* in hand. When we knocked on the door, Kai answered.

"I'm so glad you made it." As he let us inside, his eyes drank me in. "May I take your coats?"

All we had were our shabby winter coats, but we handed them over. He took them and folded them over his arm just as if they'd come from royalty.

My mom thanked him, beaming. She looked stunning when she smiled like that, loose curls hanging around her face.

"You're welcome," he answered, putting our coats on a nearby rack. "Can I take that for you?"

My mom handed him the slow cooker, and then we followed him back into the kitchen we'd cleaned for this very occasion. Mr. Rush set his phone down on the countertop and greeted us.

"You look amazing," he said to my mom.

She blushed. "Thank you, Mr. Rush."

"Tonight, it's Johnson."

Kai and I eyed each other. They were acting strange, right? It was like they didn't know how to act either, outside of the employer-servant relationship. At least Kai and I had practiced.

He shrugged and pulled out a chair. "Jordan?"

I smiled. "Thank you." I'd never had someone help tuck me into a table, and I would have expected it to be awkward, but with Kai, it was easy. Exciting, even. Especially when he brushed the back of my bare arms with his fingertips, teasing me.

Mr. Rush sat down as well and said, "Let the fun begin."

I didn't know what Mr. Rush's idea of fun was, but sitting in front of eight pieces of silverware, not

knowing which one to use, did not meet my definition. As if sensing my concern, Kai said, "Dad, can
we just have a laid-back meal?"

Mr. Rush shrugged. "I don't see why not. It will
be easier without Robert anyway."

As if worried taking too long might give his dad
a chance to change his mind, Kai moved around
the table, picking up silverware that could have
lasted my mom and me a week without doing
dishes. I couldn't help but feel embarrassed,
knowing Kai had done it for our benefit.

The two people I cared about most were too
invested in the outcome of this meal for me to get
wrapped up in technicalities, though.

Kai dispensed of the silverware in the kitchen
and came back empty-handed. "Why don't we
dig in?"

"Let's," Mr. Rush said. He stood and gestured
to the buffet table.

"Ladies first."

Mom offered a small chuckle and stood,
smoothing her dress. I followed behind her, carefully placing small amounts of each dish on my
plate. That is, except for Mom's *birria*. I loaded a
bowl with that. There would be enough for all four
of us to have at least that much, and I wanted to get

my fill. Besides, none of the spread on the table looked like the types of things we typically had on Thanksgiving. I always loved indulging in way too many *tamales* and *dulce de leche* cake. The *birria* was basically insurance that we'd have at least one good thing to eat.

At the end of the buffet, I took in the desserts. Pumpkin pie, artfully topped with a swirl of whipped cream, apple pie covered in sugary crumbles, and then...

"Are these cupcakes from Seaton Bakery?" Mom asked.

I turned to the men, watching Kai, who wore a small smile. Mr. Rush shrugged. "Seems my boy has gotten a taste for them. Couldn't have a Thanksgiving dinner without them."

"He has excellent taste." My mom kissed her fingers. "*Muy delicioso.*"

But I was too focused on Kai. The guy who knew actions spoke louder than words to me had made an effort to make me feel comfortable. To be sure I had a good time.

Still smiling, I picked up one of the cupcakes and went to my seat at the table, much more at home than before.

At first, the conversation was awkward as we cut

into our turkey. Mr. Rush was an app mogul who'd wisely invested his inherited fortune and made a billion on his own. Mom was a hardworking, first generation immigrant from a cheap apartment complex in Seaton. Kai and I were the only ones who had much in common, which, as far as our parents knew, was simply going to the same school.

That's where the conversation settled for the better part of half an hour.

And then Mr. Rush turned to me and said, "Jordan, I'm assuming you want to go into the medical field after college? Nursing, perhaps?"

"Why would you assume nursing?" I asked.

"I just assumed..."

"Because I'm a woman?" He'd found my trigger and pushed it like a child with a shiny red button that said *do not touch*.

Mom kicked me under the table. *Behave,* her strappy heels said.

As Mr. Rush stuttered through his response, I pasted on my best smile and cut him off. "Actually, I'm going to school to become an oncologist."

His eyebrows rose for a moment. "Oh, very nice. Where do you plan to enroll?"

His validation frustrated me almost as much as his presumptions about me. "UCLA," I said shortly.

Kai cleared his throat. "I heard their med school's one of the best in the country."

I smiled because I knew he heard it from me. And because he was sticking up for me.

"Is that so?" Mr. Rush said, drawing his lips down in a surprised expression. "Who knew?" He bent over his food, chewing, and when I was sure my mom wasn't looking, I mouthed, "Thank you," at Kai.

He lifted one shoulder in the cutest half-shrug I'd ever seen.

Kai took a bite of Mom's dish, and his eyes widened. "Ms. Junco, this is *amazing.*"

Mom batted a hand at him. "You flatter me."

"No," he said, loading his spoon with another bite. "You have to give Mr. Wallace the recipe."

I laughed. "Mom doesn't use recipes."

"What?" Kai asked.

Mom grinned, "I've been cooking *birria* for holidays since before I knew how to spell! But I can teach him sometime if you would like."

"Yes, please," Kai said.

Mr. Rush cleared his throat. "Maybe on her day off."

The table went so silent I could hear the wind outside the windows. Mr. Rush had just gone out of his way to remind Mom and me where we belonged, and it wasn't sitting at his kitchen table. That much was clear.

Kai extended a spoonful toward his father, who'd neglected to get a bowl. "Try it, Dad."

"Isn't there pig stomach in it?" he asked.

Okay, if I was annoyed by the nursing comment, this had to be worse. "No, that's *menudo*, made with tripe." At his nonplussed look, I added, "Cow stomach. Mom makes the best *menudo*, by the way."

Mom tilted her head toward me. "Yours isn't too shabby either, *mija*."

Kai still waited with his spoon extended. Begrudgingly, Mr. Rush stood and walked to Kai. He took the spoon and put it in his mouth, clearly straining to swallow.

"Interesting," he grunted, reaching immediately for his water and taking three big gulps.

Mom kicked my leg again and narrowed her eyebrows at me.

I knew what that meant. My face was giving away my own distaste for this man. I wanted to like him, really, for Kai's sake, but come on. *Interesting?* That was the best he could do?

"What about you, Kai?" my mom asked. "What

are your plans for after graduation? Taking over the family business?"

Kai opened his mouth, but his dad answered for him, "Not until he has his degree."

"Oh," my mom said, nodding, looking between them. "Any hobbies?"

She was reaching here.

Mr. Rush grunted. "You mean other than anonymously donating funds to charities without asking permission?"

I kept my eyes down, because I knew my face would display my emotions without my permission. Kai's dad had found out about the medical debt. And he was disgruntled about it.

Mom's voice had an amused smile in it. "Sounds like you have a philanthropist on your hands."

"Dad," Kai said, "why don't I get the ice cream?" He wiped his cloth napkin over his face and went to stand.

"I can help," I offered.

"Thank you, Jordan," Mr. Rush said, frowning, but I was beginning to think that was his only facial expression other than condescension. "If you're sure you don't mind."

"I don't," I said. Honestly, it would be a relief to escape from the building tension in the room.

Kai and I stayed casual until the doors to the kitchen had closed behind us, and when we were sure we were on our own, we gave each other a look.

"Is this going how you planned?" I asked.

"Not exactly." He sighed and took my hands. "Time for plan B?"

"And that would be?"

"Having Hank fly us to Mexico and starting a new life?"

I snorted. "Now that you've donated all your dad's billions to charity? I'm not sure we can afford it."

Kai gave me a pained look. "It's just his generation. He doesn't understand that having it all doesn't amount to anything." His hand covered my shoulder, warming me.

I forced my eyes to stay on him instead of sliding closed. "And what does amount to something?"

His hand cupped my cheek, and he searched my eyes before speaking. "Having someone to love, who's not there because of birth or requirement, but because they choose to be."

He'd used the L-word so easily, but it was big to me. My heart clung to it, the fact that love was on his mind when it came to me. And in that moment, I knew that I'd choose Kai, over and over again.

When his hand fell away from me, I felt his absence just as completely as I had felt his touch.

He turned to the freezer and took out a tub of ice cream. Holding it in front of him, his said, "Back into the lion's den?"

I could only nod.

THIRTY-FOUR

MOM and I walked to our car, tugging our coats around us. When we were several yards away from the house, I whispered. "That was *awful*."

"Shh," she hissed.

I looked back at the house. "What? No one's listening."

"You never know, *mija*." She hit a button on her key fob and only one taillight lit up. "Great," she muttered.

"I can change it Saturday," I offered.

"Are you sure?"

I shrugged and put my hand on the handle. "Yeah, we'll just take my car until then."

"Thank you." She sounded truly relieved as we got in the car. After she shut the door, she ducked her head to look in the rearview mirror and shook her hair out. "Okay, you can say it now."

"What?" I asked.

She raised her eyebrows at me. "It was awful."

"Oh, the *worst*," I said.

She giggled, more lighthearted than usual, and imitated him trying her *birria*. "Interesting."

"Right!" I cried. "Who says that? I mean, 'marvelous,' or 'fabulous' maybe. But interesting?"

She shook her head, sobering. "He was kind to have us over. And his son was very polite. I like him."

My heart swelled that Mom had noticed Kai's compassion for other people. "Me too."

For a moment, we were quiet as she drove away from the house.

"Is he dating anyone?" Mom asked.

"Mr. Rush?" I sputtered. "Mom, no."

"No! His son!"

All the jest left my body, replaced with fear. My mom knew me better than anyone else. She'd birthed me. Dressed me. Fed me. Held me. How would she miss the effect just the thought of Kai dating had on me? I hoped the disappointment was gone from my voice as I said, "He's going to the gala with Merritt Alexander."

"The girl who bullied your friend?"

"That's the one," I confirmed.

"Ugh."

"Why?" I halfheartedly teased. "You interested?"

She shoved my shoulder.

"Don't hit the passenger!"

Laughing, she said, "Under different circumstances, he'd be a catch for you."

I didn't have to lie. Instead, I stuck with the truth. "I completely agree."

"I'm sorry, *mija*."

I was too.

That night, I lay in bed, staring at the ceiling and holding my phone, wondering what to send Kai. Because he wasn't texting me. Deep down, I feared it was because he'd seen my mom and me through his father's eyes. We'd gone from servants to disappointing guests, at best. Finally, I gave up looking for the perfect message and settled on an honest one.

Jordan: Tonight was bad.

Kai: I'm sorry.

Jordan: For what? You were the one who made it just "bad" and not completely terrible.

Kai: Small consolation.

Jordan: I know.

Kai: He just doesn't know you yet. It takes a while for him to open up.

Jordan: You mean there's more behind that disappointed look or the stereotyping about women in the medical field?

The texting screen was blank for a moment, and I started second-guessing my message. Had he fallen asleep? Was Kai bored? Relieved he could go to the gala with someone his dad wouldn't dread being around for fear the poor would rub off?

Finally, my phone vibrated in my hand, and I felt like I could breathe again. That was, until I read the words.

Kai: He's not perfect but he's my dad. He's the only person who's always been there for me.

Jordan: Well my mom's always been there for me, and your dad treats her like dirt.

Kai: Excuse me?

Jordan: "Interesting?" He didn't have any complimentary words to say while he was trying not to vomit? Not one in his vocabulary?

Kai: He has IBS. It was nice of him to try it at all.

Jordan: He could have said that!

Kai: He was being courteous.

I scoffed at my ceiling, glad I had Steve Harvey's voice to cover it so my mom wouldn't hear. If that was courteous for Kai's dad, I'd hate to see rude. How could someone as kind and thoughtful as Kai come from someone with as much personality as a porcupine?

But then again, seeing the guy through office doors and briefly in passing every morning didn't mean I knew him. Maybe there was a side to Mr. Rush that wasn't judgmental. I doubted it, but that didn't mean it wasn't there.

Kai: I'm sorry.

Jordan: For what? I was the one being rude. I would be upset if someone talked bad about my mom.

Kai: I'm sorry I can't get my dad to see how incredible you are.

Much to my surprise, my lips curved into a smile.

Jordan: As long as you see it.

Kai: I can't wait to see you tomorrow night. If you look half as beautiful as you did tonight, I'll be breathless.

Smiling, I bit my lip and let it slide out of my teeth. How could I say anything to even compare to his words? But then I remembered who he'd be attending the gala with, and my smile fell.

Jordan: I wish you didn't have to go with Merritt.

Kai: Not as much as me. Trust me.

That made me feel at least a little better.

Kai: Someday, we'll go to a ball together. And it won't matter who sees us together, because we'll only have eyes for each other.

The idea of it made the yearning feeling in my chest expand to painful limits.

Jordan: Sounds like a fantasy.

Kai: It is a fantasy, but wishes can't come true if you're too afraid to dream them in the first place.

Jordan: I never thought to dream of you, but here we are.

Kai: That's okay, because I dreamed of you.

Jordan: I hope you have even better dreams tonight.

As I waited for his text good night, I wondered. What would my life look like today if Kai hadn't dreamed of me? What would my life look like if my dreams hadn't left with my father?

THIRTY-FIVE

THE NEXT MORNING, Mom and I woke at our normal time to clean Seaton Bakery since we had the day off from the Rushes. Gayle and Chris were a sight for sore eyes after having spent an afternoon with our worst and most necessary client.

The bell over the door clanged as we walked in.

Gayle poked her head over the swinging kitchen doors. "Good morning, sweethearts!"

As she walked into the main area, Chris poked his head over the doors. "How are our favorite girls?"

"Great," Mom answered, walking to the counter, the cart rolling behind her.

I twirled my finger around my ear, and Gayle

laughed. "So I'm guessing Thanksgiving with the fancy pants didn't go well?"

Mom glanced back at me. "It went as well as we could have hoped." She grinned at me and chuckled. "Especially getting to see J school a billionaire on feminism."

Gayle's eyes practically bugged out. "Okay, I have to hear about this."

I grabbed a rag from the cart and a spray bottle and said, "Pull up a chair."

While Mom got out the dust mop and started on the floor, Gayle pretended to get a chair and eat popcorn. With a laugh, I began scrubbing the counter and display case, telling her all about our awful evening.

"He sounds terrible," Gayle said. "His mama should have taught him some manners."

I pursed my lips and nodded. "No kidding."

"The boy who came and bought cupcakes—was that the son or an employee?"

An excited flutter filled my chest, and I did my best to act casual. "What did he look like?"

"Cute, kind, quiet. Black hair, dark eyes."

"That's the son."

"Someone must have *launched* the apple away from the tree because that is one sweet kid."

A smile grew on my face without my consent. "What did he do?"

"Always makes small talk, says please and thank you, leaves big tips and refuses to take it back even when you argue with him."

"That sounds like Kai."

Gayle's sly smile was hard to ignore. "Did I mention he was cute?"

Mom called from across the seating area, "He's off limits!"

"Boo," Gayle said and pretended to toss her popcorn and push in her imaginary chair. "I better get back to work before Chris thinks he has to do it all himself."

"Too late!" Chris called from the kitchen.

Laughing, I shook my head and refocused on work myself. Maybe it was good Kai was off limits. If we dated in public, I'd have to deal with his dad all the time. As it was, I got Kai all to myself. Our time together was special, secluded, so we could just enjoy each other.

But then again, it led to days like today. In just a few hours, I'd be getting ready for a gala I'd be attending by myself while Kai had Merritt Alexander on his arm. Part of me wanted to skip it altogether. Kai would be living the life his father dreamed for him, while I stayed far away. Just the thought of watching Merritt flaunt yet another thing she had that no one else did made me sick to my stomach.

She didn't understand that life wasn't a game with pawns you could move around and sacrifice on a whim. Others had real feelings, real stakes that couldn't be repaired with a bottomless bank account.

But then I thought of seeing Kai in a suit that wasn't our school uniform. Of locking eyes across the room and holding our secret, our relationship, that was just between us. And of him seeing me in the dress Zara picked out. Maybe a small part of me was satisfied at the fact that he would be able to look but not touch, for the evening at least.

"Jordan," Mom called loudly, making it clear she'd been trying to get my attention for quite some time.

I jerked to attention. "Sorry, yes?"

She passed me the glass cleaner. "Wipe the display with this."

I nodded and did as she asked. We made short work of the tables, floors, and chairs. The kitchen was Gayle and Chris's domain, so when we were finished with the dining area, we said our goodbyes and headed to the apartment for a nap.

I curled on the couch next to Mom while listening to her play along with a game of Lingo on the TV. For a non-native English speaker, she was really good with words. I wondered what she could have done in another life—one that didn't involve all the heartache hers had come with. The last thing I heard before I fell asleep was her muttering that she would be way better on this show than the contestants.

After my nap, I said goodbye to Mom, packed up my stuff for the gala, and headed to Ginger's house. Her parents didn't trust her not to sneak off to the gala, so we were going to her.

My phone's GPS led me to a bungalow in the old part of Emerson. It was painted bright yellow with gnomes nestled in the rocked front yard. Maybe someday Mom and I could have a cute house like this. (I had to dream, right?) I parked along the curb, realizing I was the first of our friends to get here. On the way to the front door, I passed a sign stuck into the ground that said *BUY RIPE*. If only I could afford to.

Readjusting my garment bag over my elbow, I

went to the front door. Their doorbell was surrounded by fruit decals, and I smiled as I pushed it, thinking of the sarcastic remarks Ginger probably made about it.

A younger girl I recognized from the junior class at EA answered the door. "Hey, Jordan."

"Hi," I said and followed her inside. "I didn't catch your name?"

"Cori—short for Coriander." She pointed at two identical girls sitting on the couch in the living room we'd walked into. "The twins are named Tarra, for tarragon, and Cara, for caraway. Our parents are a little obsessed with produce." Cori gave an eye-roll so reminiscent of Ginger I giggled.

She led me past a wall of their photos, all red-headed and blue-eyed, then stopped in front of a closed door that had signs with both her and Ginger's names on it.

"This is our room," Cori explained, "but I'm not allowed to be in there. You can hang out on my bed, though, if you want. It's clean. I mean, it's made. But it's clean too. There might be some drool on the pillow, but—"

The door opened, and Ginger gave us a mildly amused look. "Cori talking your ear off?"

I gave Cori a sympathetic grin. "Not too much."

Cori tilted her head and shrugged, making her curly hair bounce. "See you around, Jordan!"

"See ya." I waved at her back because she was already off, down the hallway.

Ginger practically pulled me into her room. I could tell just by the way it was set up that she'd been loved and taken care of her whole life. There were pictures hung everywhere of a happy life worth remembering. Was this the kind of life I would have had if Juana had never been sick and if my dad had stayed?

"Okay," Ginger said, "tell me everything about Thanksgiving."

I took Cori's offer and sat on her pink handmade bedspread. "I'm pretty sure Webster's adding a picture of the night to the dictionary, right next to 'awful.'"

"Oof." She cringed and sucked in a breath. "That bad?"

"If by bad you mean Mr. Rush insinuated I was going to be a nurse by going into the medical field and he called the dish my mom makes every year 'interesting,' then yeah."

"Kai did?"

"No, his dad." I shook my head, my eyes landing on the poster of the singer Dorian Gray hanging on Cori's side of the room. "Kai was actually nice. Got his dad to take some of the silverware off the table. Did you know people have, like, fifteen forks for one meal?"

"Most I've ever had is three." She folded her arms on the back of her desk chair and rested her chin on them. "Was it awkward being around him after the whole Martín thing?"

"Not really." I looked down at my battered nails and picked at some skin on my thumb. "He's easier to get along with than I thought."

She snorted. "Probably just doesn't want you to spit in his kale juice or something."

I managed half a laugh and shrugged.

"So, anyone new on the horizon?"

"Huh?"

"Guys? Romantic interests?" she said. "I'm living through you, remember?"

I had to fight to keep my expression even as I shook my head. "No one. You?"

She shrugged. "There are plenty of hot guys at the academy. I mean, have you seen Ray Sadler?" She fanned herself.

"I think so. Isn't that the cowboy on scholarship?"

She nodded. "He's been here since freshman year, but I've never really talked to him."

"Why not?"

Her full lips turned down. "Not everyone is into the whole sheltered ginger thing. And that's even if my dad would let him look at me long enough to go on a date. Plus, I don't know what kind of farming he does and my parents are all about organic food and no antibiotics, blah, blah, blah."

I wondered what it would be like to have that kind of money that afforded you options of buying organic or not.

She shrugged. "Besides, I don't even know if my parents would let me date. I've never had to ask."

"No one's ever asked you out? Not even to a dance?"

She shook her head, keeping her eyes on the floor.

My heart hurt for her. Rory had made the same kind of comments when she was first trying to get Beckett to notice her. I wish they knew that any guy worth his salt would embrace their curves and love them for it.

Cori's voice rattled on outside the door, and it opened to Rory and Zara. I grinned at her as Ginger got up and greeted them. Callie came next, and soon it was all of us in a frenzy of curling irons and hairspray and makeup.

I'd never gone to a school dance, but I imagined this would be like prom night. It was way more fun than I'd ever imagined. Plus, the snacks Ginger pulled from her pantry didn't hurt. Some of them were weird healthy things, like seaweed crisps, but there were actually some salted caramel rice cakes that tasted good.

Once my hair was pinned into an updo that embraced my natural curl, Zara said, "Now, put on that dress! I want to see you in it!"

With everyone's eyes on me, I changed out of my clothes and slipped the dress over my head. The smooth fabric clung to my curves, every single one of them, and the low-cut neckline accentuated the best two.

Rory fanned herself while Ginger whistled.

"Stop!" I cried, blushing harder than I knew I could.

"You look hot!" Zara said.

I tugged up on the neckline, adjusting it to more

appropriate levels. "Are you sure it's not too much—
or too *little?*"

Ginger shook her head. "Let's put it this way—
if there aren't any guys in the picture now, there will
be after tonight."

THIRTY-SIX

AFTER TAKING PICTURES WITH GINGER, we rode in a limo (provided by Zara's father) to the hotel that was hosting the gala. From the way they talked about it in our FMP meetings, I knew the hotel was grandiose, but this towering skyscraper with valets and red carpet was beyond what I'd expected. To stay there just one night probably cost more than a month's rent and groceries.

Now, instead of feeling sexy, I felt bare. Would everyone see through the bold outfit to the poor, curvy girl wearing it?

Callie nudged my arm. "You okay?"

Tugging at the straps of my dress, I asked, "Do any of you have a shawl I can borrow."

Zara sent me a confused look from across the limo. "What's going on?"

My eyes stung. Not just because of the dress, but because I knew I'd be walking inside and seeing Kai and Merritt together. She'd probably be dressed in a classy, expensive gown by a personal shopper while I had cleavage showing. "What if I'm not good enough to pull off this dress?" Or the entire night.

"Jordan," Zara scolded. "You are fierce. You are kind. You are smart. Underneath all of that, you are a hottie in a thousand-dollar dress! Own it!"

My mouth fell open. "A thousand dollars?"

Her eyes widened as she nodded. "But you look like a million bucks."

A laugh escaped my lips. "You're crazy."

"And you're beautiful," she said.

The girls nodded and echoed her sentiment as the limo pulled to a stop.

Rory put her hand on my arm. "We've got you."

That meant more than I could say.

When we walked into the ballroom, my mouth fell open. There was a massive sparkling chandelier, stunning decorations, and every person looked like they stepped out of a storybook.

"This is amazing," Callie breathed.

I nodded. "You didn't see it before? We're raising money for your dad's organization."

"No," she said. "Poppy told Dad it would be taken care of, but wow."

Wow was right, no matter how much I hated to admit it. Poppy's event planner had done wonderfully—people were already mingling, clearly enjoying themselves. But now they were starting to stare. I dipped my head lower so just Callie could hear. "What do we do at these things?"

Her eyes lit up. "Food."

We went on a mission to check out each of the catering trays and agreed to meet back under the chandelier.

A tray of drinks passed by, and they handed me one. A sip told me it was sparkling water with frozen fruit to keep it cool. I held it as I walked past dozens of people in formalwear, talking and acting like they attended events like this all the time.

I also got a hold of some bacon-wrapped shrimp, which I was pretty sure had been hand-delivered by the gods. But no sight of Kai. I returned to the spot under the chandelier, seeing my friends standing with a tall, older man.

Callie caught sight of me walking toward them and extended her arm. "Dad, this is Jordan Junco. Jordan, this is my dad, the man of the hour."

He chuckled and shook my hand with both of his. "I feel like the man of the hour surrounded by such beautiful young women." He smiled at his daughter, and I could feel the love there as much as I could see it.

I ached for that. The love only a father could give, but at the same time, I was happy that Callie had it. No one deserved to live without their dad.

"Nice to meet you," I said.

He nodded, closing his eyes as he did. "Likewise."

"So, how do these things usually go?" I asked.

Callie and her dad exchanged glances, and he said, "Eat until you drop, dance to the band's music, and then fall into bed. Right, Cal Gal?"

She chuckled. "Right."

Someone clapped Callie's dad's shoulder, and he turned away.

"So," Callie said. "Dancing?"

"I'm in," Zara said.

Rory and I glanced at each other and shrugged.

"Sure," I said.

We went to the small wooden dance floor and danced to the band's cover of a pop song I'd been hearing on the radio every morning on the drive to Kai's. I closed my eyes as I moved my hips, thinking of the anticipation I felt each morning to see him. He might have thought of me as sunshine, but he was so much more to me. How had he gone from someone I barely knew to someone I couldn't live without?

And then I heard Merritt's voice. My head swiveled toward it, knowing I would see him as well.

I wasn't disappointed. He stood next to her, looking even better than the mental image I'd prepared of him. His suit framed his body in the most appealing of ways. With his hair swept over his forehead and his dark eyes as intense as ever, he was the perfect combination of intrigue and desire.

"Hi, girls," Merritt trilled to us, bringing Kai right along with her.

My fingertips ached to touch his lapels, to trace the hard line of his jaw before placing my lips on his.

"Merritt," Zara said, the distaste clear in her voice. "Kai."

"How's your night going?" Merritt asked. She

placed her hand on Kai's chest, looking directly at me. "We're having an *amazing* time."

But then I saw where his arm was. Around Merritt's waist, like he wanted to be there with her. Like it was the most natural thing in the world.

My throat clogged with emotion I didn't quite understand or know how to explain. Seeking an explanation, my gaze met his beautiful dark eyes.

There were a million words in his stare, but none of them made sense through the pain expanding in my chest. This, seeing him with Merritt, it was more than I'd anticipated. It was the confirmation of everything I'd thought or feared in a single perfect image, with her dress that flowed over her perfect body and her hair that never frizzed curling around her face, or her perfectly manicured nails standing out against the black of his suit as she laughed and placed her hand on his chest. The one my fingers had explored so recently.

I was torn between needing to stand strong in front of Merritt and crumbling on the inside, piece by piece. But that was our relationship, wasn't it? Everything we felt was carefully hidden by a façade no one could see.

I was tired of it. It hurt. Physically.

I turned to my friends and quietly said, "I need to use the bathroom."

Callie's eyes were worried. "Are you okay? Do you need us to come with?"

I shook my head, then turned to Merritt and Kai. "Hope you keep having an *amazing* time."

And then I walked away.

THIRTY-SEVEN

I COULD FEEL their eyes on my back as I rushed out of the ballroom. I knew I was being ridiculous, but that didn't make the pain flooding my chest any less bearable. Didn't keep tears from threatening to fall.

How had I been so dumb to fall for Kai? To entertain a relationship when we both knew it could go nowhere, and only end in pain? Because right now, it hurt like hell, and I had no idea how to face something no one but me could see.

I found a door I thought was the bathroom, but opened it to find a small courtyard. A burst of frigid air blasted me, but across the way, I could see standing heaters and glass double doors opening to the area. The door behind me must have been a side entrance. I quickly walked toward the heaters, feeling the tassels of the dress dance around my legs.

The biggest heater had soft blue flames dancing inside. Soon, heat reached my skin, but it did nothing for the ice in my heart. I couldn't watch Merritt put her hands all over him. Couldn't watch him *let* her. I knew it had been a forced date for him, but that didn't mean he had to enjoy it.

On a nearby street, a car revved by, reminding me of Martín. Of my terrible taste in men. I put my head in my hands and sighed.

I needed to let go of Kai. It hurt more being with him in a world where I didn't belong than it did just being on my own. I'd miss out on an amazing guy, but I'd stop risking my mom's business. Stop risking his father's judgement.

Stop risking my heart.

The door clacked open, and Kai's voice crept into the courtyard. "I've been looking everywhere for you."

"You found me," I said quietly.

He took me in for a moment, his eyes flickering with the fire. "You look stunning tonight."

A piece of ice inside me thawed. I'd wanted him to notice me so badly, and I gave myself permission to fall, just a little harder. After all, it wasn't the falling that hurt, but the landing. "The suit is good on you," I admitted.

Sitting beside me, he said, "The fire is nice."

I nodded, hardly seeing the heaters at all. All I could see was him telling me I was his *ad meliora*.

For a moment, we sat in silence that felt heavier than any debt or expectation.

"Do you want to dance?" Kai asked.

"What about your date? Your dad?"

"They're too busy trying to look good to bother coming out here."

My brain screamed no. Accepting this dance could only lead to heartbreak, to chaos and destruction of the carefully pieced together life my mom and I led atop a house of cards.

But my heart was going to be broken anyway, and it led me boldly into the flames. "Okay."

We stood, and he drew me into his chest just as easily as he drew the bow across his violin. I sagged into him, using his strong body to hold me up before the fall. His chest rose and fell against mine as we swayed to the music of the crackling fire and passing cars.

Each second that passed felt like the final gasp before crashing into ice-cold water. So necessary and so painful before the chill wrapped around your chest and squeezed.

Hot tears burned my eyes, of sadness and anger, because Merritt had done nothing to earn her life. Yet here she was with all the privilege it entailed while I hid with Kai in a courtyard, clinging to him like bites of a last meal.

A sob wracked my chest, and I backed away from him.

Concern etched his features as he reached for me. "Are you okay? What's wrong?"

I shook my head, clutching my chest. "Kai, I can't do this anymore."

"What do you mean?" He placed his hands on both of my arms, but I couldn't meet his eyes.

"This, I can't do this." I stepped away from him and looked pointedly at his hands, which were no longer holding me. "It hurts too much, and it can't go anywhere."

He stepped closer, but I retreated again. "Is this because of Merritt? You know I didn't want to come with her. I'd rather be here with you."

"No," I said. "It's because of *life*. You're a *billion-aire*. Your father expects you to be with people like her, and he expects people like me to clean the ground you walk on so we can worship it afterward." I wasn't bitter though, not anymore. I was resigned. Even if I hadn't chosen my life, it was the one I had.

Kai's calm exterior shattered, and his lip curled in distaste. "Screw what my father thinks. What's between you and me has *nothing* to do with them."

"Exactly!" I cried, my voice echoing off the stone walls of the hotel. "That's the problem. As long as they don't know we care about each other, there will always be something else—another job, another date for a gala, another college... I'm tired of the secrets. I'm tired of always being somewhere I know I don't belong."

"What if you belong with me?" he asked.

I clenched my jaw and looked toward the cobbled stone beneath my thrift store shoes. "I don't."

The hurt I felt was only magnified in his eyes as he said quietly, "You told me you were okay with our arrangement. That you wanted it this way."

I clenched my jaw, doing everything in my power to hold back tears and failing miserably. "I can't do it anymore."

And then I turned to leave, coming face to face with Mr. Rush, Merritt right behind him.

THIRTY-EIGHT

FOR A MOMENT, we stared at each other, the truth of what existed between Kai and me clear on our faces.

Kai was the first to speak. "Dad, I—"

Mr. Rush held up his hand and then scrubbed his chin. "I heard enough."

My eyes turned toward the ground as fear and loss ripped through me. It felt like every other part of me was on the ground too, standing two inches tall. "Mr. Rush, I'm—"

He shook his head. "That's quite enough, Miss Junco." He waved his hand. "You may go. And please let your mother know I won't be needing her services anymore. You can tell her why."

Desperation replaced every other emotion. "You can't do that, I—"

He didn't raise his volume, but his tone was deadly. "I can do anything I like in my home. Your time doing that, however, is over."

The complete dismissal tore whatever was left of me to shreds. I turned and left.

"Jordan!" Kai called behind me, but he didn't follow. "Dad, let go of me."

I pushed through the open courtyard door and ran into my friends. Their faces were pictures of the shock I felt.

"Was that..." Callie began, but her sentence trailed off.

Rory's eyebrows drew together. "You and Kai were together?"

Arguing voices sounded through the double glass doors behind me, booming, yelling words like "trash" and "immigrant." I stood in stunned silence as everything I'd ever doubted about myself was aired to the person I loved.

Callie put her arms around me and hauled me away, the other girls following us. "I don't understand," she said quietly, guiding us into a bathroom. "Why was Mr. Rush saying those things about you?"

The fluorescent lights hit me like a freight train, and I closed my eyes, suddenly feeling exhausted. And I was tired—of the lies, of the secrets, of this entire day. "He found out I'm dating his son. *Was* dating his son."

The bathroom burst out in a chorus of confusion and questions, trying to make sense of a situation that didn't. Their questions assailed me just as harshly as Mr. Rush's insults had.

"Stop!" I yelled. I blinked back tears and stepped away, feeling like an open wound. "All I've ever heard you guys say is how much you hate Kai. I kept it to myself because I didn't need another person judging me more than everyone already is!"

"No one's judging you but yourself," Zara said, her chin up.

"Yeah," I said sarcastically. "That's why everyone at the Academy calls me 'ship and makes fun of my car every time I pull up."

"We never did that. So why would you punish us like we did?" Zara demanded. "You were ashamed about Kai; that's why you didn't tell us."

"No, I didn't tell you because if Mr. Rush found out, my mom would lose her job. And we did." My voice was rising, shaking now. I hated the pity filling their eyes more than the accusations earlier. "So yeah, I kept it to myself, and no, I don't feel sorry about it. I wouldn't expect you to understand when you've never had to worry about where your next meal is coming from or whether your mom's back is going to make it through the next cleaning job."

Callie's lip trembled. "Is that how you think of us? Rich kids who don't have a clue? All we've ever done is try to help you."

"Help me?" I cried. "I don't need your help, and furthermore, I don't want it."

Zara raised her hands. "I'm out. I don't need to be anywhere I'm not wanted."

"Then go," I said. "If you're perfect, then go."

Her heels pounded on the tile as she walked away. She raised her hand in the air then pushed through the bathroom door.

"You too," I told the other two. "Go. I never belonged in the group anyway."

They hesitated, Rory's eyes searching mine and Callie's looking at the floor. Eventually, Callie turned and walked away, and it felt like she'd ripped a shard of my heart out of my chest and carried it with her.

Rory's eyes were watering. "I know I've made mistakes before, but I never lied to you. We deserved better."

And then she walked away too.

I blinked quickly at the closed bathroom door, trying to stem the flow of building tears. When I couldn't anymore, I fled the bathroom and ran, leaving the hotel behind.

Shucking my heels, I sprinted across the street, getting as far from the building and from my heartbreak as I could until blisters opened on my feet and I couldn't move another step. I went inside a dingy diner and sat in a booth. The people inside gave me looks, but I didn't care.

My fingers tapped my mother's number into my phone. I had no one else, but after I told her about this, I worried I would lose her too.

Jordan: Amá, I need you.

I sent a map pin of my location and waited.

Mom: Be there in fifteen.

The waitress asked if she could get me anything, and I waved her away. She could kick me out if she wanted. It wouldn't be the first time tonight. No, I'd been kicked out of the Rushes' home. Out of the friend group. And as my mom's car pulled into a parking space, I worried I'd be kicked out of her heart as well.

Her car pulling into a front parking spot was like a godsend. My heart swelled as I ran out to her.

Mom reached out and opened the door for me, her eyes full of concern. "What happened?"

I looked her straight-on. I tried to. But I burst into tears instead. I'd ruined the most important job of her career, along with my heart. Kai and I had been playing with fire, and now everyone around us was getting burned.

"Whoa, whoa, whoa, honey." She rubbed my back. "Did someone hurt you?"

I shook my head, tears dripping off the tip of my nose. "I made a mistake."

"What did you do?" Her voice was guarded now, and I saw her looking around the car. "Are the police coming?"

"No," I said, sucking in a breath that grated against my lungs. "Mom, we don't have the Rush job anymore."

She froze, her hand on Juana's necklace around her neck. "What are you talking about?"

"We were fired." The words gritted past my teeth, all three of them wrong.

Her eyes hardened. "What do you mean?"

"I fell in love with Kai, Amá. I know you told me not to, but I did, and I was trying to end it, I promise I was, but Mr. Rush found out and he said don't come back, and I—"

She cut me off, her jaw trembling. "We lost the Rush job?"

Slowly, I nodded, wishing more than anything I could give her a different answer.

"Because you directly disobeyed my wishes." Her jaw trembled, with sadness or fury, I couldn't tell.

Again, I nodded. It was like I'd fallen off a cliff and landed, covered in bruises with broken bones, only to find out I'd actually landed on a ledge that was crumbling beneath me. Now there was nothing I could do to stop my descent.

"I—" I began, and she cut me off.

"Mama, please," I begged.

"No," she said, her eyes hard. The moisture building there was the only thing giving away her hurt. "You knew how much this mattered to our future, and you treated it like it was nothing. You are my daughter, and I will always love you. *Always*. But I will *never* forgive you."

She put the car in reverse and drove us the rest of the way home, not speaking another word. I kept my tears at bay until I was in the safety of my room, and then I lost it. All of it. And I knew, without my mom and her forgiveness, I had lost everything that mattered.

THIRTY-NINE

THE NEXT MORNING when I first woke up, I didn't think of Kai or my friends or my mom. No, I thought of Merritt. I wondered what kind of bed she was waking up in—whether it had a canopy or four posters or overlooked the ocean. Did she sleep in a silk eye mask with eyelashes on the front or did she have black-out curtains that let her rest as long as she wanted? Did she make her own breakfast, or was there a maid that prepared it just to her liking?

Most of all, when she slipped between the dark space of sleep and into the muddy space of almost alertness, did she feel a pain in her chest so strong as to be debilitating?

Because I did.

I'd never been so ashamed in my life. Not when

I earned the nickname Gassy J or the first time I pulled into the Academy's parking lot and everyone looked at my car like I'd come from another planet. Not even when the richest person I'd ever met saw me half-naked when I should have been cleaning. But now, I'd given my mother yet another heartache to mourn alongside my own.

I didn't care what happened to me—whether I needed to work double shifts at fast food places or beg Lucinda for our jobs back—but I hated myself, absolutely *hated* myself, for doing that to my mom.

Just feet away, I could hear the TV playing an infomercial to a weight loss system. She had done something she never did and let it play all night long. The thought of her lying on a fold-out couch in front of our old TV with the cable she'd been so proud of made me sick.

Wanting to hide from it all in the serenity of sleep, I rolled over and closed my eyes, but I couldn't fall back to sleep. Not with my stomach roiling and my eyes burning.

Beside the bed, my phone vibrated, and without thinking, I lifted it to my face.

Kai's name flashed across the screen, slamming into me with all the force of a wrecking ball.

Kai: I need to talk to you.

The word *need* stood out against the rest. There were a lot of needs in the world—food, water, shelter—and the biggest mistake of my life was letting him give me a taste of wants. If I needed anything, it was to be as far from him as I could.

I had meant it when I said we should end things, that he should be with someone at his level. But hearing his father say those horrible things about me only confirmed that fact.

I swiped away from the message and went to an album on my phone I hadn't visited in months—the one where I kept all the pictures of Martín and me from when we were happy.

They used to cheer me up when we were together. After we broke up, they increased the pain, but now, it was like a reminder of my terrible decisions. I needed to stay as far away from men as I could get and focus on what mattered: my mom and getting her out of here. If only fixing that could fix what I'd done to her.

Feeling trapped inside my own room, I threw back the handmade quilt, slipped on some sweatpants, a sweater, and tennis shoes, and left to the only place I could think of.

Seaton Bakery appeared in my windshield like a lighthouse, but when you've done something dark, you feel like you don't belong in the light. Instead of stopping like I'd planned to, I drove. Where? I wasn't sure.

Eventually the ocean came into view, and I pulled in the empty parking lot for Seaton Pier. Outside of the tourist season, this place became a ghost town. Sure, there were a few regular fishermen, but even they knew when to give up.

After slipping my phone under my seat, I got out of my car and started walking along the wooden planks. They creaked under my feet, blending with the winter wind and softly crashing waves.

In my mind's eye, I saw Kai and I walking down this very path, holding mochas and exploring possibilities we never should have considered. Even so, it was like my body knew Kai had been here. And that made the truth hurt that much more.

I reached the end of the pier and dangled my feet over the cold, gray water like I had with Kai. With the air so cold and my heart still aching, that day felt so far away, it might as well have happened in another lifetime.

My phone may have been in the car, but that didn't keep mental images of Kai flashing through my mind. Memories of him holding me, telling me

I was like sunshine. Our light had burned out, and it was time to stop living a fantasy that could never become reality.

Kai told me dreams would never come true if you didn't wish for them. This was exactly why I didn't bother. Because it hurt that much more when reality hit and you were reminded why it was only a wish in the first place.

I sat at the pier, watching the ocean, until my stomach growled. My legs felt like lead as they carried me back over the boardwalk and to my car. The clock, still set on daylight savings time, let me know it was around lunch.

Cars filled the bakery parking lot, so I parked behind the one I knew Gayle drove. Without a ball cap, all I had was my sweater hood to cover my face, which was pointless considering they had to know who I was to give me the food I couldn't afford. Anyone who knew me would be able to tell from my face that something was horribly wrong, and I just didn't have the heart to talk about it right now.

Despite the multitude of people there, I kept my head down and went undetected until I reached the counter. Gayle did a double-take. "Jordan, are you okay?"

I tried to smile but couldn't.

She turned her head toward the kitchen. "Chris, get the register!" she yelled before taking my arm and leading me to the women's bathroom. Once inside, she locked the door and looked me straight in the eye. "I got a call from Johnson Rush this morning, trying to get me to cancel with your mom."

My heart stalled in my throat. "He what?" I croaked.

"Johnson Rush is trying to take your mom out of business."

The words entered my ears, but they scrambled before hitting my brain. What she was saying couldn't be true. "I don't understand."

"Jordan, he's offering quite a bit of compensation to anyone who withdraws services and signs an NDA about the agreement."

"You didn't..."

She smiled grimly. "If I did, I wouldn't be telling you now." Shaking her head, she added, "Your mom's probably getting cancellations from her clients as we speak."

An expletive flew through my lips as I thought of my mom, alone in the apartment, hearing the terrible news. "I have to go tell her." I pushed out of the bathroom, and Gayle followed close on my heels.

"Let me get you some food real quick."

"I need to tell her."

Gayle grabbed my shoulder. "Jordan, please. I gave up a lot of money today because I love you guys. You're like my daughter, and your mom's more of a sister to me than my own flesh and blood. Let me do this—please?"

The helplessness was apparent in Gayle's eyes, probably because I was no stranger to the feeling. I nodded. "Okay, but hurry. Please?"

"I will," she promised.

Within minutes, I had a bag full of food, and I was on my way to the apartment to sit with my mom amongst all the ruin I'd created.

I hurried into our building and took the stairs two at a time, but at our door, I stalled. My mom, the woman who'd been there for me through everything, was on her own. Her clients had probably called and cancelled with no explanation at all, but she'd know. She'd know it was all my fault.

I couldn't let her handle it alone.

I walked inside and found my mom sitting on the couch, staring at the TV. It was off.

"Mom?"

Silence.

I stepped closer, tentatively, and held up the bag from the bakery. "Gayle sent us some food. Do you want some?"

She gave her head a small shake. "I'm going to sleep."

My heart fell. She'd gotten the bad news. I could feel it, but there was nothing I could do. Except... I spun on my heel, grabbed my purse, and walked out the door.

FORTY

THE PARKING LOT for Emerson Trails held only a few parked cars. One of them had a dent on the hood and clouds of exhaust lifting from under the back bumper. I parked a few spaces away, knowing my heart needed the distance.

As soon as I pulled up, the car door opened, and Kai stepped out looking like a model for winter clothes and remorse. "Jordan," he breathed. "Are you okay?"

A bitter laugh escaped my lips. Okay? I was so far from that, I could have been on the opposite side of the world. "No, I'm not okay. Do you know what I heard this morning? Your father is *paying* people to drop my mom's services."

His eyebrows drew together incredulously. "He what?"

Anger flooded me. At what his dad had done. At what we had done. "Your father called all of my mother's jobs—probably the one's she listed as references to get yours—and they cancelled on her. If we don't do something fast, we're going to be evicted."

His mouth fell open. "My dad wouldn't do that. He couldn't."

"But he did." My voice shook. "Call him. Make him fix it."

Kai's mouth fell open and closed, for the first time losing composure, losing the knowledge of what to do next.

"Call him!" I yelled. I needed this nightmare to be over.

Wordlessly, Kai held out his phone, tapped a few buttons, and called his dad.

For a moment, we waited, the only sound in the parking lot the rumbling of Kai's car and my heavy breaths.

Finally, Kai said, "Dad, did you get the Juncos' other clients to cancel on them?" His lips turned into a tight line of anger. "How could you do that to them? They can barely pay their rent as it is." He shook his head. "This isn't about me loving Jordan; it's common human decency!" he roared. I flinched, at both his tone and the L-word, and birds took off from nearby trees, getting away from his voice. "We will not talk about this later; you'll call and fix it n—" Kai held the phone away from his ear and scowled at the screen. "He hung up on me."

Though I hated to admit it, a part of me had believed in Kai's ability to fix it. That was the last hope my heart had to cling to, but it was gone. "Being with you was the worst mistake I've ever made."

"You don't mean that," he said, stepping closer. "Things are messed up, but we can be together. I can help you make things right, I can—"

"You've done enough," I said, each word stabbing me in the chest. "You might be able to live with hurting the people you love, but this isn't a game to me! This is *my* life, *my* home on the line. And this isn't some fantasy world where you can wish a job for us into existence. This is exactly what I was trying to tell you that night. There are people like you, who have the connections, and then there are people like us who exist under your parties, under your games."

Raking his fingers through his hair, he said, "Can't you see that I care? I'm trying to help."

"You can't!" I cried. "Thanks to *your* dad, my mom lost her job and any chance of getting more clients in order to actually support us. Her old boss won't take her back because she tried to go out on her own. And my friends hate me because I agreed to keep you a secret. Love shouldn't have to hide."

"It doesn't anymore!" Desperation filled his features as he stepped closer. "Everything is out in the open—the worst thing has already happened." He gestured between the two of us. "Do you want to lose us too?"

My eyes grew hot with moisture. "There's no more 'us,'" I said. And then I pushed past him, got in my car, and drove away.

The tears didn't fall until I looked in my rearview mirror and saw him standing there. A part of my past I could drive away from but never escape because no matter the rules, he'd taken up residence in my heart.

FORTY-ONE

MY PARENTS' old alarm clock rang at seven in the morning. I rolled over and slammed the big button on top to turn it off. I missed my phone's gently chiming alarm, but this was the alternative to seeing Kai's name first thing in the morning. I didn't even want to see it to block him. Not with all this pain still leeching through every part of my body.

Mom and I should have been at the Rushes' today, working on the media room. Her other clients—everyone except the bakery—had called to cancel her jobs on Sunday. Mr. Rush had all the power he needed to destroy us, and I was sure *he* would make sure we felt like the dirt he thought we were.

I dreaded seeing my mom, seeing what my

actions had done to her, but I had to get up to go to school. It was all I had left.

The hours I spent tossing and turning left me groggy, sluggish. My feet stumbled over the loose piece of carpet the apartment complex owners had installed after a major water leak had opened in the unit above us. I fumbled through the dark, and my fingers landed on my last clean uniform.

Making a mental note to go to the community laundromat, I pulled on the skirt, blouse, and blazer. I sat on my bed to tug on the tights and even got my shoes on in my room. My feet carried me to the wood laminate door, and I stared at it, at the hole that had been there since before we moved in.

It gaped back at me, as empty as the hollow in my chest. I took a deep breath, fruitlessly trying to fill it, and stepped into the living room.

My mom was still asleep. With a last look at her figure curled on the couch under crumpled blankets, I left our house.

At the Academy, I walked down the hallway, feeling worn down and exhausted even though it wasn't yet eight in the morning.

My friends stood together in front of Rory's locker, and I looked away. Seeing them used to be something I could look forward to every day, but now it was just another reminder of all the things I'd lost because I'd been dumb enough to fall for Kai Rush.

A note written on bird stationary hung on my locker from Mrs. Bardot. *Come to my office at eight. Please and thank you! -Birdie*

With a disgruntled sigh, I pulled the note and crammed it into the top shelf of my locker. After grabbing my books, I continued toward Mrs. Bardot's office. Her door was shut, so I waited on the bench outside her door, trying to make myself as invisible as possible. I wondered who'd gotten "lucky" enough to take the earliest slot.

The door opened, and Pixie Adler walked out. She smiled cheerfully at Mrs. Bardot like she didn't have a worry in the world. "Thanks for everything."

"Of course, Pixie!" she chimed back. "Have a fabulous day. And let me know when you hear back from Cambridge." She winked.

"I will!" Pixie glanced at me. "Jordan! I missed you at the end of the gala Friday night. We raised a hundred thousand dollars for Invisible Mountains!"

Finally, a bright spot, but the success of the gala had nothing to do with me. "That's amazing."

"Jordan," Mrs. Bardot said from behind Pixie, smiling warmly at me. "Come in."

I stood and smoothed my skirt before following her. Her finch tweeted and peered at me from his perch in the cage on a small end table.

"Hi, Ralphie," I said to him.

He tilted his head like he heard me, then ducked his beak under his wing several times.

"He likes you," Mrs. Bardot said.

At least something did. "I should put that on my apps."

With a chuckle, she went to her filing cabinet and pulled out a folder. After scanning it, she set it down and settled into her chair. "Sit, Jordan. So, you're still set on UCLA. Because I think you could have a good run for U Penn. You know they have a—"

"Seventy-six percent acceptance rate into med school?" I finished for her. "Yeah." Don't remind me, I wanted to add. "But I have to live at home." I buried the thought that my mom might not want me to stay after graduation.

She frowned. "Even with a housing scholarship?"

"My mom needs help with the bills." Especially now. That might be my one saving grace, that I could get a job and work and help. All the money in the world wouldn't be enough to make up for the way I'd betrayed her, though. She'd said so herself.

Her frown deepened. "You know, honey, there are government programs. Section 8 could—"

"No," I said. "My mom would never accept that kind of help. She says it's for people who really need it."

She scratched at a spot behind her ear making her earring jangle. "I suppose that is admirable."

I nodded. It was. Even if it was inconvenient. Rental assistance could help us get into a two-bedroom unit. Maybe even a place closer to EA. But we'd made it this long.

"So, you've applied to college?" she asked.

I nodded. "And I've filled out the scholarship application and put in for the presidential scholarship."

"Good girl." She smiled, then looked down and shook her head. "It's too bad—you could have had a good shot at the Ivy League."

Except I didn't want anything to do with the kind of people who would want to go there. Forcing a pleasant expression, I said, "I think Ralphie will forgive me." I stood and went to his cage. "Is that all, Mrs. Bardot?"

"Call me Birdie," she said, and when she realized I wasn't going to follow through on the order right away, she added. "A little bird told me about what happened at the gala."

My mind flashed to Pixie coming out of her office. "Let me guess. It was Ralphie?"

She chuckled. "You are funny. A sense of humor will take you far in life."

But would it take me far enough? I stared at the cage, feeling more like the bird inside than anyone in the building.

"I hope you know that you are above your circumstances and that you deserve every opportunity you've been given at the Academy. Nothing, and no one, is going to take that away."

A fear I hadn't even realized I'd been holding eased, and I nodded. "Thanks," I said and bent toward the cage. "See you later, Ralphie."

FORTY-TWO

WHEN I GOT HOME, Mom sat on the couch, staring at the TV, except nothing was playing.

I stepped forward, making sure she was actually awake.

She was.

"Do you need me to turn on the TV?" I asked.

"It wouldn't play," she said monotone.

"Is it broken?"

Her head shook slowly back and forth. "I cancelled the cable. We can't afford it."

My heart fell. The loss of her hope, of the one indulgence she finally gave herself, was just as heartbreaking to me as losing Kai. With no apology to offer that would actually matter, I began gathering dirty laundry.

Once I had a couple of hampers full, I scrounged for quarters and went to the apartment laundromat. It was dingy, in the basement of one building across the parking lot, but there were plenty of open machines and some tables where you could sit and wait. (Leaving wasn't an option unless you wanted your clothes stolen.)

One guy sat in the corner of the room with his big pit bull on a leash. It sat and watched me with beady eyes while I finished putting my load in and went to the opposite end of the room. While my clothes spun in the washing machine, I got busy applying for jobs. There wasn't much I could do that would make enough to support us and any luxuries, but I could help with rent, maybe even some groceries.

I applied for everything that I was eligible for, not yet being eighteen. There were food service positions, custodial needs in nursing homes, even an opening that paid above minimum wage at a call center trying to sell medical equipment. Anything that would work with my school schedule or allow me to get double shifts on the weekends, I tried.

By the time the laundry was done, my shoulders were aching from hunching over the computer, and my eyes were so dry my vision blurred. I closed my laptop, brought the laundry home, and fell into a heavy, but not restful, sleep.

I woke to my parents' old alarm clock, feeling groggy and not at all ready to start my day. But I had no choice. I got ready in a fog, putting on my uniform, shoes, and throwing my hair into a messy bun. No part of this was easy. How I could hurt so much more over Kai than Martín? Kai and I had never had the labels or sharing the intimacy I had with Martín, but I felt like a live cadaver walking around with my middle sliced open and viscera exposed for everyone to see.

And this time, I didn't even have the girls because I'd ruined that too. I ached for their friendship, their comfort, their presence. My public-school friends had ditched me for going to the Academy, and, if I was being honest, there weren't many to begin with. I'd always been busy working, studying, helping Mom however I could.

I pulled into school in time to see Kai getting out of his used Honda. Out of the million steps down he'd taken from his brand-new Tesla. Hadn't he realized he'd done that with me too?

Tears slipped down my cheeks, and I wiped them away, tilting my head back against the head-rest. The car's ceiling stared back at me. Gray, dingy, drooping in some spots. There were no answers there.

I suffered through another day of school, on my own. And as I drove home, I just wished I wouldn't see my mom staring at the TV again like she had no hope.

Instead, when I walked in, I saw my mom at the counter, flipping through a stack of twenty-dollar bills.

"Where did you get that?" I asked.

She flipped through the last few and then said, "The necklace."

It was like cold water had been doused on my head and was now trickling down my spine. "Juana's necklace?"

She nodded, cold, hard, resolute. "And the TV."

I stared at the empty space where it should have been. "You shouldn't have done that. We could have come up with something else. We—"

"I'm a mom; that's what I do. I take care of my kids. Even when it's hard. Even when it hurts. Even when I'm furious. And even when it means breaking my own heart in half."

"Amá, I—"

She shook her head. "Not now, Jordan. Can you please...just give me some time?"

I blinked, hard, and nodded.

When I made it outside, I kept walking, not wanting to drive and spend any money on gas that I didn't have to. Instead, my feet carried me to Seaton Bakery, and I asked for a black coffee and a bagel. I couldn't handle a mocha or anything sweet that would be yet another reminder of what Kai and I had shared.

Plus, maybe this was my penance. Maybe I shouldn't focus so much on my own enjoyment. That was what got me in this position in the first place—worrying about my wants over my family's needs.

I zipped open my backpack, retrieved my laptop, and opened my email, hoping some job had come through. That something had finally worked out. If not, I was ready to tackle another round of applications.

Instead, I saw rejection after rejection. Weren't these things supposed to take a while? Weren't high school kids the most qualified to work in fast food? I didn't understand how I had been turned down for almost every job I had applied for.

Feeling the tears coming, I rubbed my face, begging my tear ducts for some kind of a reprieve.

"Hey, Jordan," a low voice hummed, and I

looked up to see Beckett standing there, a camera around his neck.

"Hey," I said cautiously. He was Rory's boyfriend before he was ever my friend. And Rory and I? Well... the way she looked at me, the disappointment and hurt, was still burned in my brain.

"Mind if I sit?" he asked.

I shook my head and watched as he slid into a chair across from me. He lifted his camera strap over his head and set the camera down on the table next to my laptop.

"How's it going?" he asked.

My eyes burned with ever-present tears as I managed a sardonic laugh. "I'm having the best time of my life. Can't you tell?"

His hazel eyes were sympathetic. "I heard what happened. That must have been so hard."

"Rory told you?"

He nodded.

"And the part where I kept a secret from them? Pushed them away?"

A corner of his lips lifted. "You know, you're not the only one who's kept a secret from someone they cared about. Rory has some experience with that too."

My heart twinged, one part uncomfortable and one part seen. "How did you forgive her?"

"Because I knew she had a good heart. She cared." He met my eyes, waiting until he had my full attention. "We've all fallen short of perfect before. That doesn't make us any less worthy of a second chance."

My eyes watered, and I turned them toward the table so he wouldn't see me cry. "You should have seen the way they looked at me."

"They were hurt because they love you."

The tears fell now as my lip trembled, and I nodded. I loved them too. So much more than I cared to admit. I wasn't supposed to need anyone.

He grabbed his camera. "I better get back to work. But really. Just don't give up on them, okay?"

I made a promise to him as much as myself. "I won't."

FORTY-THREE

AFTER BECKETT WALKED AWAY, I turned on my phone. I was ready for the deluge of messages I saw from Kai. But one name stood out from his.

Ginger: Are you okay?

Her name felt better than a ray of sunlight. Better than a sweet cupcake or a good grade on a test. It felt like hope.

I hurried to text her back, and this time I promised to be fully honest, even if it meant being vulnerable.

Jordan: I'm having a really hard time.

Ginger: Do you want to talk about it?

I blinked and stared at the tiled ceiling. My tear ducts might not be answering, but the universe had.

Jordan: Please?

Ginger: My parents are putting me on phone curfew soon. Tomorrow at lunch? The AV room?

Jordan: I'll see you then.

I tried to temper the hope blossoming in my chest, but it wouldn't go away. This, Ginger, was all I had right now.

I made it through the night and cautiously looked her way in videography class. She gave me a tentative smile, then looked back at the board. At lunch, I carefully entered the AV room. The girls had moved from there to the cafeteria, now that we were eating lunch with Beckett and Carson, but I still feared facing them and their judgement for the second time.

Instead, I found Ginger, a sympathetic smile on her face.

"Hey," I said, testing the waters.

She stood and wrapped me in a hug. And I promptly burst into tears.

"I'm sorry," I sobbed. "I feel like I've been crying since Friday."

Taking my hand, she sat down with me. "What happened? What's the deal with you and Kai? And why was Mr. Rush calling all the parents on the school directory about JJ Cleaning?"

My eyes flew open. "He did what?"

"You didn't hear?"

I shook my head, and now I was wondering how I hadn't. Why hadn't my classmates rubbed it in my face?

"My dad got the call last night, and he asked around—everyone ahead of us in the alphabet had gotten one."

"What did he say?" I asked, my mind still reeling.

She spread her fingers on the desk. "Basically, he said that your mother was unprofessional, that you seduced teenage boys, and that there would be consequences for working with her in the future. Honestly, if the Rushes weren't so rich, Dad said you'd have a lawsuit on your hands."

Wow. I sat back in my chair, raking my fingers over my scalp. I couldn't even believe Kai's dad would be so vindictive as to ruin my mom's—and my—reputation. "Why hasn't anyone told me?"

"Zara told me that Kai's threatening to report anyone who does for bullying, and between him being the one reporting it and the 'zero-tolerance policy' actually being enforced after what happened to Rory..."

I was speechless. But from the way Ginger was eyeing me, she had questions of her own.

"What was really going on with you two?" she asked.

I closed my eyes, and just like every other time, I saw Kai's face. I missed him, no matter how much I didn't want to. "I loved him," I admitted.

"How did it start?"

I told her about cleaning his house, my mom's rule, how he'd taken me on a helicopter ride and how I'd shown him my life. "It wasn't supposed to be anything more, but now it is. And I'm drowning," I said. "I miss you guys. My mom hates me. She can't get work. I can't find jobs. She sold Juana's necklace. We're going to be evicted if something doesn't happen soon."

Ginger looked down, deep in thought. "And it has to be something outside of the Rushes' control."

"Which is impossible," I said. "He practically owns the internet."

"Except he doesn't," she replied, her eyes lighting up. "I have an idea."

FORTY-FOUR

AFTER SCHOOL we went to Mr. Davis's office together. At the sight of us, he pulled off his "soundproof" headphones and said, "To what do I owe this pleasure?"

"We need a favor," Ginger said.

"Oof." He cringed dramatically and then smiled. "What's going on?"

Ginger looked at me and nodded. I didn't have the relationship with Mr. Davis that she did, only being at the Academy for a semester, but from how he treated my friends, I trusted him.

"My mom and I have lost our jobs, and we're applying for work but struggling. Ginger came up with an idea, but we need video equipment to make it happen." I bit my lip, on edge. What Mr. Davis said could change our lives.

"I try not to get involved in student affairs, but I've heard what happened to you and your mom." Mr. Davis shook his head slowly, compassion clear in his eyes. "I'm here to help however I can."

Relief rushed through me so strong my eyes watered. All I could say was thank you as he prepared a camera bag for us with video, sound, and lighting equipment.

My heart was thundering as we walked out to my car, thinking this was the biggest long shot in the world. I wasn't sure whether my mom would even go for it, but I had to try.

She already said she wouldn't forgive me, but if I wanted to forgive myself, I had to do my best to make it right. Helping my mom realize her dream of owning a successful business would accomplish that goal. That didn't mean it needed to look the way we first envisioned it. Hours of physical labor was hard on your body and in some ways and even harder on your soul.

But the closer we got to my apartment, the more a different kind of nerves started to rise. I'd seen Ginger's house—the cute bungalow with garden gnomes and spacious rooms that were big enough to share. Even her parents' kitchen was large, stocked with fresh produce and all kinds of expensive food.

"Ginger," I said.

"Yeah?" Her gaze was out the window, taking in the industrial businesses passing by.

"You know my house—our apartment—it isn't...like yours."

"What do you mean?"

I readjusted my grip on the steering wheel. "It's...small. And our things aren't brand new."

"I have three little sisters. Trust me, we have our fair share of messes and stains."

"But did your couch come off a curb on big trash pickup day?"

She was silent for a moment before turning to me. I met her gaze for as long as driving would allow me.

"You know I don't care about how much money you have, right?" she said. "You could be living in a box and I'd still love you."

My chest constricted at the outright way she said it. "It's not that. I just don't want you to..." My sentence trailed off. What *did* I want? Her not to judge me? Her not to think less of me?

She—or anyone else for that matter—should be

proud of my family. Of how my mom had raised me on her own, without help from the government or anyone else, and worked tirelessly to pay back Juana's medical debt, all while shouldering the most grief a parent could.

"Thank you," I said. "It means a lot that you want to help." I realized that was the one way I was different from my mom. I could accept help. I could rest in the fact that we were worthy of a good life, just for being human. That people could care about us and stick around, even if my father hadn't. Even if Juana couldn't.

We pulled up to the apartment building, and Ginger took it in, the person with a massive dog off its leash out front. The laundry hanging over balcony railings because people wanted to save money on drying clothes. The old beat-up vehicles that hadn't moved for months.

Her face was expressionless. "Ready to go inside?"

I nodded. "Ready as I'll ever be."

She shouldered the camera bag while I lugged the lighting setup upstairs. Today, Mom sat at the counter, two stacks of paper before her. Job applications, I realized as I drew nearer. One large stack had been filled out, and the smaller stack hadn't.

"Hi," my mom said, smiling at Ginger. "Are you one of Jordan's friends?"

I'd missed her smile. It was pretty and crinkled her eyes at the corners. I put my arm around my friend. "Amá, this is Ginger."

They waved at each other, and Mom nodded toward our bags. "School project?"

"Not exactly," Ginger said.

Mom looked at me for an explanation, and I launched into our idea. After I'd explained, she was quiet for a moment.

"So, you want me to clean for...YouTube?" she asked.

I nodded.

"And that will make money how?"

"It's great advertising," Ginger said. "And, after you get a certain amount of people viewing your videos, you can start showing ads. Some of my favorite YouTubers make thousands of dollars each month on those alone. And then there are courses and books and—"

"Whoa, whoa, whoa," my mom said, putting her hands in the air and shaking her head quickly. "I don't know how to do any of that."

"But we do," I said, glancing at Ginger, who nodded along with me. "You can do this. You know more about making a house a home than anyone else I know."

I could see the wheels turning in her head, along with the doubt. Finally, she said, "It can't interfere with your schoolwork. Either of you."

"It won't," Ginger said quickly, and I agreed.

"So, when?" Mom asked. "How?"

"You'll try it?" I asked, hope bursting at the broken seams of my heart.

Her doubtful expression transformed into a tentative smile. "I'll try."

I launched forward and hugged her. After a moment, she relaxed in my arms and held me back. It wasn't forgiveness, but it was closeness, and it meant the world to me.

FORTY-FIVE

OUR FIRST DAY FILMING, we got out a jar of spaghetti sauce and created a stain on several items around the house. I held the lights, and Ginger held the camera as Mom went around the apartment, cleaning the messes.

When Mom finished pretreating the shirt and handwashing it in the sink, Ginger turned off her camera and set it down. "You're a natural, Jacinda."

Mom shook her head, her hands on her cheeks. "Are you sure it was okay?"

"It was great, Amá," I said.

Ginger agreed emphatically. "Let's plan to film more the rest of this week so we can store up some videos."

Mom nodded. "After your homework is done."

We both agreed, and as Mom set about making supper, I went with Ginger down to the car. I took her back to the school parking lot where her car was waiting and got out to help move the equipment to her trunk. My car had locks, but I trusted Ginger's neighborhood better than my own.

She shut her trunk and leaned against it, shrugging her shoulders deeper into her coat.

"Thanks for today," I said, the steam of my breath illuminated by the parking lot lights. "You have no idea how much it means to me."

Her full lips spread into a soft smile. "You have no idea how much *you* mean to me. I'm happy to help."

My heart swelled, and I wrapped her in a hug. "Thank you," I said again anyway.

As she got into her car and drove away, I realized Ginger had done something better than filming a video: she'd given me hope.

Our second day of filming, Ginger's parents learned about what we were doing, and they were completely on board. They even agreed to let us start shooting videos in the store or use expired products to create stains if we needed to.

"I wish we could do more," her dad said to us on our first day filming at Ripe.

Mom spoke up. "This is more than enough. Your daughter is an amazing and talented young woman."

His red-bearded smile grew as he tucked Ginger under his arm in a side hug. "I tend to agree."

We wrapped up filming, and Mom went to the back of the store to wash up while Ginger and I packed our equipment. With all of our materials put away, we stood and meandered toward the store entrance.

As we crossed out of the baking goods aisle, we saw Rory and her mom with a shopping cart full of groceries.

"Hi, girls." Mrs. Hutton beamed.

We greeted her too, but my eyes were on Rory. She was looking between Ginger and me like something didn't make sense. Ginger and I had kept far away from the topic of our other friends, opting instead to stay busy finishing our homework so we could upload more videos. We had stockpiled them and were getting close to the big launch we had planned. But now, I wondered what they had said about me. What had Ginger said to them?

Mrs. Hutton said, "Why don't you girls chat while I finish up?"

"Are you sure you don't need help?" Rory asked. I could tell how desperately she wanted her mom to say she could use Rory's assistance, which hurt me more than I cared to admit.

"I'm fine. I'll meet you up front." Mrs. Hutton winked at us. "Good to see you, girls."

I waved goodbye, but Rory kept her gaze on the floor for a moment before looking back at Ginger and me. "What are you two working on?"

Ginger rested her camera bag on the ground. "Filming the first season of the JJ Cleaning video series."

Rory's eyebrows rose. "A series?"

"On YouTube," I said. "Now that my mom can't get any more work."

Rory frowned and said, almost to herself, "I can't believe Kai's dad did that."

"I could." And that was the problem. Once again, we were in a horrible position because a man determined he would be better off without us. But I was done with rich people—and my feelings about them—keeping us down.

"What can I do to help?" Rory asked.

Now my stare snapped to her. I couldn't have heard her right. "What?"

"I was planning to be the one to reach out to you..." She scratched her arm. "I was talking to Beckett, and he reminded me how hard it can be to come clean, especially when you're embarrassed. I'm sorry we made you feel like you couldn't tell us the truth."

I blinked, surprised. "You don't need to apologize."

Ginger looked between us like a kid on Christmas morning and then stretched her arms around both of us and squeezed us tight. "Thank God! I've missed us so much!"

Rory and I laughed, and Rory said, "Well, you'll still have to convince Zara. Callie should be an easy sell."

I didn't like thinking about campaigning for my friendships, but at this point, I was happy to do anything. I'd made a mess of us, and now it was my turn to clean it up.

"Have lunch with us tomorrow," Rory said.

My stomach clenched. "In front of everyone in the caf?"

Ginger shrugged. "Why not suggest the AV room? For old time's sake?"

344   CURVY GIRLS CAN'T DATE BILLIONAIRES

"It's a date," Rory said.

"It's a date," I repeated. And I smiled, because it felt like at least one piece of my life was slowly moving back into place. That was, if Zara agreed.

FORTY-SIX

I WANTED to sleep that night. My body was tired, aching in ways I'd never known before, but I couldn't. I missed my friends, all of them. Hopefully, Zara would forgive me. She was a fierce friend, but she didn't trust easily. And when that trust was broken... I sighed. In so many ways, we were alike. Maybe that meant she would understand.

When I arrived to video class the next morning, I sat next to Ginger, feeling jittery. "Today's the day," I said.

She lifted a corner of her lip. "No matter what happens, you have me."

The bell rang before I had a chance to thank her, and Mr. Davis stood at the board. "Now that we've wrapped up our most recent project, I want to give you time to be creative. Find a partner of your choosing, film a video, and upload it to Emerson Academy's YouTube account. You have until the end of the semester to submit at least a ten-minute video." He turned to Ginger and me and gave us a look that said, here's your chance.

We weren't going to waste it. We got to work in front of a computer, uploading the edited videos to YouTube and scheduling the first ten to drop on Friday night. Saturday was one of the highest days for engagement, and we wanted everyone in their Saturday cleaning frenzy to see my mom's videos.

Mr. Davis walked behind us and put his hand on the back of Ginger's chair. "How's it going?"

"Good," she said, hitting submit on another video.

"You got those transitions to work?"

She nodded. "Thanks to YouTube University."

With a chuckle, he said, "Going to the Ivy Leagues, are you?" He gave me a sincere smile. "I hope all this work pays off. Really."

"Me too," I said. Scheduling the videos made our idea that much more real, validated my hope that this could work. Between Ginger's video skills and my mom's easy-going demeanor, the clips were awesome. But that didn't mean they'd go viral. Or make enough to at least keep a roof over our heads until someone hired us.

Ginger and I hit that point where we had a few minutes left in class but not enough time to make progress on anything. I got out my phone to pass the time. I didn't know why. I'd blocked Kai's number. No one else texted me anymore, not really.

But since I had it out, I swiped through the screens, seeing if there were any apps I should delete.

My fingers froze on the square that held the *Rush+* app. It was a fun game. Even more addictive than *Candy Crush*. But I hadn't been able to bring myself to open it, knowing Kai had partnered with his dad on it. That the money made from the app was what gave them the power to destroy our lives.

My hand shook as I pressed and held the screen and then deleted it, once and for all.

I put my phone away, then looked at Ginger, who was now adding tags to a video. She caught me looking at her and asked, "Are you ready for lunch?"

"No," I answered.

She lifted a corner of her lips. "It will be okay."

"I hope so."

FORTY-SEVEN

THE BELL RANG, and we parted ways. Each second that passed until lunch felt too long and entirely too short at the same time. Was there ever a good time to face the people you shoved away and beg them to take you back?

I remembered the phrase Gayle always said. *The best time to plant a tree is yesterday. The second-best time is now.* Time to plant my seed and hope it grew friendship.

At the lunch bell, Ginger met me at my locker like she worried I might run. She knew me too well. We walked together to the AV room, my chest feeling tight. The second we opened the door, the other girls stopped mid-conversation. Immediately, I felt like I was walking on ice ready to shatter and plunge me below the surface.

I lifted my hand in a jerky wave, like my joints were already frozen. Callie kept her eyes down, Zara stared at me, hard, and Rory gave me an encouraging smile. Which was probably the only reason I was able to set my bag down and approach the table.

Ginger touched my elbow. "I'm going to grab us lunch. Any requests?"

I shook my head. The idea of eating now made my stomach more unsettled than it already was.

The door closed behind her, and we were silent for a long moment before Zara finally spoke.

"What are you doing here?" she asked.

For a moment, I wanted to turn and run away. I wasn't used to begging people to stay in my life. No, if they wanted to leave, good riddance. But I also had to admit that my actions had driven them away. I needed to let them know I was sorry. The rest would be their decision.

Taking a deep breath, I decided to lay it all on the table. "Two months ago, my mom and I started cleaning the Rushes' home. I don't know if you knew this, but my mom and I have been buried under my sister's medical debt to the point where we've had to work hard just to meet the payments and survive. And she told me that this job would be the one that could finally help us pay it off. But under no uncertain circumstances was I to fall for Mr. Rush's son. Kai.

"I thought, no problem. He's a stuck-up snob, my friends don't like him, and I hate everything he stands for." I blinked, turning away from their hard stares. "But I was wrong. Kai wasn't like that. He was kind and considerate and willing to do what it took to make me more comfortable in his life. He got a used car. Paid off my sister's medical debt. Spent a day with me in Seaton just to see how I lived.

"I wasn't supposed to fall for him, but I did. And because our relationship was so against the rules and I didn't think it would last, we kept it quiet. It was the biggest mistake of my life." I blinked back tears. "I lost my mom her business. I lost him. And I lost all of you."

The tears flowed heavily now, and I bent, covering my eyes with my hands.

Someone rubbed my shoulder, and I looked to see Callie standing by my side. Rory was coming next, putting her arm around me. Then Zara came to face me. She took my hands and held them, moisture welling in her own eyes.

"Jordan, I need you to hear me," she said, voice firm even with emotion. "Don't you ever feel like you have to keep secrets or hide who you are. Not with us. Okay? We love you because of your heart and fire for everything you do, not because of your mom's bank account or who you decide to love."

I smiled at her. "There's just one problem."

"What?" She seemed confused.

"I didn't decide to love Kai. If I could choose, I would love anyone else. But I can't stop loving him. No matter how hard I try." I completely broke down now because after a life of carefully tempering my wishes and expectations, I had allowed myself to dream the wildest dream of all. That someone like me could be with someone like him.

Zara took me in her arms so all three of them were holding me—keeping me together. "We'll be here, no matter what," she promised, and the other two were quick to agree.

And I knew, deep in my heart, they were telling the truth.

FORTY-EIGHT

MOM and I got out of our car in Zara's giant garage. She looked beautiful in khaki joggers and a button-up denim shirt that hugged her curves. The curves she passed on to me.

"Are you ready?" I asked her over the hood of the car.

"No," she answered with a breathy chuckle.

"Me neither," I said. Our weeks of hard work were coming true tonight with the premiere of her YouTube videos and our push for viewers. We were watching the videos as they went live in Zara's massive media room and using our laptops to contact everyone we knew, asking them to subscribe and share.

Zara's maid, Beth, met us by the garage

entrance and led us to the media room, where there was a massive table full of snacks and my friends spread out in the cushy leather couches. Carson and Beckett were there too, and it made me feel more supported than ever before.

"Hi, girls," my mom said, smiling warmly at them. "Boys." A deep part of me wished she could have been a mom to more than just me. More girls deserved to have her as their role model.

"Hi, Mrs. Junco," Callie said, followed by greetings from the others.

"What can I do?" Mom asked.

"Take a seat," Zara directed, "get your phone out, and start texting! Ginger's reaching out to influencers, I'm tapping my dad's connections, Callie's getting with her network, Rory's contacting her brother's friends and her tutoring network, Beckett has got the jocks, Carson's getting their neighborhood, and we need you two to spread the word in Seaton as much as you can."

I nodded, feeling a sense of purpose replace my nerves. We could do this. We had to.

For the next two hours, my mom's videos played on the screen. She might have been nervous about being in front of the camera, but she was a natural —warm and funny and instructive. Plus, Ginger's video talents were definitely taking her places. These clips looked every bit as professional as the other YouTubers we researched for inspiration.

"Numbers are looking good!" Ginger called from her computer. "Halfway to our goal already!"

My mom and I caught each other's gaze from across the room with matching giddy grins. If we reached our goal, we could monetize her channel and start making money. This was really happening.

Every phone in the room pinged at the same time except mine. I looked around at them, confused. "Was there a weather alert?"

"No freaking way!" Beckett said, holding his phone in the air.

Every head swiveled his way.

"What happened?" I asked.

"Look at this notification," he said, sticking out his phone so I could see the *Rush+* banner over his phone.

Level up your cleaning game with videos + more from JJ Cleaning!

With my mouth hanging open and my heart still not sure of its rhythm, I looked up to find every eye in the room on me.

"Did that go to every *Rush+* user?" Ginger asked.

"It had to," Carson said.

Beckett shook his head, amazed. "They have almost half a billion users."

"We hit goal!" Ginger cried, clicking at her track pad. "WE HIT GOAL! I'm monetizing right now!"

My eyes were watering, and I looked at my mom who had collapsed into a chair and was sobbing into her hands. We had enough viewers to start making money on something we'd been crazy enough to dream. I went to my mom and hugged her tight. Within seconds, she had her arms around me too, clinging to me.

"Is this really happening?" she asked.

"It's happening, Amá. It's happening."

"Monetized," Ginger cried from the front of the room. "The ad income should start coming in soon, and YouTube has monthly payments set to be direct deposited into your bank account!"

All of our friends clapped and cheered so loudly the noise echoed off the walls.

When the din died down, Ginger said, "You ready, Mrs. J?"

I looked from Ginger to my mom, confused enough for my tears to stall.

Mom was wiping her eyes and saying yes. She

disengaged from our hug and walked to the front of the media room, standing in front of the screen.

Her voice shook as she said, "You girls have been working so hard, and I worked on a video of my own for when we launched the channel." She wiped at the underside of her eyes, trying not to mess up her makeup, even though it was a lost cause. "I want to see what you think of it."

Mom stepped to the side, and her face came on the screen. The video was clearly shot in selfie mode on her phone.

"About a month ago, I got the worst news of my career..."

My chest tightened, knowing exactly what she was talking about, and that it was all my fault.

The mom on the video took a deep breath and continued. "I was fired from a job, my reputation was tarnished, and I had no way to support my daughter and give her even half the life she deserves."

I turned to my mom. "Amá, you don't—"

She shushed me and pointed at the screen.

"I told her..." Her voice cracked, and she rushed through the next words like if she didn't say them fast enough, she wouldn't be able to say them at all. "Baby, I forgive you. I never should have said that I wouldn't. The real question is, can you forgive me? For all the missed episodes of *Family Feud* and dinners of beans and rice and nights spent crying? For the *years* I spent grieving and holding on to you instead of letting you spread your wings?"

My throat clogged with emotion.

"So," she said on the video, "I hope you will forgive me, and I hope you know everything I do, all the hard choices I make, I do them for you."

The screen went black, and I went to my mom, arms extended.

She pulled me into a hug and rocked me back and forth. "Do you forgive me?" she asked through tears.

"Of course," I cried.

She took my face in her hands and wiped my cheeks with her thumbs. "I am so proud of you, *mija.*"

"But what about what I did? Falling for Kai was so reckless." The force of my regret was so large it still ached.

"It was reckless," she said. "But that is exactly why I'm so proud of you. You were brave with your heart. For years, I've hidden away and buried my heart behind a brick wall I called hard work, but you let yourself fall. You shouldn't have to stop yourself from loving someone. You should be able to love who you want and love with all your heart."

My lips trembled with her words. I did love him, and I couldn't stop. "But it doesn't matter now," I said. "It's over."

"Are you sure? I'm pretty sure his father didn't send a notification out to half a billion users."

My lips curved on their own, because she was right.

"I think you should invite him here so you can thank him," Mom said and waggled her eyebrows. "What do you girls think?"

My friends let out cries of agreement while Carson said, "So I'm a girl now?"

As Callie patted his shoulder, I let out a teary laugh. "I think that's a great idea."

Zara cringed. "About that..."

My eyes widened. "What did you do?"

"I might have already invited him."

FORTY-NINE

"WHERE IS HE?" I cried, already trying to wipe at my face, which I knew was streaked with tears and wet mascara.

"He should be here in twenty minutes," Zara said, extending her hand. "Let's go get you fixed up." She glanced at Carson and Beckett. "Can you two hold down the fort?"

Carson lifted his hand to his brow in a mock salute. "Aye aye, cap'n."

Callie rolled her eyes. "Are you sure you want to leave it with them?"

"Honestly," Ginger said, "our numbers are looking great. We can handle a break."

My heart was hammering faster with every second that passed, and I thought I might burst.

Didn't they know Kai was seconds from being here? "Guys!" I cried. "We're running out of time!"

Zara put her arm around me. "Let's get you ready to meet your billionaire."

"Well, technically," I began, then realized I was just wasting time. "Never mind. Let's go!"

My friends, my mom, and I trekked across the house, on a mission to Zara's room. I could see my mom's eyes as we went, taking in all the expensive features and spacious surroundings.

"So this is where you've been spending your weekends," she said so only I could hear.

I nodded, still trying to interpret the emotion behind her words.

"I'm glad you have good friends, *mija*. You deserve it."

I smiled and wrapped my arm around her. "I learned what a friend should be from the best."

Zara led us into her room, and she began barking orders—Rory to get makeup wipes, Ginger to fire up the curling iron, and then Callie to text back and forth with Carson to make sure everything was going okay with the channel.

Mom and I stood together while Zara dove into her closet, her mental wheels turning a thousand miles a minute. I could hear my mom encouraging me, but my mind was oddly blank. Thoughts of Kai had somehow overloaded my mental circuits, and all I was left to do was observe the frenzy around me and hope against all hope that everything would be alright.

Callie returned first with the curling iron and started piecing my hair apart to touch up my curls. The others followed suit, poking and prodding with makeup and clothing and perfume. It all happened so quickly, it felt like no time at all had passed until Zara stood back with a scrutinous eye and said, "She's ready."

My mom followed with, "She's *beautiful*."

I blinked my newly applied false lashes, and warmth spread through my cheeks despite fear gripping my heart. Kai was on his way, maybe already downstairs, and I was supposed to what? Look pretty?

I had no idea what I'd say, how to act, what to do. This was Kai. The guy who saw my heart instead of my size or background. He knew me better than a guy who'd dated me for months. He'd protected me to the best of his ability—and was still doing that, even at the risk of his father's wrath.

How could I ever deserve him or match him as an equal?

Rory put her hands on my shoulders, steadying me. "I know how hard it is to admit you've done something wrong and lay your heart on the line. But please, trust me when I say love is worth the risk. Every single time."

"And if it doesn't work out?" I asked, biting my lip to keep it from trembling.

"We'll be here," Zara said.

"Always," my mom agreed.

I extended my arms as far as I could and hugged everyone in reach.

Zara's hip vibrated against mine, and I jumped back.

Giggling, she pulled out her phone and held up the chat for me to see.

Kai Rush: I'm here.

FIFTY

I SWALLOWED, hard, in a failed attempt to push down the nerves in my throat.

"You can do this," Zara said. Her fingers flew over her phone's screen, and then she looked up at me. "Beth is bringing him to the patio."

"Do you need a coat?" Mom asked, looking around like she could make one appear.

Zara shook her head. "The heaters are going. Do you want us to walk with you?"

"No," I said. "I need to do this alone." My relationship with Kai started in private, and it seemed right for our fate to be determined in private as well.

"Good luck," Ginger said with an encouraging smile.

The others nodded, and I gave a brief wave goodbye before turning and walking the now-familiar path to the balcony where the hot tub and pool resided. The entire way, I pressed each of my fingers into my thumbs, trying to come up with something to say. The blood rushing through my ears drowned out any ideas.

Cautiously, I stepped onto the patio and looked around. Disappointment filled me when I realized he hadn't arrived yet. I pressed my hand into my chest, trying to still my heart.

Then Kai's voice blocked out everything else. "Jordan."

The way he said my name, full of pain and longing and...hope. It cut me to the core.

Slowly, I turned to face him. His eyes were dark, guarded despite the hope in his voice. The only warmth in his skin was the light reflected through the fire rising from glass beads.

I'd been so worried about my mom and our finances that I hadn't realized how hard this had been on him too. Guilt swept through me, but there were no words to pair with it. None adequate enough to express the depths of my regret.

"You saw the notification?" he asked.

Slowly, I nodded. "You have no idea—" Emotion constricted my throat and stung my eyes. I swallowed. "You have no idea how much it meant to me."

His expression softened, and he came closer. But not close enough to touch. "I hope it helped."

"We reached our goal. I'm not sure how it translates into dollars, but we're on our way." The relief was obvious in my voice. Just saying it made me feel lighter. Not as light as if Kai knew how sorry I was, but I couldn't bring myself to apologize out loud. Not yet. "I hope your dad wasn't too upset."

"He doesn't know yet."

I raised my eyebrows. "What will he do?"

Kai shrugged. "At this point, I don't care." Cautiously, he took another step forward and reached for my hand.

I watched his fingers come closer until the touch I'd been longing for landed on my skin. Everything in me fell apart, collapsed at his simple contact, like I'd been holding it all together, waiting for this moment to come.

"What my dad did was wrong," Kai said fiercely. "He can't judge you and your mom for my mother's mistakes and his broken heart. I don't care if I have to start from scratch or live on loans until I graduate college. I know what's right. And I know what I want." His eyes met mine, saying the word he didn't out loud. *You.*

"Kai." I put my hand on his cheek, and everything in me cried that this was right. That every second we'd spent apart was wrong and the world was just now shifting back into the right orbit.

He looked to me, his eyes open and earnest and...hurt. I'd done that. And that fact ate at me.

"I did the same thing your dad did," I admitted, hanging my head. "I judged you because of your money. And I thought you were like every guy who would hurt me or leave." Drawing my gaze up, I met his searching eyes and traced my thumb over the rise of his cheekbone. "From the first time I met you, you've been kind, strong, caring, and *here* for me. Even when it cost you your brand-new car or your time or even your father's affection." I blinked quickly, fighting against tears that would cut off the most important part of what I had to say. "I didn't do anything to deserve you, but I promise I'll spend every day as long as you'll have me showing you how much you mean to me."

With a smile, he closed his eyes and shook his head. "Don't you see, Jordan? You didn't have to do anything to earn my love. You had it. From the time you walked into the school and I saw how beautiful you are. Every day I see your strength and grit and determination and it makes my heart"—he held our clasped hands over his firm chest—"beat just a little bit harder every time you're in the room."

I rested my forehead against his, wishing my feelings for him could transfer as easily through our connection as they did through his words. But I only had three. "I love you."

For a moment he was silent, and I lifted my head, opening my eyes. His expression filled with emotion, and he grit his teeth, taking me in. Both his hands went to my cheeks, and he held me, looking at me, through me—into me—for the longest of moments.

And then he breathed those words, "I love you," and his lips were on mine. Needing, wanting, tasting, feeling, taking.

But he didn't need to take, because all I wanted to do was give all of myself to him. He had me—all of me—in every way that mattered and more.

"I love you," he said again through kisses, like

he couldn't say it enough. But he had done something better than saying the words: he'd shown me. With every movement of his hands over my body. With every delicate kiss on my skin. And with every hint of his breath on my lips, I knew. And I never wanted it to end.

FIFTY-ONE

I LAY with Kai on one of the patio couches, and he held me to his chest, stroking his thumb back and forth over my shoulder. I'd never felt happier than I had in this moment, more at ease, with my lips still dancing from the way he'd so thoroughly kissed me.

"What do you think everyone is doing?" he asked.

I raised my eyebrows to look up at him. "Probably anxiously waiting to hear how this went. Or trying to spy on us."

He chuckled low. "Should we tell them the good news?"

"That...?"

"We're in love," he said. "And admitting it."

I smiled. That action was getting easier by the second. "I suppose so."

As we walked into the house, he wrapped his arm around my waist, and all of me warmed at how close his body was to mine. I wasn't sure where, or when, but I couldn't wait to explore these feelings with him, together. Not as forbidden lovers but as two people in an actual relationship.

I led the way to Zara's media room, and when we opened the door, we saw everyone snacking and watching a movie.

The second they caught sight of us, the cheering and squeals commenced. My mom rushed to us and kissed both of Kai's cheeks before giving me a hug. Kai's hand never left mine the entire time.

"Get in here and watch the movies, lovebirds!" Ginger yelled, tossing a few kernels of popcorn our way.

"You don't need to ask me twice," Kai said, putting his arm around my shoulders and kissing the top of my head.

I grinned up at him. "Me neither."

We sat in a cushy leather chair toward the back, curled as close to each other as we could get in front of my mom and friends. I tried to pay attention to the movie, I did, but with Kai tracing a slow pattern up and down my bare arm with his fingertips, I could hardly focus.

When his hand fell away from my shoulder, I stared at him. "Why'd you stop?" I whispered.

He held up his phone, and I read the screen.

Incoming call from Dad.

Taking a deep breath, he stood, and I followed him out of the media room. I could feel the others' eyes on us as I closed the door behind us, but this was important.

My chest was tight as he swiped the screen and turned the call to speaker.

The second the timer started, his dad began his tirade. "I don't know what's gotten into your head, young man, but you had no business sending out a notification to *half a billion users*. It was reckless, off-brand, and most of all, a betrayal to me."

"What about how you betrayed me?" Kai asked, his voice cool.

Shock flooded through me at the quiet strength in his voice. He was standing up to his father, business partner, an actual billionaire, and the man who held Kai's financial future in his hands.

"Excuse me?" Mr. Rush said, his voice just as dangerous.

"I know Mom left you. Betrayed you. But you've sheltered me for far too long, trying to keep me from getting my heart broken. The only thing you succeeded in doing was making sure the only girl I've ever really loved couldn't be with me."

Brave. That was what Kai was. I took his hand and squeezed.

"What do you know about love?" Mr. Rush demanded. "You're eighteen years old."

"More than a man who's spent his life too afraid to find it."

The line was silent for so long I wondered if he had hung up. Kai met my eyes, and I gave him a questioning look, but he turned his gaze back to the screen, watching the seconds tick by.

Finally, Mr. Rush cleared his throat. "I've raised you by myself for eighteen years."

Kai tilted his head toward the phone, his voice softening. "I know. And it's always been just us. But it's not anymore. I'm ready to start living my life, and that includes falling in love, even if it means risking my own heartbreak. I don't want to lose you, Dad, but I'm tired of going behind your back just to be happy. I'll lose every dollar I have before I lose the chance to live a life I can be proud of."

His dad let out a frustrated grunt. "There's a difference between service and martyrdom."

The anger in Kai's voice was almost palpable. "You destroyed their reputation, Dad. Our relationship was just as much my fault as it was Jordan's."

"Can we talk about this at home? Man to man, not father to son."

Kai's jaw clenched. "I'm not interested in a smoke job."

"I'm not interested in giving one."

For a long moment, neither of them spoke, and then Kai said. "I'll see you tonight."

They said goodbye, and Kai tucked his phone into his pocket. He studied me for a moment. "You're worried."

"I'd be lying if I said I wasn't."

His dark eyes filled with concern, and he dipped his head to the side. "What are you concerned about?"

My throat felt tight, and I shook my head. I didn't want him to think I distrusted him, but after all we'd just been through...

"Tell me," he breathed.

I blinked quickly. "What if..." My voice cracked. "What if he convinces you I'm not worth it?"

"He could never do that. Do you understand

me?" Kai put his phone in his pocket and drew me into a tight hug. "I love you too much."

I linked my arms around his waist and breathed into his chest. I believed him, with every part of me. "I feel the exact same way."

FIFTY-TWO

THE NEXT MORNING, my mom and I sat in Seaton Bakery, eating a late breakfast of muffins and mochas. It was like our lives had returned to their normal pattern, only better. With less waking up at four in the morning. Even though the check hadn't come in yet and her views hadn't yet amounted to enough to fully support us, things were looking up.

Mom's phone rang from its spot inside her massive purse, and she glanced at it before shaking her head and reaching for her muffin.

"Take it," I said.

"Are you sure?"

I nodded.

She pulled it out, her eyes widening.

"Who is it?" I asked, leaning forward to try and see the screen.

"Johnson Rush."

My mouth fell open. "Why would he be calling you?"

With a shrug, she said, "Should I answer?"

Hurriedly, I nodded, moving across the table so I could sit next to her with my ear to the phone.

"Hello?" she said, sounding composed but cold. Perfection. My mom was goals.

"Yes, Jacinda?" He was clearly uncomfortable.

She wasn't giving him any slack. "Yes?"

"I, um, I mean." He took a deep breath. "I wanted to call and offer you your job back."

Mom and I stared at each other, mirrored shocked expressions on our faces.

I started whispering, "The nerve of this a—"

She held her hand up and mouthed, *I got it.* "You have some nerve." She winked at me. "You humiliate my daughter, insult her, threaten her living situation by ruining my reputation, and you call to see if I want my job back?"

"I suppose I should have started with an apology," he said, seemingly repentant. "As a single parent, I'm sure you would go to the ends of the earth to protect your daughter."

"Of course I would protect her, but that rarely calls for cold-hearted revenge."

"I've already scheduled an email to send to everyone I called, apologizing for my actions and recommending your services. I have also given my son my full blessing to date who he chooses."

Her eyebrows rose. "It seems you've had a change of heart."

"If I'm being completely honest, I didn't have a choice."

"What do you mean?"

I leaned closer to hear his answer.

"It was my son," he said. "He made it very clear no amount of money could buy his loyalty."

Mom's shoulders seemed to relax. "You've raised a good young man."

"If only in spite of me," he replied. "Have a nice day, Ms. Junco."

She hung up the phone and turned to me.

"So that means?" I asked.

She shrugged, a slow smile on her lips. "You chose the right guy?"

I laughed. I supposed I had.

Kai had a busy morning, with a dress rehearsal for the winter orchestra performance the next evening, so I met the girls at Waldo's for lunch. I'd just eaten with Mom, but I was happy for the chance to spend time with them. Even though we'd only fought for a couple of weeks, it felt like we'd been apart forever.

I pulled up next to Chester's pristine old car and got out. Inside the diner, I could see my friends sitting in our usual booth toward the back, but I had to stop and say hi to Chester on my way.

He smiled at me, his eyes twinkling. "How are you, my girl?"

"Good, and you?"

He shook his head slowly. "The missus wants to get a cat."

"What's wrong with that?" I asked. "I'd love to have a kitty, if I had more time for one."

"Well, I'm more of a dog person myself, less temperamental."

I laughed. "That is true. So it's a no go?"

He shook his head, a wry smile shaping his lips. "I might not be a cat person, but I'm a Karen person."

My own lips lifted in a dopey smile. "You're getting one?"

He nodded. "Sometimes, when you love some-one, it means doing things you'd never imagined, just to see them smile. I guess something about a cat person and a dog person, it just works."

"Let me know if you ever need someone to cat sit," I said.

"I will."

As I walked toward my friends, I thought about true love and how it took risk and compromise. I'd done the craziest thing of all—given Kai my heart. Maybe, something about a curvy girl and a billionaire just worked.

Callie and Jordan waved at me, and Ginger and Zara turned around in the booth to grin at me.

"Hey," I said with a wave.

Ginger and Zara scooted over so there would be room for me on their side, and I sat down. "What's new?"

Rory raised her eyebrows. "You mean other than the fact that the most powerful man in Emerson sent out an apology email to everyone in the school directory?"

"Or," Zara said, "that a billionaire is dating a 'ship in The Curvy Girl Club?"

"Or," Ginger added with a grin, "that your mom is going viral?"

My cheeks warmed. "This is crazy, isn't it?" It almost didn't feel real.

"Totally," Callie said. "But that's what makes it awesome."

I laughed. "I guess you're right."

"What's the plan for tonight?" she asked.

"Kai's taking me on a date—he won't tell me where yet. Or what we're doing." I winked for good measure, even though I really had no idea.

Zara ran her tongue over her toothy grin and shimmied her shoulders while Callie blushed furiously.

"Get it, girl!" Ginger said, laughing.

We spent the rest of our time together just enjoying ourselves and each other's company. I may have gotten the guy, but it wouldn't be nearly as enjoyable without having The Curvy Girl Club back together again.

FIFTY-THREE

KAI KNOCKED on my door at seven that night. Dressed in fitted black pants with a tight, dark blue sweater, he looked moody and intense and hot. Like, really hot.

Mom peeked around my shoulder to get a glance at him. "Hello, Kai."

He waved with a soft smile. "Hi, Mrs. Junco."

Mrs. Gutiérrez called to us from the kitchen. "*Necesito verlo!*"

Kai scrunched his eyebrows in the cutest way, and my mom opened the door wider to show Mrs. Gutiérrez leaning against the counter with a bowl of popcorn.

"Want to come in?" Mom asked.

He nodded, and instinctively, my chest tightened at the idea of having him in my house. Of showing him how we lived, especially now that we didn't have a TV. But I knew we had nothing to be ashamed of. Especially not with Kai.

I looped my arm around his and stood by his side as he walked in, his expression unreadable.

Mrs. Gutiérrez looked him up and down with a sly smile on her lips. "*El es tu nóvio?*"

"*Sí.*" I grinned. He was my boyfriend, and I couldn't be happier about that fact.

"*Hola,*" Kai said. "*Me llamo Kai. Mucho gusto.*"

Her toothy grin grew even wider, revealing the pink of her dentures. "*¡Habla espanol! Que bueno, Jordan.*"

I turned to him, just as surprised. "You speak Spanish?"

"I've been learning," he said. "I'm thinking it would be good to pair with my business major at UCLA."

"What?" I asked.

"I just got my acceptance letter."

My face might as well have been a heart-eyed emoji. How had I gotten so lucky?

The microwave dinged, and the popcorn inside

made a few last pops. Mom went to it and shook the bag. "Want some?"

"No thanks," he said. "Movie night?"

Mom and Mrs. Gutierrez made matching offended expressions.

Kai's face fell. "What did I do? Are you guys against televisions or something?"

Laughing, I shook my head. "You *never* say no to food in a Latino household!"

"Oh!" He seemed to relax. "Please, give me all the popcorn. Leave none for yourselves."

Mom shook her head, laughing, and let him take a handful from the bag. "Doña and I are just having a girl chat." Then she held up a book on the counter with a hot guy on the cover. "I have a hot date with Fabio afterward."

He chuckled and looked at me. "Are you into that too? Because that's a little hard to live up to."

Laughing, I shook my head. "Nah, I'm more into the brooding billionaire type."

"Looks like I'm your guy," he said with a playful wink.

My mom gave us a sly smile that made me blush. "You two have a good time," she said. "*Ten cuidado.*"

"We will be careful," Kai promised.

Then she leaned against the counter next to Mrs. Gutiérrez. "But don't have *too* good of a time."

"Bye, Mom." I pushed Kai toward the door. "I'll see you later. *Adios, Doña Gutiérrez.*"

We walked down the uneven stairs to the parking lot where Kai's Honda waited.

I smiled up at him. "You know, you don't have to keep driving that thing."

Shrugging, he said, "It's kind of grown on me."

"You should have a doctor check that out."

"Ha ha," he said and opened the passenger door for me. "I'll just wait eight years for you to look at it. Now, get in the car."

"So pushy."

He leaned over and looked me right in the eyes, all humor gone from his expression. "I'll be doing more than pushing tonight."

My stomach swooped and my skin pricked into goosebumps at his words, excitement flooding through me. I bit my bottom lip, looking up at him.

He reached up and pulled it free with his thumb. "That's too hot. I have a whole date planned, and we'll never get to it if you keep doing that."

With a breathy chuckle, I settled into my seat and buckled in. "Let's get on with it then."

He grinned at me. "Happily."

As he pulled out of the drive, I asked, "Where are we going?"

"The marina."

"For what?"

"Mountain climbing."

I gave him a look.

"There may be a boat involved," he said slyly.

"A boat."

"Okay, maybe it's closer to a yacht."

"What? We're not flying to Hawaii in the helicopter?" I teased.

With a small smile, he shook his head. "That's date three, at least. I wanted to take you on a good, official first date."

"Time for lesson two," I said. "Most people just go out to eat and watch a movie."

"Most people don't get lucky enough to go out with someone like you."

Butterflies danced in my stomach. "I'm the lucky one."

Shaking his head, he began driving toward Brentwood Marina, holding my hand the entire way. Perfect first-date etiquette.

He parked near a dock strung with twinkle lights. It was beautiful, like something out of a fairytale. My eyes fell on the yacht floating at the end of the wooden planks—a large white boat barely moving with the waves.

After Kai opened the door for me, we crossed the bridge hand in hand to step onto the ship.

"Are you driving?" I asked.

He shook his head. "No, I'm having supper with you."

"So you did pay attention to the first date handbook?"

He laughed, waggling his eyebrows. "Baby, I wrote it."

I'd only seen glimpses of this Kai, the care-free one who laughed and played with me. I loved it.

Taking my hand, he led me inside the ship's private dining room. A single table stood apart from the rest, covered in a white tablecloth with votive candles standing out in the dim lighting.

"Do you like it?" he asked.

At the tone in his voice, I realized something. "Are you nervous?"

For a moment, he was quiet, but he held out a chair for me and helped me sit at the table. "I want to be the boyfriend you deserve. And I want to make up for hiding you away when I should have been showing you off."

My heart warmed, and I reached across the table for his hand. "You were about to throw away your entire inheritance for me, and you're talking about not being the man I deserve?"

His lips turned up, and it struck me how much I wanted to kiss him.

"Okay, I see what you're saying," he said. "And for the record, I'll never understand how I got so lucky to be with a girl like you."

"We both got lucky," I said. "But it took a lot of hard work, too."

He smiled. "Totally worth it."

With a laugh, I looked out the window at the dark sky passing by and the city's lights getting smaller in the distance. We were getting farther from town, out by ourselves.

A server came and brought course after course of delicious food—but only a fork, spoon and knife sat on the table for me. Could he be any more perfect?

I pushed my empty dessert plate away and said, "I so should not have gotten seconds on that cake."

"Nonsense," Kai said.

I smiled and shook my head. "So, what now? A string quartet?"

"Well, I did bring my violin if you wanted to hear me play, but I had another idea." The boat came to a stop, and Kai said, "Right on time."

"What's going on?" I asked.

His dark eyes, full of warmth I knew was love, found mine. "Ever since we spent that day together at the pier, your name's been written on my heart. Is it okay if we write it in stone?"

My mouth fell open at his words, and I looked out the window and saw the ships lights illuminating palm trees. "Is this Walden Island?"

"Yes," he answered simply, taking my hand in his.

I stood and followed him off the boat. We walked across the sand to a trail and reached the caves. This time, my heart was beating so loudly I could have sworn he heard it.

"My parents wrote their names here," I said, "for their honeymoon. Can we find it?"

With a smile, he got a flashlight out of his pocket and said, "I think there's something you should see." Carefully, he crawled over the stones and helped me to a spot at the far end of the cave.

Like he knew the spot exactly, he panned the beam over the rocks until we saw a crude carving.

J+J+J+J

My eyes stung, and I covered my mouth with my hands. "All four of us?"

"Your mom told me they came out each time after their daughters were born to add to their story."

A tear slid down my cheek as I thought of them, a young couple promising love when they didn't know the heartache that would come. "But it didn't end well."

Kai set the flashlight down so it shined on the walls. The light reflected softly on his face as he took my hands. "A love story doesn't have to last forever for it to change the world. Your parents' marriage wasn't perfect, and I hate that your dad left, but look what came out of it. They gave me you."

I leaned into his arms and held him tight. It was easy to want to erase the past, the heartache those letters represented. But then we would have been erasing the love too, the potential.

He pulled back and wiped the tears from under my eyes. "Happily ever after may have ended with them, but I want it to continue with us."

My lips trembled in a smile. "I'd love that."

He reached into his pocket and retrieved a small chisel. After taking off the cover, he set to work, carefully forming the beginning of a new story. Ours.

EPILOGUE

GINGER

My friends each looked stunning in their dress clothes for the winter orchestra recital. Jordan's eyes were wide as she took in the performance hall, decorated to the hilt for the event.

"Is it like this every year?" she asked, still craning her neck back to take in the artwork on the ceiling.

"Yes," I said. "It's like the Academy's last hurrah before Christmas."

She shook her head in wonder. "Our school just had the choir sing a few Christmas songs in the auditorium."

Zara laughed. "Welcome to Emerson."

"Should we find our seats?" Jordan asked. "It looks like they're filling up pretty fast. Plus, my mom ditched me for one of her clients." She jerked her thumb over her shoulder.

I swiveled to look in the same direction to see Jordan's mom sitting with a junior's good-looking—and totally single—dad. "Think there's something going on there?"

Jordan shrugged. "I hope so. It's about time she dated someone."

"She's a total MILF," Zara said. "She'll find someone."

I laughed and shook my head. "You two find your seats. I'm going to interview some people backstage before I start the live stream." I lifted the Wi-Fi-enabled camera around my neck as proof.

"Nerd," Rory teased from behind me.

I swiveled to see her and Beckett together, holding hands and looking absolutely adorable. "Ugh, you two are way too cute."

She smiled up at him. "He is pretty good-looking."

"Yeah, yeah," I said. "See you later."

I turned and walked toward the stage, where I knew I could get back access to the preparation rooms. I did have to go take pictures, but part of me was happy to have a mission, to not have to sit surrounded by friends who had happy relationships and guys who liked them.

Most of the time, I was fine without a relationship. There were videos to work on and homework to do. And I hardly had time for anything else between that and helping my parents out at the store. But I'd be lying if I said I never thought of having more. Because I did. Every time I saw Ray Sadler in videography class, my cheeks got warm. He was good-looking, respectful, and I'd be lying if I said I hadn't checked out his muscles a time or two. But guys like that didn't date girls like me.

I caught sight of the orchestra director, watching as the woodwinds tuned their instruments. "Care for a quick interview?" I asked.

He nodded swiftly. "A quick one, yes."

I held up the camera, started the live stream, and faced it my way. "Hi, Drafters! This is Ginger Nash, EA reporter, here live from the winter recital..."

After introducing myself and him, I asked him a few questions, which he answered before turning back to his students. I paused the live recording and wandered toward the practice rooms, hoping to find Callie or Kai. Interviewing one of them would be easier than talking to an acquaintance.

Through one of the doors I heard soft violin notes fading to the end of a song. I knocked on the door, and heard Kai's voice say, "Come in!"

Twisting the knob, I stepped inside. "I was hoping it would be you."

He smiled at me and set his violin on the couch. Since he and Jordan went public, it seemed like he was a new person—warm and open and friendly. Or maybe we'd just never taken the time to see him for who he truly was.

"Do you mind if I get a quick interview?" I asked.

"Sure." He shrugged. "Anything specific?"

"I'll ask a few questions, and we'll *roll* with it."

He chuckled. "Roll with it. Nice."

My cheeks warmed. I tried not to make too lame of jokes in front of people who weren't my family, but sometimes it was hard to hold back. Instead of replying, I held up the camera, started my intro, and then asked him a few questions about his last winter recital and what he was looking forward to about the show.

He did well, having had practice speaking for *Rush+*, and then we wrapped up. "That was great," I said.

"Thanks, but I lied," he deadpanned.

My eyebrows drew together. "About what?" I so did not want to have to retract a statement made on the live feed.

"I know I said I was looking forward to hearing everyone perform, but there's actually something I'm more excited to do..." He reached into his pocket and held up a delicate silver necklace. "I'm giving this to Jordan and her mother after the show."

My mouth fell open as I touched the dangling charm. "Is that Juana's necklace?"

He nodded. "Do you think it'll be okay, or should I wait?"

"Jordan's been searching for it everywhere," I said. "How did you find it?"

"I'd been to every pawn shop in Emerson and Seaton, and I finally found it at one in Brentwood." He put it in his pocket. "I'm lucky I found it at all."

My hand covered my heart. "Jordan is going to be so happy."

His expression softened. "I hope so. I'd do anything to make her happy."

"I think you already have." I gave him a parting smile before letting myself out of the dressing room, wondering how on earth I would ever find a love like that.

Want to read the story of Kai giving Jordan and her mother the necklace? **Get the free bonus scene** written from his perspective!

Use the QR code to access the free bonus scene!

Continue reading Ginger's story in Curvy Girls Can't Date Cowboys today!

Use this QR code to get to Ginger's story!

ALSO BY KELSIE STELTING

The Curvy Girl Club

Curvy Girls Can't Date Quarterbacks

Curvy Girls Can't Date Billionaires

Curvy Girls Can't Date Cowboys

Curvy Girls Can't Date Bad Boys

Curvy Girls Can't Date Best Friends

Curvy Girls Can't Date Bullies

Curvy Girls Can't Dance

Curvy Girls Can't Date Soldiers

Curvy Girls Can't Date Princes

The Texas High Series

Chasing Skye: Book One

Becoming Skye: Book Two

Loving Skye: Book Three

Anika Writes Her Soldier

Abi and the Boy Next Door: Book One

Abi and the Boy Who Lied: Book Two

Abi and the Boy She Loves: Book Three

The Pen Pal Romance Series

Dear Adam

Fabio Vs. the Friend Zone

Sincerely Cinderella

The Sweet Water High Series: A Multi-Author Collaboration

Road Trip with the Enemy: A Sweet Standalone Romance

YA Contemporary Romance Anthology

The Art of Taking Chances

Nonfiction

Raising the West

AUTHOR'S NOTE

This book was hard for me to write. Not because I have a ton going on in my life (I do), not because my fingers ached with each keystroke (meh), and not because a worldwide pandemic happened and I couldn't go write in a coffee shop every day. (But, please, God, please open up the coffee shops!)

No, I had a hard time because this subject, wealth and poverty, is something near to my heart. As I was growing up, we always had enough—food, clothing, a house—but there weren't a lot of extras. We had to work hard for what we had. Even in high school, I was one of few students working a regular job, paying for my gas, having to get my phone, and so on. It was so hard for me to reconcile why some kids had wealth and others didn't.

Since I got married young, it was important to me to be self-sufficient, so my husband and I worked hard to pay our way through college on our own and build up to what we have now. As we've experienced more, we've also seen plenty of people who have a harder time than we do. Those who don't have homes or families to lean on as a safety net. We've seen children who bounce from home to home in the foster care system and are raising several of them. And every time, I wonder *why* people who have the means to help don't.

Jordan and I are a lot alike in that way. We want to help others but have absolutely no desire to accept help for ourselves. Which creates an interesting dynamic. How can you expect people to help when you wouldn't be willing to accept it?

See? Difficult.

Throughout the course of this book, Jordan realized it's not all or nothing. Someone can be a billionaire *and* generous. Someone can be poor and still have plenty to give. And the amount we're willing and able to give will change throughout our lives.

Right now, my husband and I pour so much into our children that there's little of us left over. Accepting help from friends and family in the form of babysitting or even moral support has shown me just how interdependent we all are.

Whatever stage of life you're in, I hope you'll look for ways you can give, and if you can't give I hope you know you are worthy of help. Don't go it on your own. There is a whole world of incredible people out there. You just have to find them.

ACKNOWLEDGMENTS

Jordan and Kai's story has been such a roller coaster ride, and I'm so thankful for everyone who has challenged me on this story to make it better!

My husband, who brainstormed solutions with me,

Sally Henson, who provides excellent feedback as a beta reader and friend,

Tricia Hardin, who is as good of an editor as she is as a person,

Yesenia Vargas, for serving as a sensitivity reader and sharing of her experience,

and my mom, who I can count on for an honest review.

I'd also like to thank my narrator who has done fabulously with book one and I am so eager to see what she does with Jordan's story! I find myself thinking about how she'll perform the words as I write them!

I started writing books before I became a mother myself, and writing this story with three little boys running around has been such an adventure. I love seeing them "working" in front of a play computer or seeing a book and asking if I wrote it. They are sweet supporters and future heroes.

We also gained a daughter and two grandbabies in the course of writing this book, and proximity to her strength and resilience and vulnerability in the face of adversity has been nothing short of inspiring.

Every reader who has read, left reviews, left me comments on social media, or emailed me has bolstered me so much. Writing can be solitary and intimidating when you have a big story to tell in your mind. Knowing you were there, supporting me on the path to publishing this story, has meant the world.

For the person reading this right now, I hope you are loved, you are prayed for, and you are worthy of every ounce of love that exists within these pages.

GLOSSARY

LATIN PHRASES

Ad Meliora: School motto meaning "toward better things."

Audentes fortuna iuvat: Motto of *Dulce Periculum* meaning "Fortune favors the bold."

Dulce Periculum: means "danger is sweet" - local secret club that performs stunts

Multum in Parvo: means "much in little"

LOCATIONS

Town Name: Emerson

Location: Halfway between Los Angeles and San Francisco

Surrounding towns: Brentwood, Seaton, Heywood

Emerson Academy: Private school Rory and Beckett attend

Brentwood Academy: Rival private school

Walden Island: Tourism island off the coast, only accessible by helicopter or ferry

Main Hangouts

Emerson Elementary Library: Where Rory tutors Anna, open to students K-7

Emerson Field: Massive park in the center of Emerson

Emerson Memorial: Local hospital

Emerson Shoppes: Shopping mall

Emerson Trails: Hiking trails in Emerson, near Emerson Field

Halfway Café: Expensive dining option in Emerson, frequented by celebrities

La La Pictures: Movie theater in Emerson

Ripe: Major health food store serving the tri-city area

Roasted: Popular coffee shop in Emerson

JJ Cleaning: Cleaning service owned by Jordan's mom

Seaton Bakery: Delicious dining and drink option in Seaton where Beckett works

Seaton Beach: Beach near Seaton – rougher than the beach near Brentwood

Seaton Pier: Fishing pier near Seaton

Spike's: Local 18-and-under club

Waldo's Diner: local diner, especially popular after sporting events

APPS

Rush+: Game app designed by Kai Rush and his father

Sermo: chat app used by private school students

IMPORTANT ENTITIES

Bhatta Productions: Production company owned by Zara's father

Brentwood Badgers: Professional football team

Heywood Market: Big ranch/distributor where everyone can purchase their meat locally

Invisible Mountains: Local major nonprofit - Callie's dad is the CEO

ABOUT THE AUTHOR

Kelsie Stelting is a body positive romance author who writes love stories with strong characters, deep feelings, and happy endings.

She currently lives in Colorado. You can often find her writing, spending time with family, and soaking up too much sun wherever she can find it.

Visit www.kelsiestelting.com to get a free story and sign up for her readers' group!

facebook.com/kelsiesteltingcreative

twitter.com/kelsiestelting

instagram.com/kelsiestelting